STRINGS
of
CHANCE

by

Jeff Pryor

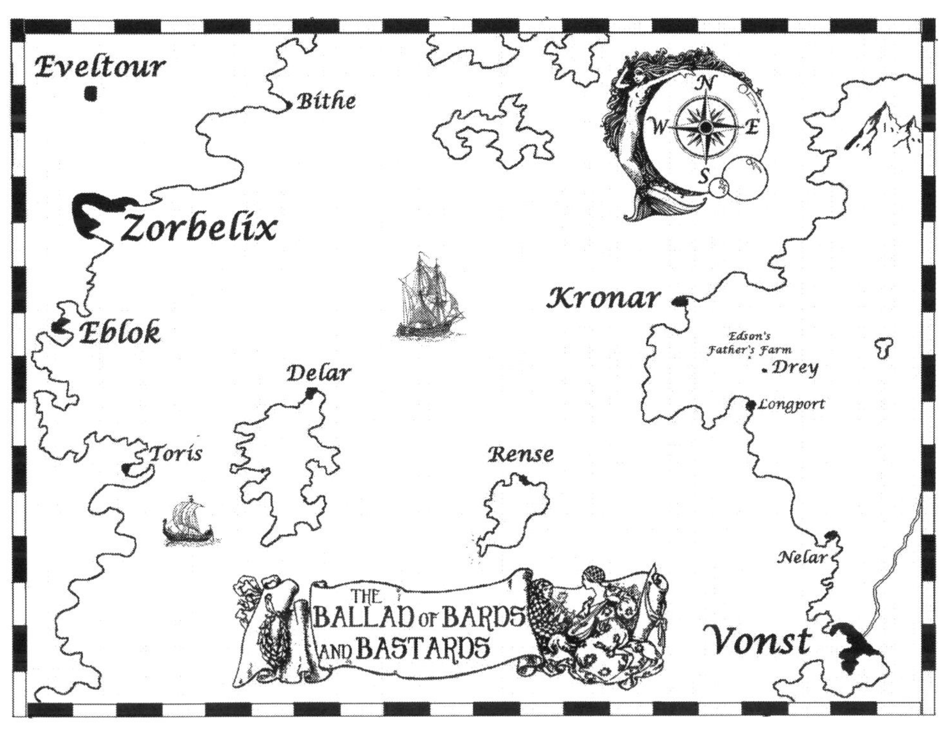

Eveltour
Bithe
Zorbelix
Eblok
Kronar
Edson's
Father's Farm
Drey
Longport
Delar
Toris
Rense
Nelar
THE
BALLAD OF BARDS
AND BASTARDS
Vonst
N
W
E
S

STRINGS of CHANCE

JEFF PRYOR

This book is a work of fiction. Names, characters, places, incidents, organizations, and dialogue are either the products of the author's imagination or are used fictitiously. Any resemblance to actual events, places, or persons, living or dead, is coincidental.

Copyright © 2019 by Jeff Pryor

All rights reserved. No part of this book may be reproduced in any manner without the written permission of the author/publisher except in the case of brief quotations used in reviews or critical articles.

STRINGS of CHANCE

The Ballad of Bards and Bastards / Act One

First Edition published May 7, 2019

ISBN-10: 1096127237

ISBN-13: 978-1096127239

Cover Art & Design by M Wayne Miller

Edited by Ashley Lachance

This one is for the entertainers in my life, and the path I briefly walked alongside them.

Life is a song, sing it well.

Scene One:

Fame Seekers and Fortune-Tellers

"Oh sing me a song, sing it today,
Play me a tune, chase my troubles away.
Oh pour me a drink, and pass it my way,
Pour me another, tomorrow I'll pay."

Edson Pye looked out at the audience as he plucked his citole and sang one of his more popular songs. It was a small crowd but that was to be expected. All the inns and taverns in Vonst featured a singer or two each night of the Midsummer Festival, and most were far more well-known than him. Still, he was developing a small following. He winked at the lass he had spent the night with. Aisley? Aedre? They had shared far too much wine for him to remember such details.

"Oh bring me a love, bring her to me,
Find me a lass, or find me three.
Oh give me the road, and wonders to see,
Give me my freedom, don't take it from me."

The lass gave him a look of disgust. Audrey? Aefre? It

didn't really matter. Tonight was his last night at the Candlehouse. He didn't know where he would go in the morning, as he had yet to find another gig. He had spent the past four years dreaming of playing in the Bardic Challenge, which was the highlight of the festival, and would perform on the streets if he had to. There were fifteen days left before the champion would be named. Edson had no chance of winning but hoped to at least make the listings. If he did, it would guarantee him solid bookings for the next year, and a chance to build his audience. He smiled at the lass. She didn't smile back, but the look went away. That was a start.

"Oh sell me a horse, sell me a steed,
Throw in a saddle and anything I may need.
Oh I see the farmer, please give me a lead,
For I met his daughter and planted my seed."

The men in the room laughed at this line, but the lass didn't share their appreciation for his lyrics. The look was back. Ashley? Alodie? He would probably never remember. She wasn't likely to warm his bed again anyway. Still, she hadn't left. That was something. He finished the number, following it with a pair of similar songs. After that, he sang one of Alwin Floyd's songs, *Edla's Rose*. Edson kept his eyes on the lass through the whole song and had her smiling again by the end. Perhaps he was going down the wrong path. Estra? Elaida? It didn't matter. He would call her Darling, just as he did with all the others.

Thinking of Alwin was a reminder of what was at stake. Edson had studied under the man, learning music, storytelling, dancing, and much more. They had traveled together for three years, before Alwin had announced that Edson was ready to travel and perform alone. That had happened at the end of the previous year's Challenge. Alwin had finished third and was a favorite to win this year. Edson hadn't seen him since they split up after the festival. He was playing in the larger inns and halls. Edson could only dream of playing in such places.

* * *

Edson sighed as he tied his last bit of catgut string into place on his citole. He had no coin left, no place to stay, and he felt a tickle in his throat from sleeping in an alley the past two nights. After leaving the Candlehouse, he had been unable to find another gig and had used most of his coins attending one of Alwin's performances. They had shared drinks after the set, but Edson had been unable to bring himself to ask his mentor to help him secure a gig.

He spent the next night singing on street corners. His earnings had bought him a bit of mutton on a piece of stale bread and enough wine to make the alley comfortable. He needed to do more. Three nights at the Candlehouse weren't enough to get him on the listings. Securing a gig was everything.

The best corners were already taken, but Edson found a spot a block away from the southern market. He wanted to earn enough for a meal before setting out to hunt for a gig. People out and about in the morning typically had a purpose though and weren't likely to stick around for a song. Leaving his citole tied to his back, he tossed his hat down and began juggling three knives from his belt. He purposely made it look as if he were struggling, making each catch and release seem desperate.

"Sorry, kind sir," he said as he caught a knife just before it would've landed in a man's shoulder. “That one got away from me.”

He tossed the knife back into the air as he backed away. The man frowned but dropped a coin into Edson's hat. A passing woman did the same, without the frown. She looked to be nearly as old as Alwin but was still pretty. Edson tossed one of his knives in her direction and pretended to trip as he rushed to catch it. He caught all three but ran into the woman. He nicked her purse strings with one of the knives before stepping back; the purse securely tucked in one of his many pockets. That was a skill he learned long before meeting Alwin.

“Pardon me, my lady,” he said, ducking his head in a slight bow. He slid his knives back in his belt and swung his citole around his shoulder. “Perhaps I should stick to songs for a while. My juggling seems to be getting worse.”

“No harm done,” she replied before walking away. Edson smiled as he retrieved his hat, which held more than enough for him to get something to eat. The purse had enough weight to promise much more.

* * *

Edson scowled as he slipped into the alley where he had slept the two previous nights. After a promising start, the rest of his day had been a disaster. With the festival in full swing, the prices of catgut and wine were more than double the norm. The coins from his pilfered purse were nearly depleted and he still had no gig. The tickle in his throat had gotten worse, forcing him to bring an early end to his evening performance. Calling it a performance was a stretch, for his only audience had been a curious tomcat.

The first bottle of wine was already in his hands before

Edson had covered half of the length of the alley. The smell of smoldering sage was the first sign that he wasn't alone in the alley. His eyes confirmed that fact a few seconds later. A man sat against the wall, a few feet from where Edson had planned to make his bed for the night. The man wore a multicolored robe and was surrounded by burning candles and scattered crystals. He had cards spread out in front of him. Edson had seen such things before. Fortune tellers were more common in Rov, but more than a few came to Vonst for the festival.

"Greetings, friend," the man said, without looking up from his cards. The sage smoke lingered, blurring the man's features. "Is this alley your home?"

"It has been for the past few nights," Edson replied. The man's accent made it clear that he was, in fact, from Rov. Edson had gone to a fortune teller just before leaving the southern city. The woman had placed her cards much the same as this man did. The Death Card had come up during the reading, nearly causing Edson to fall out of his chair. The woman had insisted that it didn't mean what he thought, but he still had nightmares about that card and what it might have foretold. "I was planning to sleep here again tonight, but I can find another spot."

"Nonsense. There's plenty of room here for both of us." The man lifted a flask and held it out for Edson. "Have a drink and make yourself comfortable."

"I've been told it's bad luck to drink with a man before learning his name," Edson said. He had never been told any such thing but wanted to see if he had ever heard of the man. Alwin had told stories of a few charlatans and con artists posing as fortune tellers.

"I've heard the same thing. I'm Braden Asbury, reader of

omens and energies, interpreter of dreams, banisher of ghosts, and student of Vedri Nelara."

That got Edson's attention: Vedri was the soothsayer to the nobility of Rov. Braden was no charlatan if he was telling the truth. Only a fool would make such a claim falsely, for Vedri was known to be a spiteful man. The flask held rum, which wasn't one of Edson's favorites. Still, it felt good on his throat. He passed back the flask after taking a seat.

"My name's Edson Pye. I, too, was a student to a master. I apprenticed to Alwin Floyd."

"I saw him perform about five years back," Braden said as he gathered his cards. The sounds of his shuffling echoed through the alley. His fingers were as nimble as those of any of the thieves Edson had trained with before meeting Alwin. "I've never seen better."

"That was a year before he found me." That seemed a lifetime ago. "He claims that I'll be even better than him someday. I used to believe that, but this festival is proving him wrong."

"Words such as that don't come easily to one as accomplished as Alwin Floyd." The cards flew effortlessly from his fingertips, forming a fresh spread. "You have it in you to be one of the best. I can help with that."

"Why would you help me?" Every instinct told Edson to run away. He had decided long ago to ignore such internal warnings, but this seemed different. "You don't even know me."

"The cards know you." Braden's eyes rarely lifted. On the few occasions when they did, the sage smoke seemed to purposely gather to obscure Edson's view of the man. "And I know the cards. Do you want my help or not?"

"How can you help me?" Edson regretted the question as

soon as he asked it. If he had any sense, he would already have left the alley and fortune teller far behind.

"I can alter your path slightly through my magic. What is it you truly want?"

"I just want to play my music." Magic! Edson didn't trust magic at all. It was one of the few traits he had inherited from his father. Still, the festival was passing by quickly, and he needed a gig. "A woman to keep me company would be nice too, but I'd settle for a gig for now."

"I might be able to help with the gig, if that's what you truly want," Braden said as he passed the flask back to Edson. "You're on your own with the woman though."

"That would be incredible." Edson didn't believe for a minute that Braden could actually change his future, even if he had studied under Vedri Nelara. If the man could wield magic that powerful, he wouldn't be sleeping in an alley. Still, it was worth a try. If it worked, Edson would have a gig, if not, there was always the rum. "I have a few good songs already, but none have caught on. A gig would help with that."

"Is that what you truly want though?"

"Of course," Edson replied after swallowing a mouthful of rum. After passing it back, he went to work on the cork in one of the bottles of wine he had bought. He could only stomach so much rum. "I want to be the most famous singer in Vonst. I can't do that without a gig."

"So, the gig is simply a means to the end. What you truly want is the fame. I can help with that too."

"What's the price for this?" Everything had a price. Other than Alwin, nobody had helped Edson without a price since he left his father's home. "What's in it for you?"

"My master sent me here to practice my skills." For a brief second, the smoke cleared just as the fortune teller's eyes lifted, giving Edson a quick glimpse. In that moment, he saw only honesty and a desire to help. This was a man he could trust. "I was told to seek out those who need my help. I think you are one of those. Will you let me help you?"

Edson nodded as the cork slid free of the wine bottle's opening. He lifted it for a drink as Braden gathered his cards and began to shuffle them. The wine cleared Edson's thoughts and ushered the doubts back into his head. He took another swallow and watched the fortune teller, who placed four cards, face down, between a pair of crystals. He looked up, but the smoke had gathered once more and Edson couldn't clearly see his eyes. "Pick a card to represent the path you would take to find fame but don't look at it."

Edson hesitantly pointed to one of the two cards in the middle. Braden set it aside before gathering the other cards. He reshuffled his deck before laying out four more cards.

"Pick another to represent the obstacles in your way."

After Edson picked a card, Braden again set it aside and laid out a fresh spread. Edson filled his mouth with wine.

"Choose another to represent the price you will pay to achieve your goals."

"Price?" Edson asked, the doubts taking over his thoughts completely. Why hadn't he simply walked away? "Why must I pay a price? I thought you said you were doing this because your master told you to help people."

"All forms of magic require a price be paid. Since my magic works in randoms, the price must work the same. It's not too late to change your mind. Once I look at the cards, it will be though. Are you sure you want to continue?"

"I've never been a quitter," Edson said, pointing at a card. Sometimes, it seemed as if his mouth had a mind of its own. Braden sighed and placed it with the others. He swept up the remaining cards and again shuffled the deck. After laying out another four, he closed his eyes and moved his right hand back and forth over the spread. After a few seconds, he stopped and slid one of the four over with the others, before returning the three to the deck.

He flipped over the first, but Edson didn't look. He was afraid of seeing the Death Card again. Or something worse.

"The path you were on was wrong," Braden said. "The card I chose will fix that. This path would've led you to ruin."

"It's good that we met then."

"Perhaps," the fortune teller replied as he flipped the second card. Edson took another drink of wine. "Various obstacles exist on your original path. My card will remove them but may also place new obstacles in your way. This is another part of the price of magic."

"How do I know these obstacles won't be worse than those I'm avoiding?"

"You don't, but this path will lead you to the fame you seek. Is that not what you want?"

"It is what I want." Edson took another swallow of wine as Braden turned over the third card. "Magic just scares me a bit."

"It scares me more than a bit, and I've spent much of my life learning to use it." The fortune teller stared at the three exposed cards for a moment while the sage smoke seemed to swirl around the remaining card. "The arcane is not something to be played with. Your price has been set, and you will be made to pay."

"What is it?"

"That's a question I can't answer. The price will be paid though. There's no turning back."

He flipped the final card before Edson could mouth a reply. Against his better judgment, Edson glanced at the card. It was the Death Card again! Fuck!

"Your path is set," Braden said. "Let's drink and celebrate your coming fame."

Edson wanted nothing more than to drink but had a hard time turning it into a celebration. Despite his doubts, he could almost feel the magic doing its work. While he didn't think Braden would really get him a gig, there was no telling what his magic might do. Whatever it was, Edson didn't want to face it sober.

* * *

Edson sang loudly as a modest audience had gathered around him. When he had awoken in the alley, the aftertaste of rum in his mouth was the only sign that Braden had even been there. By the time Edson had relieved himself and wiped the morning sand from his eyes, he had nearly forgotten the whole encounter.

His memory was triggered as the audience continued growing while he finished a song he regularly sang. It had never drawn this sort of response. Had Braden and his magic actually been real? Was all of this a result of his card tricks? The sun reflected off the coins in Edson's upturned hat, and the clinking of more coins being tossed in served as an accompaniment to his citole. Remembering Alwin's advice about taking advantage of opportunities, Edson took his performance to another level and danced as he began the next number.

People continued gathering. Nobody seemed to be passing him by, and the coins were piling up in his hat. At least three women were staring at him, making promises with their eyes. There were also a couple men giving him that look, but Edson stuck to the ladies. Alwin was willing to go down either path and had tried many times to convince Edson to walk it with him. He was sure his refusal was part of the reason the bard had pushed him away after only three years. Most apprentices served for at least five.

Some of the people sang along with Edson, as he danced around each of the three ladies and a fourth as well. They all smiled, but two had watching men. Such things didn't bother Edson much, but there was no need to court trouble unnecessarily. Especially with other opportunities presenting themselves. The audience continued to grow and the coins flowed unabated into his hat. He played every song he had ever written, yet still the audience shouted for more. He gave them repeat performances of some of his favorites, and threw in a couple of Alwin's more well-known numbers. The crowd grew too large for the street though, and the city watch arrived to break them up.

By then, the four women had become seven, including another with a man obviously watching. This still gave him a good selection though and he made his choice. He was about to make his move when he was approached by one of the men who had been eyeballing him as lustily as the ladies. He was an older man, wearing clothing that would cost more than the ample yield in Edson's hat.

"You sing really well," the man said. "I have a proposition for you, if you can spare me a few minutes."

"I'm sorry, sir," Edson replied. His choice was leaving. It turned out she had actually had a watcher too. Four remained though, including the others without men. "I only play for the ladies."

"You misunderstand my intentions," the man said. "I want you to sing in my hall. I was searching the streets for a replacement for the man scheduled to sing tonight. He was found dead in his bed. It seems he drank himself to death."

"Where is this hall?" Edson didn't bother asking the dead singer's name. Other than Alwin, he had never met another minstrel he liked.

"Three blocks south of the university. Tabara Hall."

"I know the place," Edson said. Alwin had played there two years back. Edson had managed to get about ten minutes alone in the hall and had been impressed by the acoustics. There were less than a dozen places he would rather play. "What's the pay?"

"Five mensers and a twentieth of the night's proceeds."

Edson would've done it for free. If he had to, he might have paid the five mensers for the chance, but he would gladly take the pay. Between his full hat and this windfall, he would spend the rest of the festival in the finest inns. Only two of the four ladies remained when he finished the negotiations, but they were without watchers. He smiled and offered an arm to each of them. His smile grew when they both took him up on the offer.

* * *

"Carry my heart, wherever you go,
And I'll carry yours as well.
Open your heart, let your love flow,
For I have already fell."

Edson plucked his citole softly. He hated this song. The pathetic number was one of his few attempts at a love song. The audience was eating it up though. Tabara Hall was full to capacity. Somehow, word had spread of Edson's performance in the streets, and he was seen as a potential challenger to the favorites fighting for the championship. Braden and his tricks seemed to be real. It could still be a coincidence, but Edson didn't care. The results were the same.

"Dance with me now, and for evermore,
And I'll save my dances for you.
Sing my song, let loose your roar,
I shall let loose mine too."

He recognized a few people in the audience. Evan Trefry, owner of the Amber Stallion, which was one of the better taverns in Vonst. A gig there would secure Edson's spot on the listings. Kodran Novius was a well-known bard and was Alwin's biggest rival. He glared at Edson with nearly as deep of a scowl as he typically offered Alwin. The man hated competition. Aileen Sager was married to the patriarch of a wealthy family. She was known for chasing and sleeping with any renown bard. Either she was here in pursuit of Kodran, or Edson had truly arrived. He wanted no part of Aileen though. There was a reason she was the one doing the pursuing.

"Join me, my dear, for all of time,
And I'll give you my love.
Hold my hand, listen to my rhyme,
It's you that I'm singing of."

The audience was swooning! He rarely even played this song but had wanted to mix in something for the noble ladies in the crowd. Their reaction to this crap was all the proof he needed. Braden's tricks had worked! Edson would be the most famous singer in all of Elraon. All of his dreams were coming true, and it had only cost him four bottles of wine. The fortune teller had mentioned an additional price, but Edson wasn't worried. There wasn't much he wouldn't do to make his dreams become reality. For that, he would even consider a tryst with Aileen.

He followed this with another love song. This one was much better and captured the audience completely. Aileen's hungry eyes watched him through the whole song, not once swaying toward Kodran. Edson was definitely the prey tonight. He surveyed the room, noting all the exits. He would do anything possible not to come close to her. Being rude to her wasn't an option, for her husband had a lot of influence. Avoiding her would be the best tactic.

Edson's next song was livelier. This seemed to please most of the audience, but there were a few calls for more love songs. The problem was that he didn't have any more of his own. No longer believing in love made it hard to write such songs, and he wouldn't play anything other than originals in this set. After bringing up the tempo, he began introducing his bawdier tunes. These brought everyone to their feet and soon had them singing along. Aileen's eyes remained locked on Edson though, and escape was beginning to look unlikely.

* * *

"She followed me for three blocks," Edson said. Alwin laughed. The two of them were sitting on the balcony of his suite, which was provided by the Cadmara Hall. That was where Alwin was playing for the rest of the festival. "I thought I was caught for sure. She moves much faster than I expected."

"Just take the plunge," Alwin said. "She wasn't so bad. Of course, we were much younger then. We both paid a price for our tryst, though I didn't learn of it until later. I'd do it again though, without a second thought."

"I'll take your word for it," Edson replied. He had a room at the Tabara Hall as part of his pay. Aileen was stalking the place though, and Edson had barely managed to sneak away. It was all a game to her, but he wasn't in the mood for playing. "I'm hoping someone else attracts her eye. I don't want to lose this chance because I'm too busy running from her."

"It never hindered you when I was pursuing you."

"That was different. With you, it was playful. Even though you were persistent, you still left the choice up to me. That isn't the case with Aileen. She'd take me whether I want it or not. You'd never do that."

"Don't think I never considered it," Alwin said. Edson couldn't tell if he was joking or not. "She won't give up as easily as I did. Unless another unknown singer comes out of nowhere, you'll be her target for the rest of the Challenge. My advice is to get it over with. She'll catch you eventually anyway. Especially now that you'll be playing the Amber Stallion."

"She'll find someone else more interesting," Edson replied. The offer for a gig at the Stallion had come in after his show at Tabara Hall. Having such a prominent gig meant Alwin was likely right, but Edson would go down fighting. "At first, I thought she was there for Kodran."

"They have their history as well. Keep your eye out for that one. He's as malicious as they come and wouldn't hesitate to shove a knife in your back now that you're a threat. He's tried to get me a few times."

"I know. I was there for a couple of them. I'm not a threat though. It's a miracle that I've gotten as far as I have. Someone probably heard that you trained me. It'll still come down to the two of you, but Kodran doesn't have a chance. This is your year."

"Perhaps," Alwin replied as he filled both of their wine glasses. He had never been one to boast and would probably celebrate a loss as much as a victory—as long as Kodran didn't win. Alwin would be miserable if that were to happen. "I've seen strange things happen here before though. You aren't the first one to rise up from nowhere. I've seen unknown singers take the prize more than a few times and nearly did so myself when I was young. Maybe you'll be one of those. Just be careful. Kodran is a treacherous man. Sleep with your knives handy."

* * *

Edson's head was pounding. He had managed to make it back to his room after drinking most of the night with Alwin, only departing when his mentor's level of drunkenness brought his flirting passed harmless play. Edson had watered his wine when they had traveled together to avoid such situations. As he awoke, he realized that his head wasn't the problem: someone was pounding on his door. Had Aileen found him? He got up and answered it. A pair of men from the city watch waited outside.

"Are you Edson Pye?" one of them asked. The other just

stood there looking intimidating. Aileen might be less troublesome.

"I am," Edson replied. "Is there something I can do for you?"

"We're to bring you in for questioning."

"Why's that?"

"They didn't tell us," the guard replied. The other one remained silent. What questions could they have? He hadn't stolen anything since cutting the woman's purse strings. Had she recognized him at one of his shows? Would they send guards over such a petty matter? "I'm sure it's nothing important."

"Let's get this over with then," Edson said. There was no way he was going to escape, even if he wanted to try. They knew who he was, so running would only prolong the inevitable. "I'm always willing to help the city watch."

Four additional guards fell in with the others, and they led Edson through the city. They hadn't restrained him but kept a tight circle around him as they walked. This was definitely over something more serious than a simple theft. He was taken to a guardhouse and led inside. They brought him to a room, which held a pair of chairs and a small table, then left him there. The door was locked from the outside. A man came in a few minutes later. He was a big man, with a receding hairline.

"Please, take a seat," the man said as he dropped into one of the chairs. Edson did the same in the other. "I have a few questions to ask you in order to clear something up."

"That's what the guards said," Edson replied. A barkeep in Rov had eyes like this man. He had always been able to see through Edson's lies. Some caution might be in order. "I can't imagine what you might have to ask me about, but I'm glad to help."

"Wonderful. First off, are you indeed Edson Pye?"

"In the flesh."

"Very good. My name is Brentley Sholl. You can call me Brent though. I've heard that you're quite an entertainer. One of the favorites to win this year. Is this true?"

"It's true that I'm quite the entertainer, but I don't think I have a chance at winning. Alwin Floyd or Kodran Novius will take the prize. I'm humbled just to be considered."

"I've been told that you were trained by Alwin."

"Yes," Edson said. What was this about? The questions seemed to be leading nowhere. "I spent three years as his apprentice. He sent me off on my own last year."

"That's unusual. Don't apprentices typically serve for five years or more?"

"Alwin thought I was ready."

"I've also been told that he likes the boys as much as the girls. Was that part of the apprenticeship?"

"No, although not for lack of him trying."

"So, he tried to take advantage of you then?"

"Not really," Edson replied casually. Was this guard working with Kodran in some scheme? "He just reminded me often of his interests."

"When was the last time you saw him?" Brent leaned in closer.

"Last night." Where was this going? "We drank together until the early hours of the morning."

"Interesting. Where did you go from there?"

"Back to my room and to bed. Why?"

"Because Alwin Floyd was found dead in his bed this morning. He'd been stabbed repeatedly. I think you did it."

"What?" Edson tried to stand, but his legs refused to work.

A lump formed in his throat and there was no stopping the tears coming from his eyes. Why? How? There was only one person who could be responsible for this. “Why would I do such a thing? Kodran is who you should be talking to. He's been trying to kill Alwin for years.”

“Perhaps you knew that you couldn't beat your old master.” Brent leaned back, shaking his head.

“This is ridiculous. Alwin was like a father to me.” The tears stung. They would never sing together again.

“Tell that to the magistrate,” Brent said smugly as he stood up. He knocked twice on the door. It was opened by a guard. More than a few stood behind him. “Maybe he'll believe you.”

Edson sat in shock for a few minutes after the door closed. The memories of his apprenticeship to Alwin flooded through his head. He didn't even bother wiping his tears, for they would only be replaced by more. Why Alwin? Why now? Everything pointed to Kodran, for Alwin had no other enemies. Anger began to overwhelm the grief but was eventually replaced by determination. Kodran would not get away with this.

Scene Two:

Songwriters and Soul Suckers

"Left alone to rot, in a cell I didn't earn,
Will they string me up or cut off my head?
Or just tie me to a stake and let me burn?
I don't know, but I wish they would decide,
If this is to be my life, I'd rather be dead.
Instead I sit alone, rotting away from the inside."

Edson wished he had his citole. Even more, he wished he was free, but the citole would do a lot to calm his nerves. Keeping a beat by clapping his hands against the cell walls wasn't the same, but he would never remember the words without some sort of rhythm. Not that it mattered. He wasn't likely to ever have a chance to perform again. Even if he did, this wasn't the type of song anyone wanted to hear. He was singing to pass the time and to clear his thoughts more than anything. Kodran had pulled off a masterful stroke, eliminating both of his primary competitors at once. He would win the prize Alwin had coveted and deserved. Somehow that seemed the greatest injustice of all.

"His prize was stolen, taken away unfairly,
Will he be avenged? Will there be justice?
Or will Kodran dance away so happily?
I don't know, but I wish I could go back,
If I could, I'd rewrite this midsummer solstice.
Instead I sit alone, watching my world turn black."

The acoustics weren't bad in the cell. He had learned where and how to hit the walls to get each note. This brought back memories of Alwin teaching him those notes. Kodran would pay for this. For all his faults, Alwin had been a kind and dedicated mentor. Edson owed the man more than he owed his own father. That debt would remain open until Kodran faced justice.

"Kodran thinks he'll get away with this,
Does he think this cell will bring my death?
Will he be surprised by my dagger's kiss?
I don't know, but I wish I could be free,
If only to witness Kodran's last breath.
Instead I sit alone, wishing I was anyone but me."

"Not one of your better performances," a woman said, breaking Edson's rhythm and concentration. He turned to find Aileen standing outside of his cell. A guard stood behind her. "Though I share your distaste for Kodran Novius. Do you really think he was involved in murdering poor Alwin?"

"I would bet my life on it," Edson replied. "He eliminated his two biggest competitors at once."

"He is the favorite to win now." Aileen had pretty eyes,

even if there was a dangerous hunger within them. A sadness too, but she tried to hide that. “Enough about him though. I came here to talk about you. Do you have any witnesses who would speak in your defense?”

“There isn't really anyone I can think of. I don't remember seeing anyone after I left Alwin's.” He barely remembered leaving, let alone the walk back to his room.

“I can help, but there's a price.”

“Are you serious? What's the price? I don't have much.”

“I think you know what I want.” That hunger in her eyes burned even brighter. “Our game of cat and mouse was amusing, but it comes to an end. I always get what I want in the end.”

“Alwin said the same thing,” Edson said. That was the last bit of advice he got from his late mentor. “He told me of your night together.”

“Nights. He was one of my first. We spent three weeks together in my country house.”

“He didn't tell me that.”

“I'm sure there were a lot of things he didn't tell you. How about it? Do we have a deal?”

“I'll give you what you want if you can get me out of here,” Edson said. He would too. He would match Alwin's three weeks if it would get him out of his cell. “We have a deal.”

“Very well then,” Aileen replied, turning to the guard. “Open the door. I'll be taking him with me.”

* * *

“If I were only ten years younger,” Aileen said. Her head was resting on Edson's chest. She had surprised him more than once during their night together. The experience hadn't been nearly as bad as he had feared. "I'd leave Thomas and run away with you. I see why Alwin liked you so much. He always liked young men with stamina."

"He and I were never lovers," Edson replied. "Not from lack of effort on his part. That just isn't a road I wanted to go down."

"You missed out. He was one of the best I've ever had. You remind me of him in some ways."

"I'll take that as a compliment." She had been with all the legends, including Farris Dent, who had been Alwin's mentor. Some called her a kingmaker, for she had been part of the rise of so many famous singers. What might she have looked like in her youth? "Is there any more wine?"

"Of course." She handed him the bottle from the nightstand. The taste surprised Edson, even though they had been drinking the same vintage all night. He wasn't used to such quality. Thomas Sager had an impressive cellar. Edson took another drink before offering the bottle to Aileen. She returned it to the nightstand. When she turned back toward him, the hunger was back in her eyes. Had it ever truly left? "Have you another round left in you, or have we finally reached the end of your stamina?"

"You're too much. No wonder your husband isn't enough for you."

"Thomas?" She laughed. "It's been more than ten years since he came to my bed. He's more Alwin's type. In fact, the two of them were a bit of a thing for a while."

"Really? Yet another thing he never told me."

"We all have our secrets."

"Speaking of which, you still haven't told me how you got

me out of jail. You said you would after the deed was done. It's been done four times now, and you're ready for another."

"That's not what I said." Her hand migrated south once more. "I told you that I'd tell the story of how you came to be freed. I never claimed responsibility."

"Wait," he said, sitting up and pushing her hand away. "Are you saying you didn't get me out of jail?"

"In truth, my role was minor, but I did help. I heard of a witness who saw you leave Alwin's house the night of the murder. I found the man and convinced him to come forward with his story. He also saw Alwin on the balcony after you'd left, and another pair of men saw you as you walked home. They both testified that, in your condition, you were more likely to kill yourself than anyone else."

"So, you tricked me into this night." Not that the night had been unpleasant. He just didn't like being played for a fool. "I did it all for nothing."

"That's hardly something a lady wants to hear." She pouted. "Especially after all we've shared tonight." The hunger lingered in her eyes. Perhaps Alwin was right, she would've had him no matter what Edson did. There was no changing it now.

"I'm sorry," he said, reaching for her. He stared into her eyes as he had each of the other times. There was immense beauty there, along with the hunger and the poorly hidden sadness.

* * *

The morning sun nearly blinded Edson as he made his way through the streets of Vonst. He had slipped out when Aileen started snoring after their sixth tumble. The woman really was insatiable.

He hadn't wanted to be there when she woke up, hungry again. There was also her husband to think about. Despite her reassurances, Edson remembered too many bad experiences with husbands.

His first stop was a fence he had dealt with numerous times before. Stinky Ed's shop was a mix of everything and anything a person might want to buy. Most of it was stolen, and all of it was overpriced. Still, he paid good coin and didn't ask questions. Edson sold the jewelry he had taken from Aileen's dresser before leaving. Her husband could afford to buy her more. The coins would give Edson a start.

The Amber Stallion would be his eventual destination, for the city watch had told him that they held his bags and citole. While he was eager to reclaim his instrument and the rest of his belongings, he wanted to get some rest and clean up before going to the Stallion. This brought him to the Hungry Squirrel, a cheap inn known for tasty food and ample portions.

Edson gave a false name as he asked for a room, offering out of habit to sing for his meals and a bed. There was already a bard scheduled for the night, so Edson was forced to pay. Even with the cheap prices, it put a serious dent in his limited funds. He would worry about that after some rest. First, breakfast. This turned out to be porridge and hard bread, along with a handful of berries. The barmaid gave him a wink as he ordered a bottle of wine to take up to his room, but Edson was far too tired to return the effort. He threw an extra pair of dulcers on the bar, which brought a smile and another wink.

Despite the attractiveness and enthusiasm of the barmaid, the bottle was Edson's only companion as he climbed the stairs to his room. He just wanted to drink enough to cloud his thoughts before he passed out. The Challenge was nearly over and was clearly going to be won by Kodran. Edson needed to secure at least one more significant gig to have a chance of overcoming the taint of being charged with Alwin's murder. People wouldn't remember that he had been exonerated, instead they would focus on the fact that he had been charged with the crime to begin with. That alone would make him guilty in some circles.

A pair of hungry eyes haunted his dreams, and he woke up with a terrible headache. Still, he was free, even if he was nearly destitute. It was a new day and a new start. A bath would wash away the smell of Aileen and the memories of the past few days. He would then reclaim his citole and find a gig. It was what Alwin would want him to do.

* * *

Edson barely got through the door of the Amber Stallion before the staff surrounded him, greeting him as if he were an honored guest. Perhaps Braden's cards still had some magic left to deal out. Hopefully, the debt was fully settled. Edson didn't think he could pay any more.

“Welcome back to the Amber Stallion, Edson,” said Tebor Neil, the manager. He hadn't been nearly as kind greeting Edson before. None of the staff had. They had treated him politely enough, but always with the implication that they were doing him a favor by letting him perform there. There was some truth to that, but Edson would never admit it. “We've moved your belongings to our best suite.”

“Thank you,” Edson said, not knowing what else to say.

“We were expecting you yesterday.” The staff walked away,

leaving Edson and Tebor alone. They were giving him a suite; did that mean he was still to perform? “I was worried you might have gone to another hall.”

“You have my citole and the rest of my gear. I wouldn't go anywhere without that.”

“Of course. We were hoping you would perform here tomorrow night. It's the last night before the voting.”

“I was hoping you'd still grant me the stage. I'd love nothing more.”

“That's great,” Tebor said as they came to Edson's new suite. It was nearly as nice as the one Alwin had been murdered in. “Take today to rest then. Your entire stay, including meals and drinks, is on the house. Be ready, for it's sure to be a packed house tomorrow.”

“I'm more than ready,” Edson replied as he stepped through the door. His citole called to him as soon as he entered the room. Sitting beside it were a pair of cases. Alwin's harp and flute were familiar instruments to Edson, but he didn't think he could play them without crying. “It'll be the best show of the festival.”

“I look forward to it then.” Tebor bowed and walked away. Edson closed the door and went through his gear. Everything seemed to be in place, including the pouch of coins he had left in his pack. Unable to wait any longer, he picked up his citole and tried the melody he had written in his cell. There was a song there somewhere, he just had to find it.

* * *

“Alwin spoke highly of you,” Jayme Naral said. He had been Alwin's booking agent. He had also nearly refused to even acknowledge Edson's existence the previous half-dozen times they had encountered one another. Now that Edson had fame, Jayme treated him like an old friend. Just another day in the life of a traveling singer. “He told me you weren't represented by anyone.”

“Not yet,” Edson replied. They were meeting in one of the Stallion's private rooms. It was Edson's third meeting of the afternoon. Alwin had primed Edson for this moment, and he had every intention of taking advantage of being unexpectedly in demand. “Though I do have offers on the table.”

“I'm not surprised.” Jayme was a small man, yet still seemed to loom. “I could probably quote those offers within a few finners. Nobody in Vonst is better suited to manage your bookings than me. I took Alwin on when he was slightly older than you. He had just been released from his apprenticeship by Farris Dent, while I was trying to make it as a booking agent. We both took a chance on each other, and it paid off. I can do the same for you.”

“Yet you didn't take that chance a year ago when Alwin released me.”

“That was his idea. He said you needed at least a year of being hungry and having only your showmanship to ease that hunger. I would've taken you on last year.”

“I was definitely hungry,” Edson said. He wasn't sure he believed Jayme, but it did sound like something Alwin would've said. “I eat well now though. What's your offer? Why should I sign with you instead of one of the others?”

“I'll give you the same deal I gave Alwin,” Jayme replied as he slid a piece of paper across the table. It had similar words and numbers to what the other offers held and made even less sense. Why couldn't they just make a simple agreement? “You'll get pretty much the same deal with every agent. With me though, you get years of experience and connections to get you on stage in places most can only dream of."

"Where would you send me for the next year?"

"Across the sea." That wasn't the reply Edson had expected. The other offers had him going to Rov, which is where most bards would flock, and where Edson had gone in his single year alone. He had been there three times with Alwin before that. "I can have you play before the king in Eblok, sing your songs in the huge amphitheaters of Zorbelix, and tell your stories to the masses at the Wizards' Fair in Eveltour."

"What about Bithe?" Alwin had told many stories about the tribes who gathered each winter in the northern city. "Can I sing there too?"

"I don't know why you'd want to, but I can arrange it."

"I've never been on a ship."

"Might as well get it over with then. If you're going to be a successful bard, you'll have to take passage on a ship at some point."

"How do I know you're not robbing me with this contract?"

"You don't," Jayme said, laughing. "In this business, we're all soul suckers. You might as well sign on with one you know."

"You have a point. Besides, I could just kill you if it doesn't work out."

Jayme laughed even harder and was all smiles as Edson signed his name on the sheet. He could laugh all he wanted, but Edson had meant his words. Jayme would die if he proved to be a thief. Edson smiled back. He was glad to have this business over with and eager to see the land across the sea for the first time. For now, though, he was anticipating his coming performance. He had been up writing songs half the night and still wasn't sure what his playlist would be. Having the contract signed took some pressure off, Edson could have a bad night and he'd still be booked for another gig.

He continued smiling as Jayme left. The full bottle of wine he left on the table rivaled any of those in Thomas Sager's cellar. There was no point in letting it go to waste.

* * *

"This one's for Alwin Floyd," Edson said before launching into a song. He fought back tears as his fingers furiously caressed the strings of Alwin's harp. He had never before played or sang as well as he had this night. The final song was his last chance to impress the judges before the voting began in the morning. He harbored little hope of winning but wanted nothing more. Denying Kodran the victory would almost be poetic justice—but such things only happened in stories.

"Fly on, fair Nightingale,
Fly far away from here.
I'll sing your songs and tell your tale,
And try to keep you near."

The Amber Stallion truly was packed. This was nothing compared to the audiences Edson would play for in Zorbelix. The thought was both terrifying and exhilarating. He was barely holding it together for this show. The harp wasn't his strongest instrument, but he had wanted to use Alwin's instruments in this tribute. The flute part was yet to come. He was more comfortable with that.

“Sing on, brave Minstrel,
Your songs shall never die.
Knives to juggle and stories to tell,
And never say goodbye.”

Aileen was in the front row. The hunger was still in her eyes, but there was something else. Pride? That couldn't be it. Satisfaction? That could never be it. Whatever it was, she looked pleased. Not that it mattered; Edson had no intention of going anywhere near her again. There was another woman he had his eye on. She was young and nearly as tall as he was. Her group was made up entirely of couples, yet she seemed to be alone. Edson planned to fix that, at least for the night.

“Ride on, lost Traveler,
Follow your road away.
I'll play your flute as a reminder,
And we'll meet again someday.”

Edson raised Alwin's flute to his lips, gliding across the stage as he played. Kodran was giving his final performance this evening too, as were most bards of note. Tradition prevented any serious contenders from performing anywhere after midnight. Edson intended to be drunk and dancing with the tall woman well before then. The day of voting was typically spent drinking, as well as the following day, when the winner would be announced and the listings would be posted.

“Everywhere, I hear your song,
It's like you aren't really gone.

I can't help but sing along,
Through your music you live on.
Everywhere, I see your face,
In my heart, I hope it stays.
It keeps me from my dark place,
Remembering brighter days.
Everywhere I hear your voice,
Singing to the girls and boys.
We'll meet again, this I rejoice,
Until then, I have your toys."

He went back to the flute and danced some more. The audience was captivated beyond his wildest dreams. Was he really playing this well, or was this more of Braden's magic at work? It was odd that it mattered to Edson. He had what he always wanted but was starting to feel like a fraud. He had taken a shortcut to get to the top, and the cost had been too high.

Returning to the harp, he went through the rest of the song in a daze. The ovation he received at the end was overwhelming, and the hunger in the tall woman's eyes nearly reached Aileen's level. Edson took a bow and let it all sink in. All of his dreams were coming true, yet all he could think about was getting drunk and forgetting about it all.

* * *

One look at the tall woman's leg, sticking out from beneath the blankets, nearly drove Edson back into bed. They had spent two nights together, and he was still eager for more. Instead, with a sigh, he strapped his citole across his back and left the suite. The winner would be announced soon. As a contender, Edson was expected to be on the university lawn, where the announcement would be made. If he won, they would expect him to play a song.

The crowd was thick by the time Edson arrived. He pushed his way about halfway through before someone recognized him and the crowd began to part. Edson tipped his cap and made his way to the front. All the favorites were there, including Kodran. He barely looked Edson's way before returning to the conversation he was having with a pair of noblemen.

"I saw your show last night," a man said. Edson barely knew any of the others and didn't recognize the man who had spoken. He had a lyre strapped to his back and a tambourine on his belt. "It was incredible. It's down to you and Kodran. The rest of us are just here to see where we fall on the lists."

"Thank you," Edson said. Alwin had given Edson lessons on the way speech varied in different regions. Those lessons did little to help, as Edson was unable to place the man's accent. Wherever he was from, Edson didn't share his hopes. Kodran would be the winner. "Going into the Challenge, I would've been happy just to make the lists."

"I'm in the same boat." The stranger passed a flask over to Edson. It held rum, which brought Braden and his card tricks to mind. Edson forced down a swallow. "I was in the right spot at the right time and landed your gig at the Amber Stallion while you were in jail. Then you got out and I was out of work for the most important night of the festival. Fate's a fickle bitch sometimes."

"That she is." Edson had heard something about this man but couldn't bring it to mind. Too much wine and not enough sleep. "She's been playing with my life for some time now. I didn't get your name."

"Donovan Allenson of Eber."

"You're a long way from home," Edson replied. Alwin's lessons hadn't touched much on Eber, or the rest of the western part of the continent of Aern. "I'm Edson Pye, but you already knew that apparently."

"Yes, but I'm glad to meet you. None of the others here will even speak to me."

"They aren't likely to say much to me either. We need a few more years before they'll accept us. They'd still gladly shove a knife in us then, but they'd at least acknowledge us first."

"Where are you going from here?"

"To your side of the sea," Edson answered. "Eblok and Zorbelix. From there I'll go to Eveltour for the Wizards' Fair, then on to Bithe."

"Be careful in Zorbelix. It's been said that nine of every ten people there are thieves, while the tenth is a murdering thief."

"Lovely. Where are you off to from here? Rov?"

Donovan laughed and nodded before passing the rum over again. Edson took a swallow before pointing at the temporary platform built each year for this occasion. The dean of the university was climbing the steps with a piece of paper in his hands. Silent anticipation took over the crowd, and each step seemed to take an eternity. Kodran looked as smug as ever, as if the ceremony was a mere formality. Even if that was the truth, Edson wished he could punch the smile off the man's face.

"This has been one of the more memorable Bardic Challenges in my lifetime," the dean began. "Marred as it was by the tragic murder of Alwin Floyd, this festival will stand out for its performances. Alwin's last rendition of *Edla's Rose* was said to be his best ever. Kodran Novius showed why he's the reigning champion with a daring version of *Her Majesty's Bedchamber*, while a newcomer, Edson Pye, dazzled audiences with fresh hits such as *The Angry Farmer* and *Nightingale*, his tribute to Alwin. Many others stood out, too many to name, but in the end, there can only be one winner. Before I name that winner, please join me in acknowledging all who competed this year."

Edson barely joined in the cheering. Alwin would never sing *Edla's Rose* again or any of his songs. Kodran was at fault, but Edson shared the blame. He had allowed Braden to work his magic, despite being warned. Alwin had died so Edson could be famous. Even if, by some miracle, he won, what would it matter? It wouldn't bring Alwin back. Edson would spend the rest of his life wondering if he had earned his prestige or simply gained it through Braden's tricks and his mentor's death. Was that any better than Kodran winning?

As the applause came to an end, the dean said thc words Edson had dreaded hearing. "For only the fifth time in our history, our reigning champion shall hold his title. Kodran Novius, you are our champion again this year."

The crowd cheered, but Edson could barely hear them. His rage drowned out all sounds, sights, and thoughts. Instinct brought the flask in his hands to his lips. The strong rum numbed him a little, as the reality of the situation sank in. Kodran was getting away with it all. There was no justice. A tainted victory would have been a much lesser evil.

* * *

A pair of sailors laughed as Edson nearly fell down. It wasn't his fault the ship moved as he stepped aboard. The taste of rum remained in his mouth, even though he had switched to wine after he and Donovan went back to the Amber Stallion. The tall woman was still in Edson's suite when they arrived, and she had joined in their night of drinking.

The listings had helped clear the dark cloud hanging over Edson's head. He only trailed Kodran and Alwin, who had received a lot of votes in honor of his lifetime of work. Given that, Edson could look forward to being a favorite when the tournament began again the following year. He would have to be doubly careful. After getting away with murder, Kodran would likely try it again. Only Farris Dent had ever won the tournament three times in a row, and nobody had ever done it four times.

"First time on a ship?" one of the sailors asked.

"How could you tell?" Edson asked, bringing another laugh from both of the men. "Do they always move about like this?"

"This is nothing," the other sailor said. Neither had shoes on, nor did anyone else Edson could see. Perhaps that was the trick. "Wait until we get out to sea and hit some weather."

"I'm so looking forward to that."

"It's not so bad once you get your sea legs," the first sailor said. He was the younger of the two. "For now, though, it's not your legs you need to worry about. It's your stomach. I hope you like the taste of everything you've ate or drank for the past few days, for you're likely to taste them all again."

"I've got a strong stomach. Years of drinking will do that to a man."

"We'll see about that," the second man said. "If you can play those instruments you carry, you'll be a popular man among the crew."

"I can manage a song or two. I was told I'd have a cabin.

Could you direct me to it?"

"I'd be glad to," the first man said. He even carried one of Edson's bags. Despite having the bent nose and scarred knuckles of a brawler, the man seemed to be a decent fellow. Perhaps the voyage wouldn't be so bad. Edson could write a few new songs, practice those already in his repertoire, and have his complete act nailed down before they reached Eblok.

His dark cloud returned a bit when he saw what constituted a cabin. Ropes held what the sailor, Tyler Drees, called a hammock. This was where Edson was expected to sleep! A small, wooden crate underneath the hammock was his spot to "stow his gear." Edson had hidden in lady's closets that were bigger than his entire cabin. On top of it all, the ceiling was too low to allow him to fully stand.

"There's a bucket in case you have to get sick," Tyler said before leaving. Edson sighed and tried to get comfortable in the hammock. After nearly falling twice, he found a position that wasn't bad. The effects of the night before helped him to quickly fall asleep. The ship starting to move didn't wake him, nor did the change in speed as they took on full sail. He slept through the shouts of the officers and the curses of the sailors. Only one thing finally disturbed Edson's sleep. His stomach wasn't nearly as strong as he had thought.

Scene Three:
Bargains and Bonuses

"I've been told that you're a bard of some significance," said Captain Janson Matia. He and Edson were seated at a table in the captain's cabin, which was almost the size Edson had expected his own quarters to be. "Is this true?"

"It is in my mind," Edson replied with a smile. The captain didn't seem to share his amusement. "I was trained by Alwin Floyd and finished third in the Challenge this year."

"I've heard of him." The captain spoke between mouthfuls. Edson had been seasick the first two days out of Vonst and unable to eat for two more days. This meal was his first bit of solid food, but he was afraid to eat too much. "Third, you say? That's not bad. Not as good as first, but I suppose it'll have to do."

"Have to do for what?" Edson avoided clarifying just how difficult finishing third was, especially since it was his first year in the competition. One of the professors at the university had remarked that he was only the second bard in the past ten years to debut in the top three.

"I need you to keep the crew's spirits up. Sing for them, tell stories, juggle, or whatever else it is that you do. We're on a deadline to reach Eblok and will only make one stop. Most of the crew will remain aboard the ship there. Normally, we'd have two stops on this voyage, and they'd be given leave in both ports."

"Do they know this already?"

"No, but they'll figure it out quick enough."

"What's in it for me?"

"You get to make it to Eblok alive." Edson couldn't tell if the captain was joking or not. The man would be a master at cards. "I'm not asking much. Nobody avoids working on my ship, even passengers. You'll help out the ship's carpenter when he needs it and entertain the crew when they need it."

"Since you're asking so nicely, I suppose I can't say no, though I don't know what help I'll be to the carpenter. The only thing I know about wood is that this ship and my citole are both made of it."

"He'll show you how to do everything he needs done. He asked for you and has never asked for any help before. I could hardly turn him down."

"I don't suppose the job comes with a bigger cabin?"

"Space is limited," the captain said. The man chewed with an open mouth. With Edson's stomach still recovering, he avoided watching. His own bowl was still nearly full, while the captain was spooning out his last bites. "You should see where some of the crew sleeps."

"I can only imagine. I'm finding that my appetite has yet to return. If there's nothing else, I'm going to return to my hammock for a bit."

"By all means. I'm expecting a performance tonight though."

"Of course," Edson said. He bowed slightly before making his exit. He had no real issue with entertaining the crew—he could use the practice—but didn't like being told to do so. He was more bothered by the prospect of working with the carpenter. People lost fingers, and even hands sometimes, cutting wood. Edson's hands were as important to him as his voice. Without them, he couldn't play his music.

* * *

"I've set my sights on the port of Bithe,
For there I shall see Lavena,
She is the one I want to be with,
Or perhaps it was Carlina."

With bare feet, Edson danced across the deck. He strummed his citole when he was singing and played Alwin's flute when he wasn't. The Merda was a cog, whatever that meant. The captain sat with the crew, watching the performance. This was Edson's first time entertaining the crew, but he was on his fourth song.

"From there I'll sail to Eblok,
Where I know a lass so fair.
We'll hide away near the dock,
For her husband's not one to share."

The song was a favorite among sailors. Nobody knew who had written it, and it was rare to find a minstrel who didn't sing it. It was tradition to include at least one original verse. Edson had rewritten all the words, other than the chorus. He left that unchanged so listeners could sing along.

“The sailor's life, the sailor's life,
Your family's the crew, the ship is your wife.
The pay is too low and the food is the worst,
There's never enough rum to quench your thirst.
If the pirates don't get you, the scurvy will.
Yet here we are, all sailors still.
The sailor's life, the sailor's life,
With a lass in each port, who needs a wife?”

Most of those watching joined in. That was a good sign. Getting the crew to sing together would go a long way toward keeping the peace. Even from his short time here, Edson could sense the tension in the air.

“Maybe I'll sail to Valotar,
Though I swore I'd never return.
My girl there is the craziest by far,
But I fear I'll never learn.”

If a mutiny were to start, there was little Edson could do. Being new to the crew, nobody was likely to trust him. He had to hope there was time before anything would happen. Otherwise, he would probably be thrown overboard with the captain. Edson knew how to win people over though. He would use all the tricks Alwin had taught him. Within a week, they would love him.

“Vonst is the next place for me,
Where the minstrels gather to sing.
I've a lass there as fine as can be,
To her I'll give my ring.”

'

He repeated the chorus three times before breaking into another song. This was another old sailors' favorite, and it brought the crew to their feet. They danced, drank, and sang along with Edson. He met the captain's eyes. The man smiled, but there was little mirth. He would be a bit harder to win over than the rest.

* * *

“This is outstanding,” Edson said. He was looking at a dulcimer made by Welby Dinan, the ship's carpenter. It wasn't as ornate as some Edson had seen, but it was still a fine instrument. “You have a gift.”

“It was our family trade,” Welby explained. All of his fingers were fully intact. That was good. The man made instruments as a hobby. This was apparently his reason for asking the captain to assign Edson to his service. “I thought I would inherit my father's shop, but his gambling debts did him in. He sold everything, but was still short. Rather than allow them to take me as payment, he put me on a ship. When the captain discovered my knowledge of woodworking, he apprenticed me to the carpenter. That ship was taken by pirates though. We were set adrift on rowboats. Captain Matia found us. His carpenter was an unskilled drunk. I replaced him within two weeks.”

“You should be making instruments,” Edson replied. “Your talent's wasted on this ship.”

“I've came to love life at sea though. I play around in my spare time. I usually try to sell off whatever I make when I get liberty.”

“Have you ever made a rebec?”

"I made two of them last year," Welby answered. Edson liked using the rebec for writing songs and had a few that didn't sound as well with the citole. "I have everything I need to make another pair. They were easy to sell."

"I would think so. If I could afford it, I'd buy one of them."

"Why don't we make them together? You can keep the one you make and I'll sell the other."

"That sounds great," Edson said. That was the answer he had been hoping for. "Do you know how to play any of the instruments you make?"

"Not really. I can keep a simple beat on the pipe and tabor but not much beyond that."

"The dulcimer is fairly easy. I can teach you a little."

"I'd like that," Welby said as he put the instrument away. "We better get back to work though. The captain doesn't abide slackers."

* * *

It was good to be off the ship. Edson's afternoon would be spent chasing down a list of things that Welby needed. Still, he hoped to find a few free moments. The odd part was, after finally getting used to moving about on the ship, Edson was having trouble adjusting to walking on solid ground again. He had nearly fallen twice on the docks.

He stopped at the first tavern he found. With nothing other than rum since they left Vonst, he had a taste for some wine. His time was limited, so whatever swill they had to offer would have to do. The only sign was faded so badly that it was unreadable. If not for a crudely depicted jug and mug, Edson would've passed the place without a thought. As it was, he hesitated for a brief moment, but what was one drink going to hurt?

A few scattered candles served as the only light, which was likely for the best. Zain only knows what kind of bugs might be crawling around this island. The place was nearly empty. Edson smiled as he approached the bar. A lute was hanging on the wall, and it surprisingly had all its strings. Why pay for a drink when you can sing for one?

"That's a beautiful instrument on the wall there," he said, keeping the smile on his face. "I'll play you any song you like in trade for a bit of wine."

"How do I know you can really play?" The barkeep was a large, bald man. He had what looked to be a knife scar across his left cheek. "We get all sorts of tricksters in here."

"I bet you do," Edson replied, widening the smile. "What if I told you I finished third in the Bardic Challenge this year in Vonst?"

"What if I told you I could shit gold bricks? Both statements are likely just as far from the truth."

"Pick your song then. If you don't like my performance, I'll pay for the drink."

"Deal," the man said as he turned and retrieved the lute. Edson was surprised to find it was in tune. Lutes were fine instruments, but every bard under the sun seemed to carry one. Edson liked being different.

"You still haven't picked a song."

"She Dances Under the Moon," the man replied. Edson fought back a groan. Of all the songs, he had to pick Kodran Novius' biggest hit. Edson could play it but wasn't sure a bit of wine was worth it. "I love that song."

“Many do,” Edson said. It wasn't a bad song. If Kodran hadn't written it, Edson would likely cover it now and then. It was good to mix things up. Using the same playlist every show was a quick path to mediocrity. He had learned the song from Alwin, who had put a new twist on it, mocking Kodran. Edson's smile returned as he began to play.

* * *

“This is too much,” Ulrik Bacher said. He was one of the loudest complainers on the ship. Edson continued working a piece of wood with a cabinet scraper. This would be the neck of his rebec, and he wanted it perfect. “I wouldn't have signed on for this voyage if I'd known there'd be no fucking leave.”

“At least Delar isn't far,” Tyler Drees replied. He was nearly as loud as Ulrik. In Edson's eyes, Tyler was the bigger threat. He seemed to be a completely different person than the pleasant sailor who had carried Edson's bag as he boarded. Tyler was likely to act, while Ulrik was all talk. “The captain has to let us go ashore there.”

“I wouldn't count on it.” Even Ulrik might be motivated to act when the captain announced that they would be sailing straight through to Eblok, skipping the island port of Delar altogether. Mutiny was a definite possibility. “He's been in a hurry since we left Vonst.”

“He'll have to find a whole new crew in Eblok if he doesn't give us a rest in Delar.”

“I don't think he cares.”

Edson frowned as the pair of sailors moved on, leaving him unable to follow their conversation without being obvious. Trouble was brewing aboard The Merda. Edson just hoped it would blow up in Eblok rather than before they reached the city of the knights. A stop in Delar would do wonders for everyone.

There was one huge part of this that Edson wasn't understanding. Why was Captain Matia in such a hurry? Edson had managed to get a look at the ship's manifest. There was nothing on board that was in danger of spoiling. None of the cargo seemed to be something needed with urgency. As far as Edson could tell, he was the only passenger, so it wasn't a case of someone offering a bonus to speed up the voyage. What was he missing? Why risk the wrath of the crew for no apparent reason?

Edson’s focus returned to his work. The neck was as straight and smooth as it was going to get. Welby had already finished his and was waiting for Edson to catch up. They would mount the necks to the bodies soon. That would be the biggest test of Edson's work. He almost regretted the voyage's eventual end; there were many instruments he would like to add to his collection.

Shouts interrupted Edson's thoughts. Another argument had broken out. It was over quickly but still served as a reminder of just how fragile the situation was. Finishing the rebec would have to wait until evening. Brandishing his citole, he broke into a song and danced across the deck, his bare feet fully accustomed to the ship's movements by now. The crew laughed and sang along. The distraction wouldn't last, but it was all Edson could do.

* * *

“It's not the prettiest thing I've ever seen, but it holds a tune.” Edson was thrilled with the rebec he had made. Sure, Welby's was far better, but that did little to diminish Edson's pride. “Thank you for this.”

"I should be thanking you," Welby replied. "Getting the perspective of someone who plays the instruments I make has helped me a lot. Then there's the dulcimer. I'm having so much fun learning how to play it that I might keep it."

"You should. You can keep a beat. Many can't do something as simple as that."

"It's simple for you. For me, it's one of the hardest things I've ever learned."

"Fair enough," Edson said. Music came naturally to him and sometimes hardly even seemed to be a skill as much as an instinct. The way Welby worked with wood was a true example of skill. "What are you going to make next? These are almost finished."

"I don't have the materials to make much. Perhaps a tambourine or two."

"I wouldn't mind having one of those. They're small and light. I'm already going to need a packhorse, if not a wagon."

"Get an apprentice and make them carry the load."

"The horse would be less work," Edson said. He wasn't ready for an apprentice yet. Perhaps in a few years, when the road started getting lonely. "What about you? Who's going to replace me as your helper?"

"I don't really need anyone," Welby said. It was the truth. The biggest task he had given Edson thus far was the shopping list in the island port of Rense. After playing his song in the dockside tavern, Edson had convinced the barkeep to send a worker to do the shopping. Instead of chasing down every item, Edson had spent the afternoon drinking and singing. With a local man doing the shopping, everything on the list was delivered to the ship at a cheaper price than Edson could've ever dreamed of negotiating. The skimmed difference had bought him a supply of wine to see him through to Eblok. The hardest part had been acting sober upon his return to the ship.

"With a helper, you'd have more time to build instruments, which is what you should be doing. Find someone young and teach him. Your family talent shouldn't end with you simply because your father liked to bet the ponies."

"I'm not as old as you think and still have a lot of good years left. Maybe someday I'll find a woman and have a son."

"I hope you do," Edson said. The prospect of such a life was horrifying. He and his father had nearly come to blows numerous times before Edson finally left. He had never returned. He had no desire to repeat that scene with a son of his own.

* * *

The crew was furious. In truth, Edson shared a bit of their anger and frustration. Despite knowing they would pass by Delar without stopping, he had held out hope that the captain would change his mind. Instead, the island was nearly out of sight, and they were sailing back into open water. Captain Matia had made the announcement just after the lookouts had first spotted land. He had refused to hear arguments and had locked himself in his cabin.

Edson had been unsuccessful in his efforts to find the motivation for the captain's haste. Even the ship's officers seemed baffled by it. If it came to mutiny, some of them were as likely to join in as they were to try to stop it. The captain didn't seem to confide in anyone. Edson's first impression had been accurate. The man would be a terrible person to play cards against.

The same couldn't be said for the rest of the crew. Edson

had slowly built up a solid reserve of coins. Most of this came from cheating at cards or dice. He hadn't taken more than a few coins from any one sailor, purposely allowing them all to win at times. He won enough to stay ahead and grow his nest egg. There was supposed to be an account set up for him in Eblok, with a payment for the first part of the tour. Jayme Naral was a sneaky bastard though. Edson would be stunned if the accounts were truly established.

First, they had to get to Eblok. Tyler Drees stood about ten feet away. He was speaking with a pair of sailors and kept looking toward the captain's cabin. It would start with him. Edson had an idea. He didn't know if it would work but had to try. Anything was better than simply waiting for the whole thing to blow up. He whistled, drawing the attention of Tyler and his companions.

"I have something that might interest you," Edson said. "I had a cask of wine hidden in the supplies I bought in Rense. I've been afraid to have more than a cup or two, but the captain can piss off. Not stopping in Delar is unacceptable. I say the four of us get good and drunk anyways. Fuck Captain Janson Matia!"

"I'd like to do a lot more than that," Tyler said, "but getting drunk is a good start. Where's this cask at?"

"Hidden with the supplies."

"Lead on then," Tyler said. Edson smiled. The first part was over, now all he had to do was get them so drunk that they couldn't possibly lead a mutiny. This would at least buy them another day and get them closer to Eblok.

* * *

"Fill up the glasses and strike up a tune,
For I've been long at sea.
I'll dance with the lasses and howl at the moon,
Won't you howl with me?"

Edson danced around the deck, pushing the crew to sing along. This was a new song, and everyone seemed to have taken a liking to it. Hopefully, it would be enough to keep the peace. Welby kept a beat in the background on his dulcimer. Almost nobody was watching either of them, for all eyes were on the captain, who stood at the wheel ignoring everyone. It was the first time he had been on deck since announcing they would pass by Delar.

"Serve me a warm dinner and I'll sing a song,
Maybe I'll even sing two.
Throw in a finner, and I'll sing twice as long.
It's the least that I can do."

If he were being honest, Edson stood more with the crew than the captain. It was bad enough that almost nobody had been allowed to go ashore in Rense. Skipping Delar altogether had fallen just short of daring the crew to mutiny. So far, they had stayed in line, but that line was wearing thin. Edson doubted it would hold much longer. All guesses put them at less than a week from reaching Eblok.

"Tap a fresh keg and I'll buy the first round,
For I've no other use for my pay.
I'll be half in the bag, sleeping on the ground,
And do it again the next day."

The captain hadn't left his cabin since making the announcement. Edson had tried approaching the door but had been blocked by a pair of junior officers. He was doing all he could to keep things under control. The captain's appearance on the deck had come as a surprise. Edson could almost feel the anger of the crew.

"Fire up the ovens, clean all the mugs,
Wipe all the tables, and beat all the rugs.
Check all the bottles, make sure none are short,
For my ship has docked in your port.
Wake all the wenches, and the cooks too,
For there is much work for them to do.
Dust off the mantles, the shelves, and the clocks,
For my ship's tied off at your docks.
Clean out the privy and stock up the larder,
If you don't do this, your life will be harder.
Tap a few kegs and prepare the stew,
For I've brought the whole fucking crew!"

There was a little enthusiasm with the chorus, but most eyes remained on the captain. As Edson reached the end of the song, the captain waved for him to stop playing.

"I know you're all furious about skipping Delar," the captain said, loud enough for everyone to hear. "I understand that. I can't tell you why, but we need to reach Eblok in five days."

Many from the crew shouted out questions, but the captain waved them off. He looked at them for a moment, as if trying to decide what he should say.

"If we make it, each of you will receive a bonus of a quarter of your pay." The crew cheered a little at this, but the captain again waved for quiet. "Failure isn't an option. If we aren't there in five days, it won't end well for any of us."

There was again a chorus of questions, but once again the captain refused to answer any of them. Edson shouted a couple of his own. Finally, once the crew quieted, the captain spoke up once more. "That's all I can tell you. You'll have to decide for yourselves if you believe me or not. Five days will go by fast. I suggest we put all efforts into making sure we make it in time."

Scene Four:
Knights and Knockers

A dozen knights waited on the docks as a pair of crewmen tied The Merda to the moorings. Did this have something to do with the captain's urgency? One of them stepped forward after the gangplank was put in place. Captain Matia faced him from the ship.

“Greetings, captain,” said the man Edson assumed was an officer. Edson listened closely to the man's words. Alwin had captured Eblok's accent perfectly in his lessons. Would the reminders ever stop bringing pain? “We're here to escort a Master Edson Pye to the palace. I was told he would be on this ship.”

“You were told correctly,” the captain replied. An escort to the palace? That couldn't be good. “I was told I'd receive a bonus for delivering him here on time.”

“I have a letter of credit here.” The officer took a piece of paper from his pouch. Edson was stunned. He had been the reason for the captain's haste all along. Why couldn't the man have simply told him this? “The king is honored to have a master bard as entertainment for his daughter's wedding.”

Entertainment? Wedding? Jayme Naral had said something about playing for the king, but nothing about all this. Why all the secrecy? Still, it was an opportunity one couldn't pass up.

"I'm Edson," he said, stepping forward. "If you'll give me a few minutes to gather my things, I'll be right there."

"Very well, my lord," the officer replied. Edson smiled and rushed to his cabin. His bags were already packed. He grabbed them and went to Welby's workshop.

"I was beginning to wonder if you'd come for this," Welby said as Edson arrived. He held out one of the two tambourines they had made together. "I'm guessing this is goodbye."

"I'm afraid so," Edson replied. "It seems I'm to perform at the royal princess's wedding. An escort is waiting for me on the docks."

"You're moving up in the world. Just don't sing the songs you've been singing to us. Kings have chopped off heads for less."

"I'll be on my best behavior. What about you? Are you staying on or looking for a new berth?"

"I'll probably snoop around a bit and see if any better opportunities are out there. Before this voyage, the captain has always been honest and fair with me. I'm guessing he was paid to keep quiet, whatever the reason."

"I was the reason," Edson said. He still wondered why this couldn't have been handled better. It's not like he would've refused a chance to play a royal wedding. There had to be something he was missing. "The captain was paid a bonus for delivering me on time for the wedding."

"That makes sense. I don't understand the secrecy though."

"That makes two of us. I have to get going. Thank you again for the rebec and tambourine. I'll take good care of them."

"There's nothing to thank me for. I enjoyed working with you, Edson."

"I enjoyed it as well." That was surprisingly true. Despite

his initial horror at the assignment, Edson had found a lot of pleasure working with the carpenter. “Promise me you'll keep making instruments.”

“I can't see myself stopping. I have it in my mind to take a crack at making a citole. I've drawn up the plans after studying yours.”

“I hope to see it someday. Farewell, Welby.”

“Farewell, Edson.”

There were a few brief goodbyes as Edson made his way back to the gangplank. Captain Matia dropped a pouch of coins into Edson's hands without saying more than a muffled farewell. Edson was a little disappointed but smiled as he left the ship. It was a new day, he was finally off the ship for good, and he would be performing for royalty. What more could a man ask for?

* * *

“I'm just going to explore the city a bit,” Edson explained to the guards outside the palace. He had been given an unbelievable room and pampered as he never had been before. He still hadn't met the king, or any of his family, but would perform for them in two nights. He planned to spend this night in the city, preferably in the arms of a willing and imaginative lass. “Perhaps get a drink or two. There's no need for an escort.”

“Very well then,” said the officer at the gate. “Just be careful. The king wouldn't be happy with me if something were to happen to you.”

“I'll tell him I snuck out if it comes to that.”

“Don't say that,” the man replied, with fear in his eyes. “The king would think we were lax in our patrols. That would be even worse. Just be careful."

"I'll be a perfect model of caution." Edson put on his best smile as he started walking. "I may be all night though. I'm to perform for the king in two nights and want to practice in an inn or tavern."

The officer frowned, but Edson didn't give him a chance to reply. He shouldered his citole and kept moving, not looking back until he was at least a hundred paces away. The man was still frowning but made no effort to stop Edson. That would have to be good enough.

In addition to the citole, Edson had his tambourine and Alwin's flute hanging from his belt. The rebec and harp remained in his room in the palace. He wore the worst of the clothing the palace staff had given him. They had provided him with a wardrobe that would rival Alwin's finest but had taken away all of his old clothing under the pretense of cleaning it. Thus far, nothing had been returned and Edson had little hope of ever seeing any of it again.

He was uncomfortable in all of the new outfits, especially the one he wore. This was quickly remedied with a stop at a tailor shop and a few coins from the pouch Captain Matia had provided. It had held a dozen pranters and mensers, as well as a pair of tulners. Each of the tulners was worth slightly more than the other coins combined. If the captain had given similar bonuses to everyone, his chances of maintaining a full crew had greatly increased. Just how big had the bonus been for arriving on time?

Those thoughts were left behind as Edson walked the crowded streets of Eblok. Scents of roasting meats, nuts, breads, and pies filled the air, mixing with the sounds of hawkers shouting out the benefits of their goods, hagglers trying to save a few finners, and children playing and shouting. After being on the ship for so long, Edson welcomed the variety and bustle of the market.

A cutpurse made her way through the crowd, nicking purses and slipping deft fingers into loose pockets. She was good, but he had been better at her age. The sheer luck of having Alwin pass by while Edson was singing a song—to a lass he had hoped to snuggle with—had taken him away from that life. Would chance rescue this girl as well, or would she suffer the inevitable fate of most career criminals? Life in a labor camp would be a hard way to go.

The first two inns he came to already had a bard performing. Edson drained a goblet of wine at each and moved on. The third was simply called Marla's Place. The sign featured a painting of a buxom woman serving mugs to a group of ogling men. Edson smiled and went inside. It was clean, without the smell many such places shared. Edson kept his smile on his face as he was greeted by a woman he assumed to be Marla. She was a little older than depicted in the painting, but there had been no exaggeration on her cleavage.

"I was hoping you might be in need of a bard tonight," Edson said, trying to keep his eyes up so he didn't look as desperate as the men shown on the sign. After his time at sea, this was difficult. "I'll play for my drinks, dinner, and a room for the night."

"Can you play *She Dances Under the Moon*?"

"I can," Edson replied, forcing himself to keep the smile on his face. Of course she would ask for that one. "I can play all sorts of songs. I'm a man of many talents."

"I bet you are." She smiled back at him in a manner that promised to put those talents to the test. "Let's start with that song though. Play it to my satisfaction and you've got the gig. We'll see what else you're capable of after that."

* * *

"With lances long and voices strong,
The knights join in this song.
Sing along, sing all day long,
For a knight can do no wrong."

Edson was performing for a small audience, which included the king and queen, but none of their children. A collection of noblemen and ladies filled the rest of the tiny hall. Edson sang an old song, written by a knight who was long dead. With the knights' staunch adherence to tradition, Edson didn't dare change a single lyric or note. There had been some truth to Welby's remark about kings and chopping off heads.

"On horses tall, they'll never fall,
The knights protect us all.
Heed their call, without stall,
For a knight's word is law."

A night in town had been just what Edson needed. Marla tested him in ways he had never imagined, both in and out of her bedchamber. He was considering sneaking out again for a visit but had a meeting scheduled after the performance with one of the king's attendants. She was responsible for planning and coordinating the princess's wedding and wanted to meet with Edson to discuss his role. Though he hadn't met her yet, he was dreading the appointment. Nearly everyone he had talked to told him horror stories about her unwillingness to budge on anything. He wouldn't be told how to do his show.

"The knights, the knights,
Dressed in blue and white.
Protectors of the light,
Such a glorious sight.
More solid than any rock,
As dependable as a clock.
Bred from special stock,
For the honor of Eblok.
The knights, the knights,
Defenders of all that's right.
The knights, the knights,
Oh, what a glorious sight!"

The king and a few of the men sang along. Edson had been introduced to King Jondar just before the performance. He was a tall man, with a deep, booming voice. The queen was his opposite; she was petite and timid of voice. His accent was local, if a bit refined, while she seemed to be from one of the trading cities of the Zorbelix Alliance. Both had expressed how pleased they were that he would be performing at their daughter's wedding rather than going to Rov, where most other bards of note would be. Edson was still getting used to being considered a bard of note by others. He had thought as much of himself for a long time. It was good to see others catching on.

The remainder of the show went well, and Edson found the king's attendant waiting for him as he exited the hall. She wore a high-collared dress, cut to hide any figure she might have. Her hair was tied back, with no ribbons, bows, flowers, or any other type of decoration. She was all business, just as he had heard. Still, she was cute. Perhaps this wouldn't be so bad.

* * *

The door squeaked as it closed, bringing a grimace to Edson's face. He was trying to avoid attention as he left the room of Aigneis Bain, the king's attendant. She had been quite the surprise once the doors were closed. Hopefully, she would be less demanding after their shared night together. Their conversation had started with her reciting a list of rules nearly a page long. He wasn't to speak to anyone, eat or drink anything during the show, play sets longer than a half hour, or play any songs written by Farris Dent. It seemed he had offended the king's father in some way, and his songs had been forever banished from being played in Eblok. Edson hadn't planned on playing any of his songs but found the idea of banning songs to be offensive. If not for kings and chopped off heads, he might have considered adding a Farris song to his main performance.

His thoughts were on Aigneis and Marla as he finally came to the hall that held his room. He barely looked as he turned the corner and nearly ran into a young woman who was waiting outside of his door.

“I'm sorry, my lady,” he said, coming to a stop. She was tall, with long, dark hair. Her eyes were familiar, but he couldn't place them. Something told him that she was trouble but that had never stopped him before. “I didn't expect anyone to be standing here.”

“Are you the singer?” she asked in a demanding tone—one Edson recognized it immediately—she was used to getting what she wanted. Who was this woman?

“Yes. Edson Pye's the name. I also play numerous

instruments, juggle, tell stories, perform sleight of hand tricks, and dance, but you may call me the singer, my lady."

"Well I also write poetry, am able to do advanced mathematics, speak four languages, and share your ability to dance, but you may still call me my lady."

"A wit as sharp as your beauty. I'm impressed. I didn't get your name."

"I didn't give it. My lady will suffice for now. I'm not interested in forming a friendship with you. I just need to know if you can truly sing."

"I've been told my voice is quite lovely," Edson replied. Was this the princess? One of her maids? "I would love to give you a private performance."

"That's what I was hoping for. It wouldn't be proper for me to be in your bedchamber. Perhaps one of the royal gardens?"

"Lead the way," Edson said. "I already have my citole."

This woman wore a dress that highlighted her form, rather than hiding it like the one worn by Aigneis. Edson fully enjoyed his view as he followed her through the palace. She looked back once and smiled, increasing the sway of her hips from that point forward. Edson wasn't complaining.

They eventually reached a small garden where they were alone. The woman sat on a bench, while Edson searched his mind for a song. He finally settled on *Edla's Rose*, for all the ladies loved that one. As he began, she got up and began to dance, coming closer with each following verse. Halfway through the song, she began dancing around him, her fingers lightly brushing against various parts of his body as he played and sang.

"Who are you?" he asked after barely managing to finish the song. "Are you the princess?"

"Would a princess do this?" she asked before licking his neck.

"I suppose not." Were all the women of Eblok like this? He had never had such luck with the lasses. "What's your name?"

"I already told you, my lady will suffice. If you need to know more, we can stop this right now."

"I was just asking. I'm more than happy to call you darling."

"Call me whatever you like," she said, grabbing hold of his shoulders and pulling him toward her. Their lips met, and her hands went lower. Darling it would be, just like all the others.

Their lovemaking was almost frantic, and she had more energy than Aigneis and Marla combined, which was saying a lot. Edson was worn out after and was beginning to doze off when a shout came.

"Who's that in the garden?" A man's voice shouted, putting the young woman into a panic.

"You have to get out of here," she said. "My father will have you killed if you're found with me."

"Who's your father?" Edson asked, pulled his trousers on, and fumbled for his shoes. He was afraid he knew the answer. The sounds of footsteps and plants rustling meant that whoever had discovered them was coming their way.

"The king," she said, confirming his fate. He would lose his head this time for sure. "Run out the back way. I'll distract whoever is coming."

Edson grabbed the rest of his clothing and ran like he had never run before. He didn't stop until he was in his room with the door closed. It was then that he realized he had left his citole behind.

* * *

Edson entered the first tavern he found, not even bothering to read the name on the sign. There was no time for such petty concerns. If he was going to lose his head, he was going to be drunk when the executioner took his swing. The place was empty apart from a pair of knights, who Edson vaguely recognized from the palace. He sat down at the opposite end of the bar and threw a handful of coins down.

"What's your pleasure?" the barkeep asked.

"Two flagons of whatever will get me drunk the fastest," Edson replied. His first thought had been to flee Eblok, but he didn't want to leave his citole behind. It had been a gift from Alwin, and Edson would never be able to afford another one. How had he been so stupid as to run away without it?

"That bad?"

"Worse," Edson said as the barkeep set two copper mugs in front of him, filling them both with a somewhat clear liquid. Edson took a hefty drink from one and nearly spit it back out again. "What is this?"

"It's called vodka."

"I've never heard of it."

"I received a couple barrels of it a few weeks back," the barkeep replied. "I like it mixed with a little juice, but some like it straight. Do you want some juice?"

"No," Edson replied. He didn't want anything that didn't have alcohol in it. "Just bring me a bottle of red wine. I'll use that as my juice."

The barkeep took a few of the coins before retrieving the bottle of wine. Edson left a pair finners and returned the rest to his pouch before going to work on the wine and vodka. He was halfway through each of them when one of the knights called out to him.

"Aren't you the singer the king brought in for his daughter's wedding?"

"Yes, I am. Edson Pye's the name." Lying wasn't really an option.

"I thought so," the man said. "Sing us a song. We're leaving in the morning for Voctoro."

"I don't have any of my instruments with me." Edson sympathized with them. Voctoro was one of the last places he would want to go. Although the dwarves were said to be good singers, the thought of living underground was terrifying.

"Just something simple then," the other man said. "We just want something happy to think about for a few minutes."

"I can respect that," Edson replied. He threw a few more coins on the bar and motioned the barkeep over. "Pour each of these men a bit of this vodka stuff."

Edson moved down the bar next to the men and sang them one of Alwin's ballads. It was a sad song but had a happy ending. They laughed together and drank their vodka. The soldiers bought the round after that, and they began singing together. By the time the barkeep kicked them out, they had gone through nearly a quarter of Edson's repertoire.

* * *

Once again, the pounding wasn't in Edson's head. Someone was knocking. The half dozen knights he found waiting outside his room brought the morning after Alwin's murder to Edson's mind.

There was no Aileen to pull him out of the fire this time. He considered running, but they had the way blocked.

"We've been ordered to escort you to King Jondar," one of the men said. There it was. They knew it had been him with the princess. He had heard it said that a person lives for a few seconds after their head is cut off. Edson couldn't think of a more horrible way to go.

"Right now?" he asked, struggling to come up with a way to get out of going. "I was kind of busy."

"The king doesn't wait for any man. You can come along willingly, or we can drag you. It makes no difference to me."

"I suppose I can free up a little time." If he was going to die, it might as well be with a slight bit of dignity. "Can I at least piss first?"

"Just hurry up," the man replied. "Don't even think about trying to crawl out a window or trying something equally stupid. I left a few men watching, just in case."

"Of course you did," Edson muttered under his breath as he went to the chamber pot. There were a couple swallows left in one of the bottles of wine he found along the way. He wouldn't have a chance to get drunk again before losing his head, but he could at least calm his nerves a bit. The guards formed a circle around him as they left, blocking any chance he might have to run away. They refused all his attempts at conversation along the way, and he soon found himself being led before the king.

"We've brought you the singer, your majesty," said the only knight who had spoken. He bowed and backed away with the others. Edson found himself under the glare of the king. He had never gotten on well with fathers and didn't suppose adding a royal title was going to make things any better.

"Thank you," the king said. "You may leave us."

"Of course," the man replied with a bow. He and the others left, leaving Edson alone with the king and two of his personal guards. Both looked like they would have no problem removing Edson's head if the king ordered it.

After a few moments of painful silence, the king spoke: "The wedding has been canceled." He scrutinized Edson's reaction before continuing, "It seems my daughter was caught frolicking in the garden with a thus-far unidentified man, which her betrothed took as an insult. Now I'm not only out the cost of a wedding we won't have, I've offended a potential ally and am stuck with a daughter nobody is going to want. On top of that, I paid a fortune to have you brought across the sea, and now don't even have a wedding for you to play at."

"I am sorry to hear that, your majesty," Edson replied. He fought back a smile. The king didn't know! "I'm sure your daughter will have other suitors though. I've heard she's quite beautiful."

"You heard the truth. She's also headstrong, stubborn, difficult, and a whole lot of other things. Whoever marries her is going to have his hands full."

Edson couldn't argue with that. He almost envied the man, whoever it would end up being. He couldn't think of anything to say, so simply nodded.

"I don't know where you're headed to next, but you're welcome to stay in your suite as long as you'd like. Your payment was made in advance, but I've instructed one of my attendants to give you a bonus for your troubles."

"Thank you, your majesty. You honor me with your generosity in such trying times."

“Think nothing of it. You deserve to be treated fairly. It's not like you were the one rolling around naked with my daughter in the garden.”

Edson nearly choked at that, and could only bow and back away, as the king moved on to other matters. Hopefully, the bonus would cover a new citole. If not, at least Edson still had his head.

* * *

“You didn't waste any time running out of my room yesterday morning,” Aigneis said as Edson came out of the king's hall. She seemed to have been waiting there for him. “I thought we would spend the day together.”

“My stomach was upset and I didn't want to wake you,” Edson replied. It was the truth, just not the whole truth. She handed him a pouch. “What's this?”

“Your bonus from the king. Didn't he tell you about it?”

“Yes, I just didn't expect you to give it to me.” He hadn't expected to ever see her again.

“What will you do now? Will you stay for a while?”

“Probably.” That was a lie. He planned to be gone as soon as he could find a horse to buy. “I'm not invited to guest with kings every day.”

“That's good,” she said. Her smile completely changed her face. “I was hoping we could spend some more time together.”

“I'd like that,” Edson replied. That wasn't a lie but also wasn't likely to happen. He couldn't risk being around if the king learned the truth. “I was going to clean up and get something to eat.”

“I have a lot to take care of with the wedding being

canceled. Maybe we can get together later this evening though."

"I'll be counting the minutes." He gave her a wink and his best smile.

"You're such a rogue," she said. Still, she gave him a kiss before leaving that had him reconsidering his plans for departure. One more night couldn't really hurt. A pair of knights happened to walk by then, bringing Edson back to reality. Aigneis was a wonder, and he would miss his citole, but better to lose them both than his head. He raced back to his suite. When he threw open the door, the princess was waiting inside the room. He quickly closed the door behind him.

"I was wondering if you'd ever return," she said. His citole was on the bed beside her. He wasn't sure which he was happier to see. "Is my father still angry?"

"I think he will be for some time," Edson replied. Why was he still here? He had coins, his citole, and a chance to get out of Eblok alive, yet he couldn't leave. She was too beautiful, and he still hadn't even learned her name. "Why are you here?"

"We never got a chance to finish what we started."

"You're going to get me killed."

"Some things are worth risking one's life for. Don't you think I'm such a thing? Don't you think I'm worth it?"

"You're worth more than a wretch like me." Edson picked up his citole and put it with the rest of his things in the corner. He had everything ready in case he had to flee. "I'm nobody. I was a street thief before Alwin found me. Your father plans to find you another husband. You shouldn't risk that by being here with me."

"What fun is life without risk?" She began removing her robe. She had nothing on underneath. "Have you decided yet? Am I worth risking your life for?"

Edson didn't think twice. In life, there are times when one must take chances. This was one of those times.

* * *

Edson was on his feet seconds after the princess left his room. She still refused to give him her name. Not that it really mattered at this point, for he intended to be out of the city within the hour. There was one person he wanted to say goodbye to first. He owed her at least that. Lugging his bags and collection of instruments through town quickly set him to looking for a horse trader.

He found one right away but wasn't happy with what they had to offer. Most looked to be overworked beasts of burden. He would be lucky to get halfway to Zorbelix on any of them. He found another a few blocks away and bought a piebald mare for a somewhat reasonable price. The pouch Aigneis had given him held more than he had expected. Still, it never hurt to be frugal, for that left more coins for wine.

Marla was washing dishes when he arrived at her inn. Edson stood behind her, watching for a few moments. She had a lovely behind and came with none of the added troubles the princess, or even Aigneis, brought to the table.

“Are you just going to stand there staring at my ass all morning?” she asked. How had she known? “Grab a towel and start drying.”

“I'm not so sure that's a good idea,” Edson replied. He typically broke more glasses than he successfully dried. She turned and gave him a glare that had him reaching for a towel. “I suppose I can be careful. Just don't get too angry if I break something.”

"What brings you here? Leaving already?"

"The wedding was canceled. I wanted to say goodbye before I leave for Zorbelix."

"I heard about that. There's all sorts of gossip going around. I half-assumed the whole mess was your fault."

"Don't joke about such things," Edson said. Marla looked at him and laughed, shaking her head.

"I was just joking, but now I'm not sure. You're as red as a ripe tomato. Did you seduce the princess and steal her virginity?"

"She was hardly a virgin."

"It was you! I knew it. I'm surprised the king didn't have your head chopped off."

"You're not the only one. He doesn't know though. I'd like to keep it that way, if you don't mind."

"He and I don't exactly travel in the same circles," she said before laughing again. "Though I suppose I could make a trip up to the palace on audience day. Once a month, anyone may go before the king."

"You wouldn't!"

"Probably not, but it wouldn't hurt for you to be extra nice to me just in case."

"I went out of my way to come see you before leaving," Edson replied. He thought she might be teasing him, but it was hard to tell. "Plus, I'm helping you with dishes. How much nicer do I have to be?"

"I can show you once we're finished here. If you have time for it, that is."

"I'll make time for you." The plate Edson was drying slid through his fingers and crashed to the ground, breaking into a half dozen pieces. "Sorry, it slipped."

"I guess you'll have to make up for that too. Keep it up and you'll never get out of here."

Edson smiled but was careful with the remaining dishes. She took his hand after and led him upstairs to her bedchamber. It was morning when he finally retrieved his horse from the stable. He was on the road a short time later. Leaving was harder than he thought, as all three of the women he had met in Eblok tempted him to stay. Each was special in her own way, and each was equally hard to leave behind. In the end, attachment to his own head, and a desire to keep it attached, forced his hand.

Scene Five:

Lollipops and Lovers

Princess Marla Bain, the piebald mare, proved to be as much of a handful as the three women Edson had named her after. It started about three miles outside of Eblok, when she moved to the side of the road to graze, and refused to move. Edson tried coaxing her, forcing her, bribing her, and even begging her, but nothing would get her back on the road. She only started moving when he finally climbed down from her saddle. She stayed just ahead of him, forcing him to run to keep up.

If not for the fact that she carried his reclaimed citole, along with the rest of his instruments, he would've given up and just let the horse go. Most of the morning was gone by the time he caught up to the mare. This time, she cooperated for a bit longer but eventually refused to move again. He didn't want to repeat the chase from earlier, so he waited her out. After nearly half an hour, she trotted down the road as if nothing had happened.

On the third stop, he learned the trick. While waiting out Princess—the shortened name being most apt for this fickle horse—he grew bored and took out his citole. Her ears perked up as soon as he started playing. Her head started swaying back and forth, seemingly with the beat. Her legs started moving, slowly at first, but they were soon going down the road at a steady pace. Princess was dancing, while Edson was playing and singing.

That went on throughout the afternoon and into the early evening. As long as Edson was playing or singing, Princess kept moving. The moment he stopped, she did too. Finally, they came to a small town. This time, Princess kept moving when Edson's song ended. She seemed to be as excited as he was when they stopped at the only inn Edson saw. A crude sign hanging from a bit of wrought iron named the place: The Broken Jaw Inn. It was bigger than one might expect in such a small town, and there was no music coming from within.

He walked Princess around back and left her with the stablehands, after giving them an extra dulcer to take good care of her. Perhaps she would cooperate more in the morning if she were pampered a bit. After his misadventures in Eblok and the troubles with Princess throughout the day, he was ready for a little pampering himself. He considered simply paying for a meal and room and calling it a night, but habit took over as he entered the inn. Rather than even asking, he gave in to the inevitable and broke into *She Dances Under the Moon* as he walked into the common room.

The room was nearly full. As he wrapped up the number, Edson was gifted with cheers and howls for more songs. The first of his three knives went in the air as he swung his citole around to his back. He juggled and strutted across the room, before catching the knives and bowing to more cheers. His best smile was on his face as he turned to face the innkeeper; the big man was nearly as round as he was tall. A lass, who Edson assumed to be the man's daughter based on the resemblance, stood next to him. She wasn't quite as big but was well on her way to getting there.

“I'm Edson Pye, a bard of great fame,” Edson said, looking

the man in the eyes. “In trade for enough wine to keep me playing, a hot meal and another in the morning, along with a room for the night, I'll keep everyone dancing and drinking until the early hours of morning.”

“I've heard of you,” the big lass said. “You killed your master so you could win that big competition across the sea in Vonst.”

“I was falsely accused,” Edson replied. Would that rumor follow him for the rest of his career? “All charges were dropped when multiple witnesses came forward. As far as I know, the killer still hasn't faced justice.”

“I knew I heard of you. Father, can he play here? I never met anyone famous before.”

“All I have left is a small room,” the innkeeper said. “It's yours if you want it. We're serving roasted duck tonight. I'm sure the cooks can come up with something in the morning.”

“Let's not forget the wine,” Edson said. That was the most important part of the bargain. “I could use a bit to clear the road dust from my throat. It's going to be a long night.”

“Of course,” the man replied. He turned to his daughter. “Grab a bottle of that stuff your uncle made. It's the best we have.”

Edson unpacked his instruments as he waited for the wine. He doubted he would use the harp but readied it just in case. Alwin's second lesson had covered being prepared for all possibilities. His first had emphasized the need to put everything one had into every show. There were no nights off for a true bard.

“Here you go,” said the big lass as she handed Edson a mug filled with a dark red liquid. He tried a sip first. Surprised at how good it was, he emptied the mug and returned it to her hand.

“Thank you,” he said, while picking up his citole. “That was just what I needed."

"I'll pour you another one," she replied.

"You're reading my mind now." Edson smiled before turning to face his audience. They cheered as he started with Alwin's biggest hit, *Three Fools in Love*, a humorous song about three naive suitors chasing after the same woman. He followed that with one of his own, *The Angry Farmer*. The big lass was waiting with a full mug. Edson was already feeling the kick of the first one, so he simply took a swallow before setting the mug on a table.

He played on, with the audience growing bigger and louder with every song. The place was soon filled beyond capacity. Edson kept playing and the mugs kept coming. Somewhere along the way, he stopped to plow through a plate of the duck, and nature called a couple times, but those were the only interruptions. He closed the show out with *Minstrel on the Road*, adding a nearly ten-minute instrumental to the middle of the song, during which he managed to use every instrument he owned, including Alwin's harp. The audience ate it up. By the looks of things, nobody left before the end, and every one of them came to their feet to cheer his performance.

Edson was overwhelmed by the reaction. He was finally being recognized for his talent. Was it true recognition though, or was this just another effect of Braden's card tricks? At this point, Edson no longer cared. The price had been paid already, and there would be no refunds. Alwin wasn't coming back to life. All Edson could really do was try to make the most of things.

He nearly fell as he left the stage. How much wine had he drank? The big lass was there to help him though and to hand him another mug. He smiled as he leaned against her. She had pretty eyes. How hadn't he noticed that before? Her voice was sweet too, and he wondered if she could hold a tune. Some of Alwin's songs were duets he had written with female bards. Edson had never had such an opportunity.

"This wine is really good," he said. He tried to set the empty mug down, but the table moved out of the way and the mug fell to the ground. Since when did tables move on their own? This was a strange place. Still, the wine was good, and a nice lass was holding him up so he wouldn't fall down. She started to move, so he moved with her. They stopped at the bar, where she poured another mug. At least the bar wasn't moving. "I have to put away my citole. The king can't find it or he'll chop off my head."

"This is the last mug for you," she said. He smiled and took it from her hands. "You're barely able to stand. I already told one of the barmaids to put your instruments in your room."

"There's a barmaid in my room?" he asked. He tried to stand without leaning against her and nearly fell. "She'll have to wait. I just need a little support. Dance with me."

"There's no music playing."

"I'll sing a song."

"No, you're too drunk."

"Nonsense," he replied as he kicked his heels up to do a jig. Someone moved the floor though, and he crashed to the ground. The big lass reached down and pulled him back to his feet. He laughed and started singing.

"That's it," she said, grabbing him tightly. "You're going to bed."

"I'm not that easy," he protested. "You'll have to woo me first."

Someone moved the floor again, or he would've broken free of her grip. As it was, he nearly took her to the ground. She held him tighter and pulled him up the stairs. He was singing the whole way and trying to dance. She opened the door and pulled him inside, closing the door behind them. The room was pitch black, and they nearly fell onto the bed. Edson laughed and kept singing.

* * *

Edson covered his eyes to block out the light. Someone cruel had pulled back the curtains in his room, and the sun was rudely interrupting his sleep. He had to piss anyway, so he got up to take care of both problems. He was midway through addressing the more pressing of issues, when the innkeeper's daughter walked into his room. His back was turned to her, and there was no stopping the flow, so he continued filling the chamber pot.

"You're finally up," she said, as if it were already midday. He didn't remember much after his set ended but knew it had been a late night. "Good. Everyone is downstairs with the priest. They're all waiting for you."

"Priest? For me? You're going to have to give me a bit more than that."

"We're to be married, silly. Don't you remember?"

"Of course, I remember," he said, though it was a lie. Telling a woman that you didn't remember agreeing to marry her wasn't likely to end well, especially when her extremely large father owned the inn you were staying in. Still, marriage? The very thought made Edson's skin crawl. The big lass was cute enough, and he had spent nights with his fair share of plump women without complaint, but he was nowhere near ready to settle down. He doubted he ever would be ready for that. "I'm just feeling a little rough this morning. Your uncle's wine did a number on me."

"You'll be fine once you get something to eat. The cooks are making a huge feast. Everyone's working on getting the place ready."

"Just give me a few minutes to clean up, and I'll be right down."

"I'm so happy we're doing this," she said, wrapping him in an embrace that brought back some of the memories of the night before. "I thought you only promised to marry me to get my dress off."

"Would I do such a thing?" He not only would, he could remember making and breaking such vows numerous times. "Do you think so little of me?"

"I'm sorry," she said before giving him a sloppy kiss. Her hands reached between his legs, but he pulled away.

"None of that now. You'll have to wait until tonight. Speaking of waiting, you better get down and keep everyone happy. I'll follow in a few minutes."

"Hurry up. I can't wait to be married to you!"

"I promise you that I'll move as fast as I possibly can."

He kept that promise too. As soon as the door closed, he ran straight for his bag and instruments and hauled them to the back window. There was a drop, but he was willing to risk it. He tossed his bag first, hoping it might cushion the fall of his instruments, if not him. The rebec went next. It was wrapped in leather and seemed to survive the drop. Alwin's harp followed. It was in a case and seemed fine. Alwin's flute and the tambourine Edson had made were in his bag. He held his citole as he jumped. He landed on his feet but nearly fell. As it was, he twisted his ankle. After gathering his bag and instruments, he limped to the stable.

Princess Marla Bain had her own stall and looked to have

been cleaned and brushed. She greeted him with what seemed to be a smile, as if she were amused by the whole situation. Edson smiled back and grabbed her saddle. He quickly tied his instruments and bags in place and climbed up on her back. The door was open, so he urged her forward. She, of course, wouldn't budge.

"Not now," he said. "I can't sing to you until we're on the road. Someone will hear. Get me out of town and I'll sing until my voice is gone."

She smiled again but still wouldn't move. There were other horses but that would take too long and was likely to lead him to a rope and a high branch. He reached into his bag and pulled out Alwin's flute. Putting it to his lips, he played as low as he could. Princess was having no part of that. She stomped her hooves and showed him how loud she wanted the music.

"Fine then," he said as he slid the flute back in place and swung his citole into his hands. "Let's give them a show. If we get caught, you'll be my wedding gift to the lass, and I'll never sing to you again."

He broke into *The Angry Farmer*, singing and playing as loudly as he could. Princess danced out of the stables and pranced onto the road. People streamed out of the inn and began to shout. Edson kept singing and Princess kept dancing. He would sing all the way to Zorbelix if he had to.

* * *

Edson was in a foul mood as he entered the capital city of Zorbelix. Since leaving the Broken Jaw Inn, he had lost his taste for alcohol. He blamed the big lass, suspecting she was some sort of witch, who had placed a curse on him.

Tall buildings lined the streets as far as Edson could see. Alwin had told Edson that Zorbelix was huge, but hearing about the place and seeing it were two different things. He had to find Jayme Naral's associate, Thierry Gant. All Edson had was a street name and number to go by. He asked a passerby for directions but only received a shrug and half-grin. After wandering for nearly half an hour, he found a cartographer's shop. It took Edson awhile to find the street he was looking for on the map he bought, as it was on the other side of the city.

After nearly being roped into a marriage he didn't want, Edson had avoided playing at inns for the rest of his journey. Paying for his room and meals, along with wine he couldn't bring himself to drink, had wiped out his bonus from Eblok. He was down to a few coins from his own stash. Covering the cost of a room before getting paid wasn't an option.

Fortunately, Princess Marla Bain seemed to be too preoccupied by the sounds and sights of the city to even think about being her normal pain in Edson's ass. Despite his mood, he was fascinated with the city too. Vonst was nearly as big, but there were far more people packed in Zorbelix. He would do well here. A sign on a nearby wall caught his eye. Was that his name? He moved closer to see.

COMING ATTRACTION
Exclusively at Brensworth Hall
FOUR NIGHTS WITH
EDSON PYE
Famed Bard of Vonst & Favorite to win next year's
BARDIC CHALLENGE
Limited Seating Available

Edson smiled as he read the billing. It felt good to see his name in print, not to mention being referred to as a famed bard. He found Brensworth Hall on his map. It wasn't far from where he was already heading, so he diverted his path in order to pass by the venue. He noticed dozens of other signs throughout the city, heralding his coming performances. It was good to be appreciated. His jaw nearly dropped when he saw the place. It was enormous, far bigger than any performance hall in Vonst. It was more of an arena than a hall.

“How can my voice possibly carry enough to reach all those seats?” he asked nobody in particular. Rows of bench seating circled a central stage. It would take thousands of people to fill the place.

“A wizard cast a spell upon the stage,” said a nearby woman. She had a musical voice. The hood of her cloak and her long, dark hair combined to hide her face. “Any sounds made there are amplified to carry far enough to reach everyone. You can hear the performances from out here even.”

“That's incredible,” Edson said. Why wasn't there anything like this in Vonst? “I've never even heard of such a thing.”

“Are you performing here?”

“It looks that way. I saw signs on the walls on my way through the city. I just knew I'd have a gig or two here. I didn't expect all of this.”

“Are you Edson Pye?”

“Yes.”

“I was wondering if I'd get to meet you before the shows,” she said as she pulled her hood down. She was beautiful! Her eyes were a shade of green that he had never seen before, and they took his mind into a swirl of chaos that he was determined to explore. “I'm Fayme Lobel. I'm to be your opening act for the four shows.”

“Opening act? Is that a thing here?”

“Only for the bigger shows. The crowds gather early and get restless. Giving them an opening act keeps them in line.”

“You have a beautiful voice,” Edson said. He was trying to avoid her eyes. A man could get lost looking there. “I'd love to hear you sing once I'm settled in. I have to find a man named Thierry Gant.”

“His office isn't far from here, I can show you the way, if you get down from your horse and walk with me.”

“Gladly,” Edson said. Princess was starting to get restless anyway. He hoped she wouldn't make him sing to get her moving again, though it might be worth it if Fayme were to join in. “I feel as if I've been in the saddle for days.”

“I've never ridden a horse before,” she replied as they started walking. Princess followed along without complaint. “I'm a little afraid to try.”

“It's not so bad once you get used to it. I could teach you sometime if you'd like.”

“I'll think about it. Did you really almost win the Bardic Challenge? I've always dreamed of trying to compete there.”

“I was lucky,” he replied. She had probably heard all the details. “People know me now. I'll have to be better next year.”

“You're too modest. Word of your shows reached all the way over here. That doesn't happen with many bards.”

“I'll have to take your word on that,” he said. Jayme had likely played a large role in his fame reaching across the sea. “I still say I was lucky.”

They came to Thierry Gant's office, and Fayme went her

own way, leaving Edson with instructions to an inn where she would be singing later in the evening. He was anxious to hear her voice in song. Even more, he was eager to collect his pay and learn about the four shows.

* * *

Edson's hands were shaking and his whole body seemed to itch. He hadn't been this nervous since his first gig. Brensworth Hall was packed, which meant there were over fifteen thousand people in the stands. Fayme had dazzled them with an incredible set, leaving Edson with the fear that he would be upstaged by her. She had it all: beauty, brains, and a voice to make a canary cry in shame. Edson was falling fast and hard. The thought had him considering running far away, but he was stuck. An opportunity to play shows like the four here in Zorbelix would never come his way again if he left. His career would be all but over.

There was also the pay to consider. Edson's cut of the ticket sales would net him more than he had earned since Alwin had sent him off on his own. Thierry Gant had also arranged for Edson to be the performing musician and host of the Fireball Competition at the Wizards' Fair in Eveltour. Edson would make nearly as much in that one night as he would in the four Zorbelix shows.

First, he had to get through this show. Fayme took her bows and the staff began changing the stage. All of Edson's instruments were put in place, including a pipe he had bought off a street vendor. It was easier to play than the flute and added another dimension to his show. Fayme had incorporated two backup musicians for her performance. Edson was intrigued by that possibility.

He was wearing an outfit mostly picked out by Fayme. She had taken him shopping to prepare for his shows. His boots were made from the hides of something called an alligator. Based on how Fayme described the creature, Edson hoped to never have to explain the boots to one. His shirt was silk and puffy, and in his eyes, ridiculous. She had insisted though, and he was finding it impossible to say no to her on anything. He was wearing pants of some sort that combined with his stockings to be called hoses. They looked even more foolish than his shirt, but again, Fayme had gotten her way. A feathered hat topped it all. Edson barely recognized himself in the tall mirror that stood backstage.

As he stared at himself, an image of Alwin seemed to form in the mirror, just for a brief moment. He smiled, and it faded away. Was it a sign that Edson's mentor was pleased with his opportunity, or was it that he knew Edson would fail? It had to be the former, Alwin had always wanted the best for Edson. The image was a reminder of what waited back in Vonst though. Kodran would face justice, or Edson would bring it to him personally.

“I've got them warmed up for you,” Fayme said as she stepped off the stage. Edson could only smile. He was afraid he would lose his dinner if he tried to speak. “Show them how a real bard does it.”

The applause thundered in his ears as he walked across the stage. Was he a real bard or just a fraud made popular by the card tricks of a magician? It was time to find out. A fog came out of the stage, and lights flashed from the ceiling, all part of the effects added by the wizard who had amplified the sound in the hall. Edson was prepared for that, having rehearsed on the stage twice over the past week. That hadn't prepared him for the audience. They would tear him apart if he failed to put on a good show.

His instruments were lined up for him. The harp, rebec, and citole were on stands and had been polished to a shine. Alwin's flute and Edson's new pipe sat on a bench beside his tambourine. They would be the instruments of his destruction. Someone, perhaps Fayme, had left a bottle of wine and a filled goblet. Edson was still reluctantly embracing his sobriety and feared the consequences of straying from that path. Still, it might calm his nerves. He took a sip and was surprised to find he enjoyed the taste again. Another sip gave him courage, and he took up his citole.

"This was the song that started it all," he said before launching into the song he had been singing to a lass when Alwin first found him. He hadn't sung it in ages but had discovered it was popular here in Zorbelix. The audience responded, singing along and cheering loudly. The showman in him took over, and he followed Alwin's advice, putting everything he had into the show. It was as if he became a different person on stage. His doubts were gone, replaced by a confident swagger and a refusal to put on a bad performance. The audience screamed louder with every song. Women, and some men, threw clothing at him. Many were dancing naked by the end. He closed with his tribute to Alwin Floyd. The audience cheered for more, but Edson had nothing left to give. He nearly collapsed into Fayme's arms as he left the stage and was barely able to make it to his room. The continued screams and cheers for him to return to the stage made it all worth it.

* * *

"You sing the second part," Edson said. "Wait for me to nod before you come in though."

"I remember crying myself to sleep,
Wondering if you were really there.
I remember and I start to weep,
As I run my fingers through your hair."

Edson played a few notes on his rebec before nodding to Fayme.

"I remember thinking you were a dream,
Something I made up in my head.
I remember and I want to scream,
As I hold you tightly in our bed."

They were in Edson's suite at the Duchess, a high-end inn Edson wouldn't have normally looked twice at. He could afford the finer things in life now and wanted to give them all to Fayme. For the first time in many years, he was writing a love song that he believed in. In a short time, Fayme had become his everything. He was lost in her eyes as he sang the next verse.

"I remember holding your hand,
Thinking that you were the one.
I remember and I understand,
As I realize my search is done."

Fayme stared back at him. They hadn't been apart for almost a week. With most lasses, Edson would've found a back door long ago. He had no desire to leave her, instead he was trying to figure out a way to ask her to come with him when he went north to Eveltour. She reached out and put her hand on his cheek before singing the next verse.

"I remember touching your cheek,
Wondering why you took so long.
I remember and I cannot speak,
As I lose myself in our song."

They wanted to do a duet for the show later that night. It would be Edson's final performance in Zorbelix. Tickets were going for as high as a thousand mensers. Fayme claimed it was the most in demand ticket of the entire season. Edson would be glad when it was over. He waved his hand for Fayme to join him for the chorus.

"It's all happening so fast,
I'm looking forward at last.
Before you, I was an outcast,
With you, I wash away the past.
Sing with me, sing to me,
Make me feel like I'm truly free.
Play with me, play for me,
Make me see what can truly be.
I can't change what came before,
I've already closed that door.
In your arms, I have hope for more,
I'm ready for what life has in store.
Sing with me, sing to me,
Make me smile, make me happy.
Dance with me, dance for me,
Make me see the me that you see."

They both laughed after the chorus. It was coming along but still needed work. Edson poured them some more wine. His abandonment of alcohol had ended with the first performance at Brensworth Hall. He and Fayme had spent half the night drinking and the other half in each other's arms. His moments of sobriety had been rare since. Any thoughts of a curse placed on his head by the big lass were long forgotten.

He had other concerns now. Alwin's appearance in the mirror before Edson's first performance had only been a beginning. Edson was now seeing his mentor's ghost on a regular basis and was afraid he knew why. Alwin had learned of Braden and his card tricks. Edson wouldn't be free of his ghost until Kodran was brought to justice.

"Are you doing *Three Fools in Love* tonight?" Fayme asked. "I'd like to do it but won't if you have it in your set list."

"Go ahead," Edson replied. It had been on his list, but he had plenty of others to choose from. "I'll do *Edla's Rose* instead."

"Thank you." She opened her mouth as if she was going to say something, only to close it again and look away.

"Spit it out," he said. He wasn't one for holding back and wanted her to feel comfortable speaking with him about anything. "What's on your mind?"

"I'm just wondering what will happen after the show. You have your gig in Eveltour, while I have a few performances booked here. Will we ever see each other again?"

"Of course. You're welcome to come with me. You can open up for me at the Wizards' Fair."

"I can't back out of my commitments but thank you for asking. You should return here after instead of going north to Bithe. There's nothing there besides barbarians. Plus, it will be cold by the time you get there, you'll be stuck until spring."

"I already planned to winter there," he replied. "I too have commitments that I can't back out of. You should join me, or at least meet me in Vonst for the Bardic Challenge."

"I'll try to get to Vonst. There's no way I'm going to Bithe."

"That will have to do. For now, we have each other and a song to finish. It won't be long before you're on stage."

"We have a little time," she said, placing her hand on his and looking into his eyes. He was instantly lost again.

* * *

Edson was afraid to move. The ghosts dancing around him didn't seem to be harmful, but he wasn't taking any chances. It wasn't just Alwin anymore. Anyone Edson ever knew who had died was there, including his mother. There were people there who he didn't even know had died. Were they really dead, or was this all in his mind?

Nobody else seemed to see the ghosts. Edson had mentioned them to Fayme, but she had laughed at him. She insisted he was simply feeling the effects of the wine, which was infused with henbane. The ghosts seemed real enough to him though.

They were at the after-party, celebrating Edson's final performance in Zorbelix. Everyone who was anyone in the city was supposedly there, but Edson didn't care about the living guests. He smiled and attempted to make polite conversation when forced to but otherwise avoided everyone, living or dead. He wanted the party to be over so he could be alone with Fayme. He would try one last time to convince her to come to Eveltour with him.

"Dance with me," a woman said. Edson had to look to see if

she was alive. It was Joceline Gant, Thierry's wife. Edson almost wished it had been a ghost instead. Joceline had come to the party in place of her husband, who had gone ahead to Eveltour to make the final arrangements for Edson's performance. She had mentioned how lonely she would be in her big bed to Edson five times already. If not for Fayme, he might have considered her obvious offers. He couldn't be rude to her though. Her husband was too important to Edson's career.

"I'll try," he said as he stood up. A group of local musicians played in the background. They weren't bad. "I've had far too much wine, so I may step on your toes from time to time."

"A little pain adds a certain excitement to things," she replied. Fayme smiled at Edson from across the room. She found Joceline's advances to be amusing. "I could teach you all about such things."

"I'm sure you could. Your husband might not like that though."

"Thierry? I'm sure he's enjoying the company of a young barmaid or whore somewhere right now. We've never denied each other our pleasures."

"It wouldn't be right," Edson replied. His mother's ghost was frowning at him. Did she know Joceline was married? "Besides, I'm with Fayme."

"You two are too much alike for it to ever work out. You'll figure that out eventually."

"She's everything I've ever wanted. I just didn't know I wanted it."

"Young love," Joceline said with a laugh. "Thierry and I were like that at first. Things change over time."

They made light talk as the song went on. Fayme joined

them on the dance floor, in the arms of an older man. Edson fought back jealousy, while Joceline simply smiled and gripped him a little tighter. The ghosts danced around all four of them, but again, Edson seemed to be the only one who noticed them. His mother was dancing with Alwin now. Edson closed his eyes but that only made things worse. He could still see the ghosts but not the living people.

"Come and find me when it all falls apart with Fayme," Joceline whispered in Edson's ear as the song came to an end. "I'll pick up the pieces and help you forget all about her."

She left him with a kiss on his cheek. Edson returned to his seat, but Fayme and the older man stayed on the dance floor with the ghosts. Edson poured another glass of wine. Henbane or not, he needed a drink. The band started a new song, this time doing one of Alwin's older hits. His ghost turned to watch the performance, seemingly amused, while Edson's mother danced with the ghost of a man who had been Edson's father's friend.

"Dance with me," another woman said. This one was a ghost. She was the girl Edson had been singing to when Alwin had discovered him. Edson hadn't known that she had died. He couldn't even remember her name. She was older now, as he was. "Sing for me."

Edson closed his eyes, but she was still there. She was younger though, as she was when he had last seen her. He was younger too, and they were back in Vonst. She was everything to him. He wanted to show her how much she meant to him, so he stood and sang a song. People gathered around to watch, but Edson didn't care about them. He sang to the girl alone. Halfway through the song, a tear ran down her face. A man appeared behind her and sliced her open with a knife. The man smiled and vanished. Edson screamed and was back in Zorbelix.

Everyone, both living and dead, was looking at him. The ghost of Edson's mother clutched her chest and fell to the ground before vanishing. Other ghosts died or were killed, before disappearing from Edson's sight. Finally, the only remaining ghost was Alwin. A person appeared beside him and drove a knife into his side. Edson screamed and rushed forward. The killer vanished with Edson failing to see who it was.

"No," he screamed as Alwin's ghost faded from view. Fayme was at Edson's side by then. She took him in her arms and led him away. Edson went along, not caring where they were going. He grabbed a bottle of wine from a table they passed. Everything was going to be fine, as long as he had Fayme to look out for him.

* * *

Edson nearly fell as he made his way to the window. He pulled back the heavy drapes, exposing the lie of the dark room. It was no longer night—or even morning—by the looks of things. Fayme was nowhere in sight, but the evidence of their wild night was on full display. Wine bottles were scattered about the room, along with the contents of Edson's bag. How had that happened?

Fayme wasn't in the other room either. Where had she gone? Hopefully to get breakfast. Edson felt as if he hadn't eaten for weeks. He rummaged through his clothing, looking for something remotely clean to wear. He found his coin purse. It was empty. He frowned and opened the hidden flap in his bag. The pouch he kept there was gone. In its place was a piece of paper. Edson's hands shook as he read the note.

Edson,

I'm sorry it had to end this way. I will always remember our time together fondly, but I have my own dreams to pursue.

I hope you understand. I took your rebec to remember you by.

With sincere love,

Fayme

Edson screamed. He went to his citole case, where he had stashed more coins. That pouch was gone too, as was the one he had hidden in the nightstand. Every coin he had was gone. More importantly though, Fayme was gone. Joceline's words from the night before rang in Edson's ears. How many times had Edson feigned love and left similar notes behind after rummaging through a woman's jewelry box? How many women had he left wondering if he had ever loved them at all? He and Fayme were too much alike, and he had realized it far too late.

Was this another part of Braden's magic? The big lass's curse? Did it even matter anymore? Edson had nobody to blame except himself. He had agreed to play Braden's card games, he had drunk the big lass's uncle's wine, and he had been dumb enough to fall in love. What had it gotten him? Fame? So far that had landed him in jail, forced him into the arms of Aileen, nearly gotten his head cut off, and almost stuck him in a marriage he wanted no part of. Fortune? Fayme had stolen every coin Edson had. He would earn more in Eveltour but had to get there first.

One of the wine bottles was half full. That was as close to

breakfast as he was going to get. He finished it as he gathered his things. The bottle he had taken from the party was still full, but he wanted no part of the henbane. It went in his pack for a more suitable occasion. He had to be out of the suite by the end of the day. He had nowhere to go, and only one person he could turn to. With Thierry Gant in Eveltour already, his wife was Edson's only option. Joceline had told him to come to her when it fell apart between him and Fayme. Had she expected it to happen so soon? He sighed and took one last look around the room before grabbing his things and leaving the place behind.

He went to the stables to claim Princess Marla Bain, only to discover that he owed twenty-three mensers for her time there. He promised to return later in the day with the coins. He would steal them if he had to. Princess was all he had left. First, he would go to Joceline, and do whatever it took to get an advance on his pay for the Eveltour show.

* * *

Edson was tempted to leave Alwin's harp behind. Despite already discarding half of his clothing, and anything else he wouldn't absolutely need, Edson's bag and instruments seemed to weigh as much as a large plow horse. Having Princess to carry his belongings had spoiled him. It was going to be a long trip to Eveltour if he couldn't find a way to pay her stable fees.

He had learned from one of the barmaids that Fayme had left before dawn. She hadn't told anyone where she was going. Edson doubted he would ever see her again and, at this point, wasn't sure he wanted to. She had filled the void in his heart, only to brutally empty it again. He had been taught a lesson he thought he had learned long before. Love only happened in stories and songs. In this world, all one could hope for was a bit of pleasure. Edson couldn't even afford that.

A street vendor was selling sausages on sticks. Edson tried to trade a song for one but had no luck. The smell was almost too much. He considered trying to steal one but was afraid of what getting caught might mean for his reputation and career. The same concern had stopped him from approaching an inn about securing a gig. Going from playing Brensworth Hall to pleading for a job at an inn would make him appear to be desperate. He was, but nobody needed to know that.

Finally, he reached a point where he could go no further. He dropped to the ground in an alley, laying his things beside him. His shoulders and back were throbbing from carrying the weight, and his feet were starting to ache. There was no way he would be able to carry this load all the way to Eveltour. Some way or another, he would have to get Princess back.

"Why did you do this to me?" he shouted, as if Fayme were there to answer. She was probably long gone from Zorbelix. If not, she would be in hiding. Either way, Fayme and his fortune were gone. His rebec too, which hurt nearly as much. At least she had left his citole.

Everything he had been through began crashing down on Edson's shoulders. He didn't even try to stop the tears flowing from his eyes. He cried for Alwin, for his mother, for the girl he had sung to when Alwin found him, for the women he had wronged, and most of all, he cried for Fayme. He hated the person he had become, as that same type of person had driven a dagger into his heart and exposed the farce his life had been. He couldn't hate her without hating himself.

"Are you alright, mister?" a small girl asked. Edson hadn't even noticed her approach. She looked to be around four years old, if that. There was something in her hand as she reached out toward him. "Would you like a lollipop?"

"Nothing would make me happier," he replied, forcing a smile to his face. He hadn't been much older than this girl when his mother had died. He took the candy from her hand. "Thank you."

"Were you crying?" the girl asked. The lollipop was the best-tasting thing he had ever had. How long had it been since he had enjoyed one of these? "I always sing when I feel like I'm going to cry. It cheers me up."

"Singing cheers me up too. What songs do you sing?"

"The Toad and the Bullfrog is my favorite, but Sister Maleth says I shouldn't sing it."

"She's probably right." It was nearly as bawdy as some of Edson's worst material. "What about *Three Crows in the Road*? Have you ever sung that one?"

"With my father before he died," the girl said. "It was his favorite."

"It's one of my favorites too. I'd love to sing it with you, but I'd need to know your name first. I don't sing with strangers."

"Sister Maleth says I shouldn't even talk to strangers. How will I ever meet anyone new if I don't talk to strangers?"

"That's a good question. I guess if we know each other's names, we won't be strangers anymore."

"My name is Kari Charon. What's yours?"

"I'm Edson. Edson Pye."

"You're famous! What are you doing here in an alley?"

"Talking to my new friend. Do you play any instruments, Kari?"

"No, but I want to."

"Take this," he said, pulling the pipe from his bag. He could get another later. "I'll show you how to play *Three Crows in the Road*."

"Thank you," she said. Her smile did more for Edson than all the praise he had received after his shows. He spent most of the morning with Kari, singing and teaching her how to play the pipe. He even taught her *The Toad and the Bullfrog*, after making her promise not to play it where the sisters could hear. Though the instrument barely weighed anything, his pack seemed immensely lighter when he finally continued his journey to see Joceline Gant.

Scene Six:
Apprentices and Assholes

Edson put on his saddest face as Joceline opened her door. She smiled, as if she had been expecting him. Had it been so obvious that Fayme would leave him? How had he missed the signs?

"Aren't you a sad, little puppy dog," she said, opening the door wider and motioning for him to enter. "Did the bad woman leave and break your heart?"

"She did more than that," he replied as he stepped in and she closed the door. The entryway was nearly as big as the suite Edson had stayed in. "She took everything I earned for the four shows here in Zorbelix. I have nothing left."

"That is bad. Will you be able to travel to Eveltour?"

"Not unless I can find a way to pay the stable fees for my horse and buy some feed for her. I can sleep outside and sing for my supper the whole way there. I was hoping you could give me an advance from your husband's accounts."

"He doesn't give me access to the business accounts," Joceline said. "How much do you need?"

"Fifty mensers should do it," Edson replied, purposely inflating the number by a good bit.

“That doesn't seem to be nearly enough to get you all the way to Eveltour. I was about to have something to eat. Join me and we'll come up with a better number.”

“I thought you couldn't get to your husband's accounts,” Edson observed. When had her hand come to rest on his arm?

“I said that I don't have access to his business accounts. I said nothing about our personal accounts. Thierry gives me full discretion on household spending. I can think of quite a few things you can do for me around here.”

“I'm not very good at fixing things or yard work.”

“Who said anything about such tasks? You seem to like adding additional meanings to my words. I'm a simple woman. I think we both know what I want from you.”

“What about your husband?”

“We talked about that last night. He wouldn't mind.”

“What about Fayme?”

“What about her? She's gone.”

“I still love her,” Edson said. Was that the truth though? Had he ever truly loved anyone? Could he? “I can't stop thinking about her.”

“Think about her all you want. I don't care. Imagine it's her you're with instead of me. It won't make my experience any less pleasurable.”

Joceline moved in and kissed Edson. He didn't fight it and soon was kissing her back. Fayme had made the decision to leave, Edson had no choice other than to move on. As far as he could see, Joceline was the only path open for him to do so. He couldn't walk to Eveltour.

* * *

"It was twenty-three mensers this morning," Edson said. The stable master wanted twenty-five now. Edson was sure he was skimming.

"That was this morning," the man replied. "The horse has been here all day."

"Fine," Edson said as he counted out the extra coins. Joceline had given him three hundred mensers. It would be more than enough to see him through to Eveltour, providing he was careful. He was never careful. "I'll take my horse now."

"I'll see if we can get her out of her stall. She's a stubborn one."

"Tell me something I don't already know. Take me to her, I'll get her moving."

"If you say so. Just watch your step. We sweep the stables regularly, but the horses have no discretion with their droppings."

"It's not my first time in a stable. I'll be fine."

Princess's ears perked up as Edson approached. It had been nearly a week since he had last come to visit the horse. He hoped she would be too pleased to see him to put up much of a fuss. It seemed to be working, as she was friendly as could be, right up until he tried to get her to come out of her stall. The stable master and his helpers laughed as Edson begged and pleaded. Finally, he took out his citole and began to play. Princess danced out of the stall, barely stopping to allow Edson to climb into the saddle.

The horse was having no part of him stopping his music. Edson gave up and put on a show from her back as they rode through the city. Children followed along, laughing at the dancing horse. Remembering the girl with the lollipop, Edson played *Three Crows in the Road*. The children sang and danced, which only encouraged Princess.

Finally, they came to the Shady Tree Inn, which stood at the northern edge of the city. Edson wanted to sleep there for the night and get an early start in the morning. A few coins paid for a room for him and a stall for Princess, along with meals for both of them. Edson was tempted to share hers after one taste of the chicken stew he was served. The meat had a texture unlike any chicken he had ever eaten. The potatoes were undercooked and earthy, while the carrots were soggy. The whole thing was over-peppered. Edson forced down enough to silence the angry growls of his stomach and turned to the bottle of wine he had splurged on.

The innkeeper had offered to provide his room and meal for free if he would play a couple songs, but Edson had refused. He had to arrive in Eveltour with his reputation intact. Playing in a common inn on the road would be fine but doing so in Zorbelix would make him the butt of countless jokes. He would be much better off simply drinking until he passed out.

* * *

"I fell in love a short time ago,
With a girl who was so fair.
She stole my heart and stole my soul,
With her green eyes and wavy hair."

Edson stood on a street corner. The only instrument he carried was his tambourine, so he kept a beat with that and his stomping feet as best he could. The only audience was three empty wine bottles and the full one he had just opened.

"I loved her and she loved me,
At least that's what I thought.
But all of those kisses I'd thought were free,
Turned out to be something I'd bought."

Underneath it all, that had been all this was. Fayme had pretended to fall in love with him in order to get his coins. What was the difference between that and a whore?

"I smiled and told her I loved her,
She left me holding the bill.
For I'd found a whore when I wanted a lover,
If she'd have me, I'd be with her still."

A passerby tossed a coin in Edson's empty wine goblet. He almost laughed but came just as close to crying. If her actions made her a whore, what did that make him?

"I wanted love, but found only heartbreak,
Falling in love was my first mistake.
My second was thinking that she loved me,
For that was a lie, as anyone can see.
So now, I no longer believe in romance,
Give me a new partner each night for my dance.
And if I'm alone when it's my time to die,
Fetch the whore to kiss me goodbye."

A man and a woman passed by as he finished the chorus. The man frowned, but the woman's eyes lingered as they passed. If Edson wasn't so drunk, he would steal her away from the man for the night. That was all he was good for. A night of fun and a broken heart in the morning. If that was the way it was going to be, then he was determined to be the one doing the breaking. Being on the other end was too painful.

He drank the last of the wine. Hadn't he just opened that bottle? Was there a hole in it? The lights were still on in the Shady Tree Inn, so Edson fished in his pouch for a couple coins. He would just have to tighten his belt a little more on the journey to Eveltour. That was a problem for another day.

* * *

Edson and Princess Marla Bain were having a competition to see who could be more stubborn. The horse wouldn't move unless Edson played a song, which he refused to do because of a splitting headache. This left them stuck in the road, less than fifty paces from the Shady Tree Inn. It was a wonderful start to Edson's day.

In fairness, the day had been bad even before Princess's antics. It had started with an eager housekeeper, anxious to prepare Edson's room for the next tenant. That had been followed by a dispute over Edson's bill and the number of bottles of wine he had consumed the night before. There was no way he had finished seven bottles. When did innkeepers become so dishonest? Had Edson simply avoided this in the past by singing to cover his bill?

He might have paid the bill without complaint if he had been allowed to get a full night of sleep. Who gets up before ten anyway? He had skipped breakfast, not wanting to chance the cooks from the night before working a double shift. To make matters even worse, a light rain was falling. His citole and Alwin's harp were wrapped tightly and wouldn't see a drop, but the day was only going to get worse for Edson and Princess.

"Are you Edson Pye?" an older man asked. He had a woman and a young lad with him. Edson had never seen any of them before.

"Yes, but I'm not performing today. My last performance in Zorbelix was two nights ago."

"We're not here to see you perform," the woman said. She shoved the lad forward. "This is Porter. He's a singer. We were hoping you might take him on as an apprentice. We're willing to pay a fee."

"An apprenticeship to a bard can take five years or more," Edson replied, fighting back the refusal he had almost given. He wasn't ready for an apprentice, but a fee would allow him to be comfortable, rather than frugal, on the journey to Eveltour. "I'll be sailing across the sea in the spring. There's a good chance that I won't be back in Aern any time soon."

"We understand all of that," said the older man. "There are no true bards on this side of the sea."

"I can't guarantee his safety," Edson said. He wouldn't guarantee much of anything for that matter. "There are dangers on the road, and some of the places I play aren't the safest in the world."

"I can take care of myself," Porter said. "I've taken lessons in sword fighting."

"Impressive," Edson said, though he thought the opposite. He had no intention of being in any fights, especially ones involving swords. "I'm leaving for Eveltour now. How long would it take you to be ready?"

"I just have to get my horse out of the stable and grab my

bag," Porter replied. "Does that mean you'll take me?"

"If we can come to terms on a fee, I'll give you a try."

"You mother and I will handle the negotiations," the older man said to Porter. "Go get your horse and things. We'll have it worked out by the time you get back."

Edson smiled as Porter left. For a reason Edson couldn't figure out, they were desperate to have Porter leave with him. It was time to find out just how desperate they were.

"I'm trying to come up with a fair number," Edson said. That was a complete lie. Any number he suggested would be far from fair. "I'll have to provide food and boarding for him and his horse for up to five years, plus pay for his passage across the sea, and eventually back. Then there's my time. I'll have to work with him every day, especially at first. Did you have a number in mind?"

"I haven't put much thought into it," the man replied. That meant he could afford the price, no matter how high it was. "How much did your father pay when you were apprenticed?"

"I have no idea." Edson's father had always been a miser. There was no way he would ever have paid an apprentice fee, especially for something such as music. "Besides, that was years ago, and there was no ship fare to factor in. I'm thinking three thousand mensers up front, plus another two thousand per year. That should cover all expenses, plus a little for my time."

"You won't be able to contact us for the future payments," the man said. He tossed a heavy pouch to Edson. "I'll make this easy. There are fifty tulners in the pouch. I'll also give you letters of credit for another fifteen thousand mensers. That should buy us a little more reassurance that you'll look after the boy."

"That sounds fair," Edson replied. He had thrown out a high first offer, thinking it would be negotiated down. Instead, the man had increased the amount and was paying up front. If he had known it would pay so well, Edson would've taken on an apprentice long before this. “Say your farewells to Porter when he gets back. I have to go buy extra supplies for the road, since I'm no longer traveling alone. I'll return here when I'm finished.”

Ceding the competition to Princess, Edson sang a happy number. Princess seemed to laugh, before dancing down the street. Edson laughed along with her. The day was starting to look much better.

* * *

“You're too quiet,” Edson said for at least the fourth time. He had been trying all afternoon to get Porter to talk, but the lad still wouldn't say more than two words unless asked a direct question. “You'll have to get over that if you're going to be a successful bard. The stage is no place for shyness.”

“This is my first time away from home.” That had been obvious from the start. Edson would gladly wager what was left in the pouch from Joceline that the lad's bag had been packed by his mother. He would double the bet on there being a packet of sweets hidden away as a reminder of home. “I'm still a little in shock.”

“Why were your parents so anxious to ship you off with me?”

“Conrad isn't my father,” Porter replied. That connected some of the dots. “When my half-brother was born a few years back, it was only a matter of time before I would have to go. Mother told me they would be apprenticing me to a master bard this year. I didn't believe her. I guess I underestimated how badly Conrad wanted me gone.”

"I won't have any problems collecting on these letters of credit, will I?"

"He wouldn't risk you bringing me back to him. Conrad inherited a fortune. Whatever he paid you is nothing to him."

"What happened to your father?"

"I have no idea. Mother would never tell me who he was or anything about him."

"From my experience, fathers are pricks." Edson could barely remember what his father looked like anymore. Would they even recognize one another if they passed on the street? Did it matter? "I doubt you really missed anything. Let's move off the road a bit and make camp for the night."

According to Edson's map, there was an inn a few miles away, but he wasn't ready to deal with people yet. It was bad enough being saddled with Porter. There had been one unexpected perk to taking on an apprentice. Princess had taken a liking to Porter's horse and had been on her best behavior. Edson hadn't been forced to sing or play all day.

"This spot will do," Edson said a short time later. There was enough flat space in a small valley for them to be comfortable. Edson set Porter to gathering wood, while he took the packs and saddle off of Princess. There were enough small branches laying around to get a fire going before Porter brought back his first load. Edson kept the fire small, just big enough to build up coals for cooking. He had splurged on a pair of bison steaks and some potatoes. They would eat at inns most nights, but Edson prided himself on being able to cook a decent meal when he needed to.

He opened a bottle of wine as the meal cooked and offered some to Porter, who declined. What kind of bard refused wine? The lad had a lot to learn. Edson tried to remember Alwin's first lesson, which seemed like a lifetime ago. He had tested Edson, trying to see what his strengths would be. That would be a good place to begin. Patience would be needed as the lad would be raw. That meant more wine. Edson had a small cask and five bottles. He hoped it would be enough to see him through the next day. Music was always better with wine. Then again, not much wasn't.

"Let's have a look at your lute," Edson said after they had eaten and Porter had cleaned the dishes. The second bottle of wine was half gone, and Edson felt he had built up a sufficient reserve of liquid patience. "I haven't played one of these in some time. Nearly every bard in Vonst plays one, which is a big part of why I picked up the citole. I wanted to be different."

"It was a gift from my mother," Porter said as he handed Edson the instrument. It was a beauty, as far as lutes go. Porter's mother had likely spent a fortune on it. "She gave it to me last year. She was the one who introduced me to music. I was taking lessons from a man named Marcus, but he left to visit his family."

Edson played one of Alwin's early hits. The lute was tuned perfectly, and Edson's fingers glided along the frets. He could get used to playing an instrument of this quality. Perhaps he would use some of his earnings to find Welby and commission him to make a new citole. That and another rebec. Thinking of that brought Fayme to mind and started Edson down a dark path that only wine could divert him from. He returned the lute to Porter and took up the bottle instead.

"Let's see what you have," Edson said, preparing himself for the worst. "Play me your favorite instrumental. We'll do some singing in a bit. I just want to hear you play for now."

He played a song Edson had never heard. It started slow but built in tempo and volume until it reached a hectic, but pleasing, conclusion. The lad was gifted. He had no flare, but he had skill. The rest would come with confidence, which was the true thing Porter needed.

"That was good," Edson said. Too good. If Edson wasn't careful, the boy was likely to show him up. The second bottle of wine was empty. Was Porter sneaking drinks when Edson wasn't looking? "Let's hear you sing now. Do you know the words to *The Toad and the Bullfrog*?"

"The tavern song?"

"Yes. Do you know the words?"

"Of course."

"Sing it then, I'll play the music."

Despite being a bawdy tavern song, it had a good beat and a catchy hook, which was likely the reason why the little girl, Kari, had loved the song. It also required a good range if one were to sing it properly. That, and the reminder of the little girl who had saved him from himself, was why Edson had picked it.

Edson played the song on his citole, but the rebec would've been better. The lad came in at just the right time and nailed the pitch. His voice was strong and didn't waver when he needed to hold a note. There were a few spots where his tempo was slightly off, but otherwise the lad was perfect. How was that even possible? Edson had been terrible when he first started. Who was this man who had taught Porter?

"That's enough for tonight," Edson said when the song was finished. He could only imagine what else the boy was capable of. He could probably juggle four knives while dancing and singing. The cork finally came out of the third bottle. Edson didn't bother filling his goblet. Drinking from the bottle was faster. "We'll be hitting the road early tomorrow morning."

* * *

"Make sure they brush Princess down," Edson said as he grabbed his citole. They were far enough from Zorbelix for Edson to put on a performance. He wasn't worried about the pay but would haggle just to keep the innkeeper honest. "After that, bring our bags in. Be careful with Alwin's harp. Not even Conrad could afford to truly replace that."

Edson left the lad to his tasks. The Fallen Log Inn wasn't even on Edson's map. Finding it had been a pleasant surprise in what had been mostly a miserable day. It had rained off and on most of the day, stopping just long enough each time to give the illusion that they would actually dry off. The only other real bright spot had been watching the lad try to juggle. At least there was one thing he couldn't do.

The inn was a large, log building. It stood three stories tall and had an attached stable. Edson had his citole on his back as he entered. He held three colored balls in his hands. They went into the air as he approached the bar. He juggled them with one hand, keeping the other free for wine.

"Greetings, friend," Edson said to the gray-haired barkeep. "I noticed that you have no entertainment this evening and thought I might be able to fill the void."

"Crowd's light tonight," said the barkeep. Edson didn't argue, but he had played for smaller audiences. "I can't pay any more than a room and a meal."

"Throw in my wine for the night and you have a deal."

"I've drunk wine with bards before. That's a price I can't afford to pay."

"You're a smart man," Edson said. "How about a room for me and another for my apprentice, and food for both of us. He'll be in with our bags any moment."

"I can do that, as long as you're buying your wine."

"Deal." Edson would have played for free if not for the principle. He threw one of the tulners from the pouch on the bar, while deftly keeping the balls in the air. "That should cover most of the night. I'll take a bottle now to get me started."

"I don't want a drunkard driving off my customers," the man replied. He reached under the bar and grabbed a bottle. "Take it easy on this."

"I'm insulted by that," Edson replied. He may be a drunkard, but he would never drive off an audience. These people would get a show to rival the four he had put on in Zorbelix. He raised his voice to allow everyone to hear him. "I'm Edson Pye. I once drank a bottle of wine standing on one foot, while juggling flaming torches, in high winds. I filled Brensworth Hall in Zorbelix four times and was drunk for every performance. If you have any complaint with my show, you can keep the tulner, and I'll give you another. Just don't deny me my wine."

"Easy, friend. I'm just looking out for my patrons. I didn't know who you are. I've heard of you. The first bottle of wine's on me."

"Thank you," Edson replied. He kept the balls in the air as he emptied the goblet the barkeep had filled. "Keep it coming."

The lad was coming through the door as Edson turned to face the audience. Porter might have a magical voice and natural ability with his lute, but Edson had stage presence. He had confidence, and knew how to work an audience. Tonight would be the lad's first real lesson. Edson swung his citole around into his hands, and the show began.

* * *

"Are we going to have a lesson today?" Porter asked. They had made camp early, as there was nothing close on the map. Edson had just opened his first bottle of wine for the day, and the lad was already becoming an annoyance.

"No," Edson replied. "I'm going to get drunk. If you'd join me, you might really learn something."

"Either that, or we'd both be useless."

"Useless? That's what my father always said I'd be. It's good to finally live up to his expectations."

"He sounds like a smart man."

"He was an ass," Edson said before taking a drink of wine. "I'm sure he still is, if he's still alive. He'd probably like you though."

"What's that supposed to mean?"

"Nothing bad. The opposite, in fact. He was always on me for everything I did wrong. You never do anything wrong, so he'd probably like you."

"Yet you don't."

"I barely know you," Edson said, yet there was some truth to Porter's words. Underneath it all, Edson didn't like him. Something about the lad reminded Edson of someone, but he couldn't figure out who. Then there was the lad's natural talent. He would be one of the great bards. Edson had dreamed of that himself and held out hope that he would be remembered among the best, but Porter would outshine him within a couple years. "I'm not used to the idea of having an apprentice yet. It's going to take some time."

"You'll never get used to it if you don't work with me," Porter replied. "I just want to learn."

"How about we make a deal then? You drink with me tonight, and we get to know each other. Tomorrow, we'll begin your lessons."

"As long as you promise to stick to that, I'll try some of your wine. I don't know if I'll like it though."

"Have you never had a drink before?"

"I tried something called beer once. I didn't care for it."

"It's not my favorite," Edson replied. It was too heavy for him. He could enjoy wine before, during, and after dinner. With beer, he would pass out from gluttony before drunkenness, which was his preferred reason for passing out. "Though Alwin once took me to visit some monks who brewed a recipe that would make me consider giving up wine."

"Conrad always said that alcohol was the ruin of good men."

"Conrad's an ass too. Fuck him."

Porter actually laughed at that. Edson couldn't remember seeing the lad do that before. Hopefully, the wine would open him up a bit. The bottle Edson had opened was too bitter for someone not accustomed to the subtleties of a good wine, so Edson opened a bottle of cheap red instead.

"Try this," he said, passing the bottle over to Porter. "Take a little sip and let it sit on your tongue for a moment."

Porter's face puckered up slightly with the first taste, but he smiled at the end. He took a bigger drink before passing the bottle back. Edson stayed with what he had been drinking. He always started the day with his best wine. After a bottle or two, even the cheap stuff tasted good.

“That's not bad,” Porter said. “It's almost like juice.”

“Have some more,” Edson said, passing over the bottle. This was what he missed the most about traveling with Alwin. Singing with him was incredible, and Edson had loved the lessons, but none of that beat getting drunk together in the middle of nowhere. They talked about things Edson had never shared with anyone else. He didn't know if he and Porter would ever share such a bond, but one thing was certain, they would never do so sober.

They talked for a bit about their musical influences. Edson was pleased that Porter listed Alwin among his favorites but wasn't happy when Kodran joined him on the list. After a bit, Edson had finished his bottle of wine and took the bottle of red for a swallow, rather than getting up to get another bottle. He took a drink and was surprised at the taste. This wasn't the red! It was the last bottle of henbane-infused wine, and the lad had already drunk a third of it. Edson laughed and tipped back the bottle. It was going to be a fun night, and he had a bit of catching up to do.

Scene Seven:
Witches and Wizards

"The hardest part is getting close enough," Edson explained. He was trying to explain to Porter how to pick pockets, but the lad was having no part of it. "People are suspicious of strangers. If their eyes are on me though, they won't be watching you."

"It's stealing though," Porter replied. "It's wrong."

"What about those who stop and watch our shows in the street without leaving even a finner. Isn't that stealing?"

"That's different."

"Is it really? Our music is our trade. If I went into a tavern and helped myself to the wine, you would call it stealing. If I had a smith put new shoes on Princess and refused to pay that would also be theft. Where's the difference?"

"It's just different," Porter insisted. "You told me yourself that you play mostly because you love the music. The same isn't true for the barkeep or blacksmith."

"I've never heard of a good blacksmith who didn't love their trade, and most barkeeps I know do better with the lasses than I do on my best days. Let's see if you still feel this way when you're wet, hungry, and haven't a coin to your name. Morals are a great thing to have but so are a full belly and a warm bed."

"I guess, though I'd have to be starving to even consider resorting to thievery."

"You'll get there at some point if you want to be a bard. It's not the life of glamour most think it is."

"That's one lesson I've already learned," Porter said. They came to the top of a hill and saw Eveltour in the distance for the first time. Multicolored towers took on all sorts of shapes and seemed to compete to reach the sky. This was a city of legend, built by magic during the time of the Council of Nine. Mergerok, the only surviving member of the Nine, lived in the tallest of the two hundred towers that made up most of the city.

"That's a sight I'll never forget," Edson said as they stopped to take in the scenery. "That's also the biggest lesson for today. Perhaps the best part about being a bard is getting to see the wonders of the world, but you have to remember that you aren't just seeing them for yourself. Soak in this vision, remembering the special details that stand out. Use those in the future if you ever have to describe Eveltour in a song or story. Learn to make your audience feel like they're visiting the places you describe and you'll go far."

"What about the visions I had a few nights back? Am I to describe those as well?"

"I already said I was sorry," Edson replied. He certainly hadn't meant to have the lad drink the henbane-infused wine. They had spent the night chasing each other's hallucinations. Edson's visions had included another appearance by Alwin's ghost, who was angry at Edson for the lad's condition for some reason. "I never would've given you that wine if I'd known what it was."

"I'm just giving you a hard time. I actually had fun for the most part. Are you nervous about your show?"

"Any man who says he isn't nervous when dealing with wizards is either lying, a fool, or a lying fool."

"Will we get to watch the Fireball Competition?"

"I'll be hosting the event," Edson said. He wasn't even sure what that meant but knew he was being paid a lot. That was all that really mattered. "You'll be helping me, but I'm sure you'll get a chance to watch."

"I'll have to watch," Porter replied. "As you said, I'm not just seeing it for myself."

Edson laughed and urged Princess forward. Her cooperation continued, as did their journey.

* * *

The streets of Eveltour curved around the towers and gardens of the city. Edson was thoroughly lost within twenty minutes. Porter was no help. The lad resembled a country yokel on his first trip to a city, with his head turning back and forth and his jaw hanging wide open. Not that Edson blamed him. Where most cities would have singers and jugglers entertaining passersby, Eveltour had magicians. They weren't doing sleight-of-hand magic, like Edson dabbled in, but were instead using real magic for entertainment. It was both horrifying and thrilling at the same time. Could a bard even make a living in such a place?

"How is a person supposed to find their way through this maze of a city?" Edson asked. It was complete madness. None of the streets went straight for more than a hundred steps or so, and there were few signs to show what the street names were.

"Just ask one of the golems for help if you're lost," a man

said. He pointed at a statue across the street. Edson and Porter had passed by dozens like it, in the oddest places and poses. “They can give directions or even guide you to your destination. Just tell them where you want to go. They'll also carry loads or help with simple tasks. At night, they pick up trash and sweep the streets.”

“Are you serious?” Edson was sure the man was messing with him. It was probably a popular local joke to play on people from out of town. Then again, this was a city built by wizards.

“Completely. There are thousands of them scattered throughout the city. They would help defend us if anyone was ever foolish enough to attack Eveltour.”

“Thank you for your help, sir.” Edson decided it wouldn't hurt to see if the man told the truth. The worst that could happen was the man and his friends getting a laugh at Edson and Porter. Getting laughs was a large part of Edson's job.

The statue was of a man who looked to be of noble bearing. Edson approached cautiously. Princess sniffed at the statue as if she knew there was something odd about it. Edson could almost smell the magic himself.

“Statue,” he said loudly, “I'm lost and need help finding my way.”

“Please say directions if you want directions,” the statue said, in a deep, monotone voice. Princess voiced her displeasure with the statue talking and backed away a couple steps. “Please say guide if you want to be guided to your destination.”

“Can you guide me to where I need to go?”

“You have chosen to be guided. Thank you. I am pleased to be of service. Please tell me where you wish to be guided.”

“Incredible,” Edson said, unable to believe what he was seeing.

“I do not know where that destination is. Please select another destination or give me a new command.”

“I want to go to the Crystal Cavern Inn and Tavern,” Edson said. That was where he was supposed to meet Thierry Gant.

“The Crystal Cavern is located on Nightshade Lane. If this is your destination, please say yes.”

“Yes, that's where I want to go.”

“Thank you. We will begin our journey in one minute. If you would like me to wait longer, please say wait.”

“Don't wait, I want to go now.”

“You have requested that I wait. I will remain here until you are ready to go to the Crystal Cavern Tavern. When you are ready, please say ready.”

“I'm ready to go now.”

“You have indicated that you are ready. Thank you. We will begin our journey in one minute. If you would like me to wait longer, please say wait.”

“This thing is useless,” Edson said. “What kind of fool would design such a thing?”

“I think it's incredible,” Porter said, still gaping. Edson couldn't really argue, though he was a little frightened of what else the statues might be capable of. One thing was certain, he would be a happier man once the show was finished and he could leave this city of wizards.

The statue started moving a few seconds later. Princess wanted no part of following, even when Porter's horse went ahead. Edson was forced to take out his citole and play a song as they went. She didn't dance this time, but the music worked to get her moving. Edson urged her forward and they caught up to Porter and the statue.

* * *

"Many years have passed without mention of Zelkof or the black star, yet Mergerok remains vigilant to this day." Edson was finishing a telling of *Wizard's Demise*, which was a story originally penned more than a century before. Nobody knows who wrote the tale, or if it was a true depiction of the fall of Zelkof and the Council of Nine, but Mergerok had never challenged it. Most storytellers, including Edson, would put in subtle changes to keep the story fresh.

The audience stood and cheered. This was the second of three shows Thierry had arranged in addition to the already scheduled hosting of the Fireball Competition. Despite the smaller venues, Edson was making more in Eveltour than he had in Zorbelix. He and Porter would live well in Bithe through the winter.

"That is how the Council ceased to be." Edson didn't believe much of the story. Thierry had insisted he tell it, which was a good call. Anything involving Mergerok seemed to be popular in Eveltour. "And that concludes the first set of my show. I'm going to leave you with my apprentice, Porter Rence. Please give him a hand."

The audience clapped with little enthusiasm as Porter came onto the stage. This was the lad's first test. Edson had kept him out of the first show but wanted to see how he would handle being in front of an audience.

“When I've fought my final battle and it's time for me to die,
Lay me across my saddle, and hold your weapons high.
Celebrate me in my glory, for this is no time to cry.
Sing my song, tell my story, and give me a proper goodbye.”

Edson had picked the song for Porter to sing. *Soldier's End* was an old song and had numerous versions, depending on where it was being sung. Fortunately, one of the versions Alwin had taught Edson was the one favored in Eveltour. He had passed it on to Porter. It was serving two purposes. The first was highlighting Porter's amazing voice. Since beginning to work with the lad, Edson's attitude had changed greatly. He now saw the lad's inevitable success as an extension of his own, rather than a threat to it. The second purpose was to put the audience in a somber mood. Edson had started that with his telling of *Wizard's Demise*. Porter would nearly have them in tears by the time he was finished. Edson would open with a series of songs he had picked to lift everyone's moods. The emotional swing would make the performance even more memorable.

“When I die take up my sword, wield it proudly, wield it true,
Say a prayer, say a word, say whatever comes to you.
Set my body upon a pyre, give me my honors due,
Say a prayer, light me on fire, if you die, I'll do this for you.”

The lad was hitting the notes perfectly. The only thing Edson would fault him on was his reluctance to look up at the audience. He needed to get over his shyness. If he could do that, his apprenticeship had the potential to be as short as Edson’s had been.

“He has a beautiful voice,” a woman said. She was a few

years older than Edson, yet wasn't wearing a wedding ring, which was the local custom. Her blond hair had a slight red tint to it, and her eyes were as deep a shade of blue as Edson had ever seen. "Where did you find him?"

"Zorbelix," Edson replied. "This is his first time on stage."

"That's impressive. You must be proud."

"I am, though I had little to do with it. He just needs some confidence."

"I can help with that," the woman said. "In my experience, the root of most men's confidence lies between their legs. Has he even been with a woman?"

"I don't know," Edson said. She was only interested in the lad. "The topic never came up. We're staying at the Crystal Cavern, perhaps you and a friend could come by for drinks after the show?"

"Perhaps we could."

"We'll be there either way," Edson replied. The kid was coming to the end of the song, and Edson hadn't even gotten a drink yet. "If you'll excuse me, I need to hit the bar and get back on stage."

She smiled and sent him on his way. Edson put the odds at even that she would show up at the Crystal Cavern. The odds of her bringing a friend were far less. This led him to the dark-haired woman at the end of the bar, and a night he would remember for a long time.

* * *

Edson had never been so happy to finish a show. He took his bows, and even did two encores, but nearly ran off the stage at the end. The dark-haired woman had promised to show him around the city. He had already forgotten her name, but that was nothing new. The important thing was that she had stuck around like she promised. Not all women did that. Fayme hadn't.

"Drinks before we leave?" Edson asked as he approached her. "My throat gets a little raw after shows."

"We can't have that," she replied. "I have wine in the carriage. We can open a bottle."

"You say all the right things. Lead the way, darling."

Edson looked back on the way out. Porter was packing away the instruments and would make sure everything got back to the Crystal Cavern, where he would hopefully be surprised by the blond woman. She was most likely right about his confidence. Edson's first experience had done wonders. Porter needed the same.

"Where are you staying?" the dark-haired woman asked. Her carriage was an elaborate thing, which had no horses or other beasts of burden to pull it. Would the statues push or pull them around the city? That seemed unlikely.

"The Crystal Cavern," he replied. The entire tower was carved from a large crystal. The innkeeper claimed it had been brought there from another world by a powerful wizard. Edson didn't know enough about such things to know if it was true or not, but he had never heard of such a crystal anywhere on Elraon.

"I like that place."

"It's a little odd, but the beds are comfortable." Sometimes a little nudge was all it took.

"I wouldn't know," she said as they sat down in the carriage. Edson was surprised when it started moving on its own. The dark-haired woman laughed and took a bottle of wine from a compartment. The carriage ride was much smoother than riding in a horse-drawn one. It was almost as if they weren't even moving at all.

“Is there anything not done by magic here in Eveltour?” Edson asked. If he could get past his distrust of the arcane, the place would be wonderful.

“Many things are still done with manual labor. Much of the magic you see, such as the golems or this carriage, is old. A large portion of it came from Korci, and the knowledge of its workings vanished with him.”

“I never believed most of the legends about him. Since coming to Aern, I've started to question that. Every city seems to have stories and statues of him.”

“I would imagine that would be most true in Eber and the surrounding area. He spent most of his time there, and it was the last place him and Trig were seen.”

“I started writing a song about the two of them but never finished it. I should plan a trip there in the near future.”

The small talk and light flirting continued between the two of them as they toured the city. It really was a beautiful place, though most of it terrified Edson. Even without considering the carriage, statues, and streetlights, it wasn't possible to go more than half a block without a glaring reminder of those who had built it all. After a while, he barely noticed things that would have once amazed him.

“What is this place?” Edson asked. They had stopped at one of the largest towers in the city.

“This is my home,” the dark-haired woman replied. “I thought I'd show you what a real bed feels like.”

“As I said earlier, you say all the right things. Lead the way, darling.”

The door opened as they approached. More magic, but

Edson was starting to expect such things. The entranceway opened up to a large sitting room. A bar on the far wall seemed to be well stocked. Elaborate carvings and paintings covered the walls. Everything about the place screamed wealth. Who was this woman? Was there a husband? While such things wouldn't normally bother Edson too much, it was different in Eveltour. If there was a husband, there was a good chance of him being a wizard.

"Pour a glass of wine and sit down," the dark-haired woman said. "I'm going to change into something more comfortable."

Edson smiled and went to the bar. Everything was of the highest quality. He filled two glasses with wine and took a seat. Music began playing. Surprisingly, it was one of his songs. He jumped to his feet when the singing started—it was his voice! Just then, the dark-haired woman walked back into the room, stopping as if to give him a view. She was wearing only a black slip that barely covered anything.

"I thought hearing yourself play and sing might relax you," she said. It was actually nice to hear himself as others did, but he was uncomfortable with the fact that magic had obviously been used to copy his voice. There was a lot of potential for such magic though. Selling copies of his performances at shows could make him a rich man.

The dark-haired woman regained his attention: "I tend to make men nervous."

"I don't know why that would be," Edson said. "Everything else in this city has made me nervous, but you haven't."

"I have a bit of a reputation," she said as she started walking toward him. "Most men avoid me, other than the brave and the foolish. Which are you, Edson?"

“I've never been called brave, but I've been called a fool more than a few times.” She stopped about four paces away from him. She raised a hand and the lights dimmed. Edson's wine glass floated from his hand and came to rest on the table next to her glass. What was this? Was she some sort of witch? Edson tried to ask her, but his jaw wouldn't move. He tried to stand, but something was holding him in place.

“I'll let you move again in time, darling,” she said. “You see, I like to play a little rough. It wouldn't do to have you trying to run away.”

Edson again tried to speak but still couldn't. The air rippled, and the buttons on his shirt came undone. Flames leaped from her fingertips and shot toward him, stopping just short, yet close enough to burn much of the hair on his chest. She closed the distance between them and placed her hands on his shoulders. Intense heat flowed from her fingertips. It seemed to go right through his skin, before racing through his body. He nearly went into shock as his internal temperature rose dramatically. Just when he thought he was going to pass out, the pain stopped. She sat beside him and caressed his hair. Tears ran down her face, as if she were the one who had suffered the pain.

“I'm sorry,” she said. “Let me make it up to you.”

She began kissing and touching him. He was still unable to move, but she climbed on top of him and did all the work. After, she cried once more. The pain began again a few minutes later and lasted deep into the night, intermixed with brief moments of pleasure. Edson's music played in the background all the while and he began to hate his own voice.

* * *

Edson leaped out of the carriage as soon as it came to a stop in front of the Crystal Cavern. If he wasn't obligated to play another show, and to host the Fireball Competition, he would have run straight to the stables, climbed on Princess's back, and never looked back. As it was, he was stuck in Eveltour for a few more nights. He doubted he would ever return.

While there had been some pleasure the night before, there had been much more pain. Something was seriously wrong with Seynia, for that was the dark-haired woman's name. Edson would never forget it again, though he wished he could. She had left his body covered in small cuts and bruises, and his mind covered with worse.

The blond-haired woman with the blue eyes came out of Porter's room as Edson came up the stairs. Her friend followed. She had light brown hair and moved like a dancer. They both gave him a look that had him further regretting his decisions the night before. Had they both spent the night with Porter? The lad had all the luck.

"I believe the boy may have a bit more confidence when he wakes up," said the blond-haired woman. She winked and kept walking, with her friend gliding alongside her. He was definitely a fool. Never brave, always the fool. Someone had to play the role though.

Edson tried taking a nap but kept seeing the night before in his mind. Finally, he decided to have breakfast. The ground level of the Crystal Cavern held the kitchen, two common rooms, and a half-dozen private rooms. He found Thierry in the smaller of the two common rooms.

"I'm surprised to see you out and about so early," the man said. He had a full spread laid out before him. There was ham, sausages, potatoes, eggs, fruit, and some sort of cake that smelled incredible. “I saw you leaving with Seynia the Scorpion last night. I'm surprised you can even move. You're a braver man than I am.”

“I'm a fool,” Edson replied. “I should never have come here. I could've done another three or four shows in Zorbelix instead.”

“That's true. You probably would've sold them out too. Then, when you return next year or the year after, everyone would've already had a chance to see you. Because you only did four shows, those who attended will talk about it, and those who missed it will be eager to buy tickets for your next tour. Always leave them wanting more.”

“Alwin often said the same thing. I'll probably go to Rov next year but might come back to Aern the following year. Porter has to see Rov at least once.”

“He's a real find. Is anyone managing him?”

“He'll be my apprentice for at least three years,” Edson replied. He would keep the lad at least a day longer than his own apprenticeship had been, simply on principle. “Until then, everything he does goes through me.”

“That's fair.” There was disappointment in Thierry's voice. “We'll be working together again during that time. If you steer him my way when he's ready, I'll cut you in on his first three years on his own. You could make a nice profit.”

“As you said, we'll be working together again. Show me that you're the best one to handle the lad's interests, and I'll negotiate the deal. I won't shirk my responsibilities to him.”

“I'm not asking you to do that. Just keep me in mind.”

“Speaking of the lad, here he comes.” Porter had a grin from ear to ear. Edson and Thierry smiled as the lad approached their table.

“I didn't expect to see you for a few hours yet,” Edson said. “I hear you had quite the night.”

“It was amazing,” the lad replied, with the grin returning immediately. “I think I'm in love with both of them.”

“Slow down a little,” Edson said after he and Thierry stopped laughing. “You have plenty of time left in life for that. If you're going to be a bard, you'll find love in every village, town, or city you visit. If you're looking to stay with one of them, you picked the wrong profession.”

“You'll never hear a truer statement.” Thierry said. “I love Joceline more than anything in the world, but our marriage wouldn't have lasted a year if we didn't allow each other to enjoy the company of others.”

“They said they might come to the show tomorrow night.” Porter sat down and eyed what was left of Thierry's breakfast. Edson waved for a barmaid, as he had given up on her coming to the table on her own. “Do you think I can do something a bit more uplifting than *Soldier's End*?”

“Your version of that was too good not to include it in the show,” Thierry said. He turned to Edson. “Perhaps he could do two songs.”

“Alwin had a song that we might be able to do together,” Edson said. He smiled as he thought of the day Alwin had taught him the song, and the dance that went along with it. It was easy to learn, and Porter was in for a fun day. Edson smiled and looked over at the lad. “If you can pick it up by tomorrow night, we'll do it as one of the encores.”

Edson ordered him and Porter a breakfast to match the one Thierry had. They discussed the final show and the Fireball Competition. Thierry also told them that he wouldn't be joining them in Bithe. One of his and Jayme's associates would manage things there, including booking passage back across the sea in the spring. Jayme would handle matters from there.

Edson and Thierry gave Porter a hard time, but he refused to give them any details about the night before. It was all fun until Thierry started asking Edson about his encounter with the Scorpion. That was one subject he hoped to never discuss.

* * *

"Three crows stood in the road,
Blocking the way for all.
Three crows, blacker than coal,
Arguing in their crows' call.
Arguing in their crows' call."

Edson danced as he sang. Porter wasn't dancing but was playing and singing along with the children on the repeated line. Their show wasn't until later in the evening, but Edson had decided to take the lad to the park and put on a performance for the local children. They had rehearsed Alwin's song and dance routine countless times, and Edson was confident that they would pull it off. The trip to the park was to relax them both and part of Edson's way of paying back the debt he owed to Kari.

"A man shouted, 'Get out of the way,'
But they refused to budge.
The fight could last for many a-day,
For a crow can hold a grudge.
For a crow can hold a grudge."

Porter hadn't wanted to do this show, but he seemed to be enjoying it. Hopefully, it was taking his mind off of the blond-haired woman and her friend. The pair had been all he would talk about and seemed to be all he could think about. This impromptu performance had been the only thing Edson could think of, other than another woman, to distract the lad.

"A woman threatened them with a broom,
The crows didn't even turn around.
A farmer swore he would be their doom,
But the crows stood their ground.
But the crows stood their ground."

The children were laughing and dancing, which only encouraged Edson. The looks some of their mothers were giving him and Porter didn't hurt either. Not that he was likely to pursue anything with any of them. He had learned the hard way that anyone in Eveltour could be a wizard. He had always thought women were witches or sorceresses, while men were wizards or sorcerers. Seynia had given him a thorough education. He had also learned that men could be witches, and that these were sometimes called warlocks. Call it whatever you want, Edson wanted to be done with all of it.

"So, if a crow should block your way,
Go around, don't waste the whole day.
And if by chance, you should see three,
Go the other way, please listen to me.

So, if a crow should argue with you,
Give up the fight, it's what I would do.
And if by chance, you argue with three,
You can't say you weren't warned by me."

The song was silly, but children everywhere seemed to love it. It was the first song Alwin had let Edson do on stage. The memories still brought pain, but not as much as they had. In many ways, they now brought more pleasure than pain. Would the pain someday just be a memory? Edson hoped so. He wanted nothing more than to bring Kodran to justice but had no idea how to go about doing that. Fortunately, he would have a winter in Bithe to think on it.

There were other matters Edson needed to think on. He would obviously return to Vonst for the Bardic Challenge, but what would come after that? He had mentioned Rov as a destination to Thierry but wasn't fully convinced that was where he wanted to go. While it was important that he take Porter there at least once, there would be two more opportunities, if not three or four. Edson was considering another unconventional path.

For today, his second biggest concern was that Seynia would be at the show later that night. Worrying him even more than that was the probability that he would be unable to resist leaving with her again if she did make an appearance. There was little he could do to prevent either possibility, which was a big part of the reason why he was singing about crows to children.

* * *

Boom!

Edson winced as another fireball exploded in the sky. He regretted agreeing to host the competition. At least his time in Eveltour would be over after this. That was the bright spot in an otherwise miserable day. The fact that Seynia hadn't come to his last show, and, thus far, hadn't made an appearance at the competition, both cheered and depressed him.

Porter's pair of lovers had also failed to return, leaving the lad in a mood. Their performance of Alwin's song and dance routine had gone well at least, especially considering it was the first time they had done it on stage. Edson planned to work out some new routines with the lad on the way to Bithe. He had a gift for Porter as well, but that, too, would come on the road.

The competition was down to four wizards. Edson didn't care who won, as long as it ended soon. Playing around with something so powerful as these explosions wasn't his idea of fun. Besides, the audience seemed to have no interest in his songs or stories. All they wanted between rounds was juggling. With Porter still struggling to pick up that skill, the whole show was falling on Edson's shoulders.

Boom!

This one didn't startle Edson, as he had been paying attention. The four remaining wizards were taking turns launching fireballs. After they had each launched three, the judges would eliminate two of them. The remaining pair would be given an hour to rest, before they battled it out to determine a winner. Edson would be free to leave then but would wait until morning.

Thierry had arranged for Edson and Porter to travel with a

pair of traders and their guards. It would add a few days to the journey but would greatly increase their chances of making it to Bithe safely. Hopefully, Princess would cooperate. The horse had ignored Edson earlier in the day, when he had visited the stables. Singing her a song hadn't even worked.

He wasn't sure what he would do with Princess, or Porter's horse, when it came time to board a ship to return home. It would likely cost him more to ship her across the sea than he had paid for her. He had somehow become fond of her though, and the lad's horse helped keep her in check.

Boom!

Edson didn't know if he had any cousins or other relatives. His father had never talked about such things. He never talked about much, other than the farm, and the many things Edson had done wrong. He had been thinking about his father far too much of late. Was he even alive? Edson's route would take him close enough to allow for a detour to find out. Did he even want to know? Did he care?

He thought of Kodran, the one man he hated more than his father. He was probably living in luxury in Rov. After winning the Bardic Challenge two years in a row, he would have his choice of gigs in any city he went to. With Alwin dead, it fell on Edson to stop Kodran from winning again. That would be another objective for both the trip and his winter in Bithe. He would play every tavern and inn they stopped at, refining his show and working Porter hard. The winter would be spent writing new material and practicing.

The show would be perfected by spring, in time for their

return to the mainland. They would tour the coast for a couple months, bringing them into Vonst just in time for the first days of the competition. With Jayme handling his bookings, Edson didn't have to arrive early to scramble for gigs. Instead, the best venues would be competing to land him. What he had earned in Eveltour and Zorbelix was nothing compared to what his take would be in Vonst.

Boom!

With each competitor having launched their first fireball, Edson was expected to entertain the audience for a few moments. The four wizards had to prepare to cast the spell again, and the judges needed time to record their observations on the round. Edson didn't bother singing, instead he launched his knives into the air and told a couple one-line jokes. The juggling went over well, but the jokes flopped as badly as his songs and stories had. It seemed the audience wasn't interested in what he had to say, be it in story, joke, or even song.

How could he be expected to entertain them with only silent juggling? They would grow tired of it eventually. Then what? They loved magic, but he didn't know any, other than sleight-of-hand tricks. He was desperate though, and tried one, making a coin seem to appear inside a woman's handbag. The audience went crazy for it. He had time for one more trick, so he made it look as if the same coin vanished from his hand and reappeared in Porter's pocket.

As the four competitors began the second round, three wizards took him aside. They pressed him on his method of magic and refused to believe his explanation that the only tactics he employed were diversion of attention and deft hand movements.

They were tricks performed on street corners in every other city of Elraon. Perhaps because of the high visibility of real magic in Eveltour, sleight-of-hand tricks were almost unheard of in the region.

Boom!

Edson was again startled, as he had allowed himself to be distracted by the questions of the three wizards. He tried answering as many as he could but had difficulty following some of the more technical questions. The wizards were eventually satisfied, after he demonstrated his tricks for them in slow motion, clearing showing how he had fooled the audience. He hated giving away the secrets but saw it as the only way to get the wizards to leave him alone.

A winner was eventually chosen, and the competition came to an end. Edson was relieved to be finished with Eveltour and looked forward to the journey to Bithe. It would be good to put this city of magic behind them. He was surprised to find Seynia waiting for him in his room at the Crystal Cavern.

"You should close the door, darling," she said as she dropped her robe to the floor. She was wearing only the black slip underneath it. Edson didn't know whether to smile or scream.

Scene Eight:
Barbarians and Barmaids

"How long do you think it will take for us to reach Bithe?" Porter asked, forcing Edson away from his memories. Had it really only been three days since they left Eveltour? He was struggling to get Seynia out of his mind. Their second night together had been much more pleasant than the first, though there had still been a few terrifying moments. "Will it take as long as it took to go from Zorbelix to Eveltour?"

"Longer," Jacob Turnstel said, saving Edson the trouble of replying. The leader of the caravan they were accompanying seemed to always be there whenever Edson opened a wine bottle but never around when the time came to buy more. "We'll be on the road at least three weeks."

"That long?" Porter groaned and stood up. They were tending a small campfire, with Jacob's drivers and guards sharing a bigger one. "We should just ride on without the caravan. We can get there much faster on our own."

"If you make it that far." Jacob filled his goblet again with Edson's wine. Perhaps Porter's suggestion was worth considering. "There's a reason I have so many guards. There's safety in numbers."

"I looked at Conrad's maps before," Porter said, "Bithe

didn't look to be that far from Eveltour."

"It's not. The problem is the hills. All of the roads wind around the many hills and valleys between here and there." Jacob sat back, lifted his goblet, and smiled. "You might as well enjoy the journey."

"I have something that should help improve your mood," Edson said. With Seynia dominating his thoughts, he had forgotten about Porter's gift. "There's a package wrapped in leather with my packs. Grab it for me."

"I've been wondering what was in that," Porter said over his shoulder as he walked toward the tent they shared. He was quickly back to the campfire with the package. "It's not more of that henbane-infused wine, is it?"

"Open it and find out," Edson replied. If he had more of the vision-inducing wine, he would give it to Jacob instead. Perhaps that would discourage the man a bit. "Just be careful."

"What's this?" Porter asked as he took a wooden case out of the leather wrapping. His eyes grew wide as he opened the case. "This is beautiful. What is it? It's not like your harp."

"Alwin's harp, not mine." It would always be Alwin's harp. "It's a lyre. You need something else besides the lute."

"This is for me?"

"I have the harp." Alwin had given Edson a similar lyre in the early days of his apprenticeship. He lost it in a night of bad dice rolls and worse wine. "Let me see it though. I'll show you how you hold it and some of the basics. We'll work on it every night."

"Thank you." Porter handed the instrument over. Edson had tuned it before wrapping it up but that was well before they had left Eveltour. He showed Porter how to hold and tune the lyre before playing a couple basic songs, including one of Alwin's early hits.

The lad was nearly shaking with anticipation as Edson passed the instrument back.

"I don't think you're doing it right," Jacob said after Porter made a crude effort at playing part of the first song Edson had played. "Music shouldn't hurt the ears."

"He'll get better," Edson said. Who was Jacob to judge? Did the man think the lad would pick up the instrument on his first try? "It's not as easy as it looks."

"I'll take your word for it." The caravan leader emptied his goblet again. The bottle they were working on was nearly drained as well. "Though the boy isn't making it look very easy."

A shout from the bigger fire told them that the evening meal was ready. The cook Jacob had hired had a complete lack of imagination. Variety was apparently not in his vocabulary and spices were obviously not in his budget. Still, Edson was hungry, so he joined the others. It was going to be a long three weeks.

* * *

Edson's arm was asleep. He couldn't do anything about it without waking the barmaid his arm was trapped under. Her screechy voice was one he would never forget. The worst part had been when she had attempted to sing. Such endeavors were best left to those with the tools needed for the job. One didn't hire a blacksmith to mend a torn shirt.

Even beyond ridding himself of the barmaid he had spent the night with, Edson was eager to be on the road. If everything went well, they would reach Bithe by the end of the day. Knowing he would be spending the next three to five months there did little to diminish Edson's excitement. Not only would he be done with

Jacob the Mooch, Alwin's stories about the plainsmen of northern Aern were some of Edson's favorites. He was anxious to compare the pictures he had painted of them in his mind to the way they really lived and to make memories that would eventually be stories of his own.

First, he had to free his arm. He had already tried wiggling it free but couldn't get past the elbow. He would have to get her to move, without waking her up. With his free hand, he grabbed the wine bottle from the nightstand. There was still a little in the bottom. It wasn't much, but it was enough to start his day. He had to twist around a bit to get it all but managed it without waking the woman with the screechy voice.

A memory came to him. She was ticklish. He brushed his fingertips against her back. She wiggled a little, but he still couldn't get his arm free. He tickled her again, and she giggled. He froze in place. Had he woken her up or had she reacted in her sleep? Either way, he was still stuck in place. Something would have to give soon, as the wine was gone. Figuring he had nothing to lose, Edson tried tickling her one more time. She laughed and rolled over, nearly wrenching his arm out of its socket.

"Good morning, lover," she said. Edson winced. Her voice was even worse sober. His arm was free, but it would be some time before he had feeling in it again. Her arms didn't seem to have that problem, as she wrapped them both around Edson and pulled him closer. She kissed his neck, and he decided he could tolerate her voice for a bit longer, as long as she didn't sing.

* * *

"Raise your flagon, for the brave and pure,
For the ones who defend us all.
Raise them high, be strong and sure,
For without them we'd surely fall."

Edson was covered in sweat. He was on his second encore and would do at least one more. This was his third show in Bithe, all of which had been sold out. Alwin had been right on the mark about winters in Bithe. With all the tribes gathered there until spring, Edson could book a show every night if he wanted to. He would do a few more performances before taking a break for a month or so. He wanted to work some new songs and routines in, including pushing Porter to write his first song.

"Clap your hands and stomp your feet,
For the ones returning from the war.
Reward them with drinks and food to eat,
For we owe them so much more."

The song was old and supposedly originated in the north. Alwin had mentioned that it was always a favorite when he came to Bithe, so Edson had added it to the show. After the first night, he made it one of the encores. Porter would join him in the next one, as they would do Alwin's song and dance routine. If the audience responded well, Edson would consider another song after that.

"Close your eyes and bow your head,
For the ones who won't return.
Remember the reason they are dead,
For we all could be next to burn."

Edson had spent the previous night drinking with a group of warriors from the Ke'yantaga tribe. They were almost exactly as Alwin had painted them in his stories. While most would describe the plainsmen as barbaric, they were anything but simple. Alwin's stories had somewhat prepared Edson for this fact but seeing it firsthand really drove home the point. Their culture was different, and the nomadic life they lived placed serious restrictions on their luxuries, but they had a society that benefited all. Elders were respected and given a place of honor, while the young were nurtured without being coddled. Everyone had a place, and everyone did their part. Edson had his doubts about such a system working in a city as large as Vonst or Zorbelix, but it seemed to work well in Bithe.

He and Porter went through Alwin's routine without a hitch, which brought a healthy enough round of applause for Edson to give them one final number. He wasn't making as much for the shows as he had in any of his other stops in Aern—the audiences were much smaller—but was still glad he had insisted on ending the tour with a visit to the city of the plainsmen. His only disappointment thus far had been the consistent spurning of his advances by the women of the city. Porter was having the opposite result. He seemed to have a different woman every other night, while Edson couldn't even convince a barmaid to snuggle a bit.

It had taken the lad awhile to get over the blond-haired woman and her lithe companion, but, since he had, Porter became a different man. His confidence had increased so dramatically that Edson was starting to wonder if he would be able to justify keeping him as an apprentice for the full three years, let alone five. Even his juggling had improved, though he was struggling to learn to play the lyre. Even considering that, the lad had enough skill now to make the listings in the Bardic Challenge. By the time his apprenticeship was over, he would be a perennial favorite to win it.

They cleared the stage together, stowing the instruments and such in Edson's room, as it was the larger of the two. Edson asked Porter if he wanted to get a few drinks, but the lad declined, as he was meeting a lass who had attended the show. Edson instead found a spot at the end of the bar and began drowning his sorrows in wine.

* * *

Edson wanted to get up and join the dancers but was afraid he would cause offense. A husband and wife of the Wahahgma tribe had invited him back to their camp for dinner and to hear the music of their tribe. The dancers were shaking rattles fashioned from gourds, which seemed to be some sort of squash. A group to the side added to the beat with drums, pipes, and pan flutes.

There was a second reason why he didn't join in. He wasn't sure he was capable of doing so. After dinner, he had joined a group of men around a fire. When they passed around a pipe, Edson again hadn't wanted to offend his hosts. Whatever they had smoked had left him feeling strange. All of his worries had melted away, and he was fully at peace for the first time since Alwin had been murdered. Edson didn't know what this was, but it was much better than the henbane-infused wine. He just felt good.

The tribe had offered him the use of one of their tents, which they called a chum, for the night. Before leaving Bithe, Edson had left word for Porter, who had been with another of his lasses, that he might not return until morning. A night of drinking and dancing, and possibly more smoking, was just what Edson needed to clear his mind. Besides, it wasn't as if any of the barmaids were going to warm his bed if he returned. Many of the Wahahgma women were beautiful, and he had caught most of them looking at him at some point during the night.

One of the younger warriors stopped his dance in front of Edson and motioned for him to stand. Once again looking to avoid insult, Edson did his best to comply. He was surprised when his feet cooperated. The same couldn't be said for his head, as a wave of dizziness struck, leaving him with blurred vision and difficulty grasping where he was.

"Hold out your hand," a voice said. It was a male voice. Alwin? No, he was dead. Father? He was only dead to Edson. Prater? Wait, was that his name? Perter? The voice hadn't sounded like him anyway. Still, Edson complied and held out his hand. Someone put something in it. It was small and vaguely round. "Put it in your mouth, chew it up, and swallow it."

"What is it?" Edson asked. At least that was what he thought he asked. Had he asked anything or had he just thought it?

"Just eat it," the voice said. "It will set you free."

"I want to be free," Edson said. He wanted nothing more in the world. He wanted to be free of guilt over Alwin's death, free from any lingering effects of Braden's card tricks, and free from the pain from his mother's death and Fayme's treachery. Were those two separate pains or were they bound together to create one large hole in his heart? Either way, he wanted to be free. He put the small disk in his mouth and began chewing. It tasted awful.

"Keep chewing. Force it down if you want to be free."

Edson chewed as long as he could before forcing himself to swallow. The taste lingered on his tongue, and he wondered if he had been poisoned. His vision was clearing, as were his thoughts. The young warrior howled and returned to the dance. Throwing caution to the wind, Edson threw back his head and howled too. As long as his feet were cooperating, he was going to join the dance.

* * *

"Where are you, Fayme?" Edson shouted into the fog, but there was no answer. He didn't know where he was, or why he was naked. In many ways, he didn't even know who he was. He knew that he needed Fayme but wasn't sure who she was. Was she a lover? A friend? His mother? He just didn't know. "Where am I?"

It seemed as if he had been wandering aimlessly for most of the night. Was he supposed to be going somewhere? If so, where? Why? What would happen if he never arrived? Would anyone care? Would Fayme? He closed his eyes and shook his head violently to stop the questions from overwhelming him, as they had at least three times already. The questions had again retreated, but the fog was still thick, both in and out of his head.

"Why did you leave me, mother?" He was shouting again, though he didn't know why. Was he really shouting, or was it just in his head? It didn't matter, as there was nobody to hear. Nobody cared about him anymore. "What did I do to make you hate me?"

"I could never hate you, Edson," said his mother. Where had she come from? Wasn't she dead? Had his father lied about that? He reached out to touch her only to have his hand pass right through her body. "Your father doesn't hate you either. He just doesn't understand you."

"How could you know that? You weren't there."

"I've always been there. You just couldn't see me."

"Why do I see you now then?"

"You don't," she replied. "You only see what you need to see. That's me for now. Some would say your third eye has been opened, but that's not the complete truth. You won't be able to see me, or the other one, for much longer. Each of us has a reason for being here. My reason was to tell you that your father loved you. I've done that. Now it's time for me to go."

"I don't want you to leave," Edson replied. She couldn't abandon him again after finally being returned. "I've missed you."

"We'll meet again. This life is only a small part of the journey your soul will take. I'll be there for the next part too."

He screamed as she faded away. The questions renewed their attack on his head, mostly surrounding his mother's visit and abrupt departure. Had she really been there? Who was the other one she had mentioned? Was what she said about his father true? Did it even matter?

"I should have brought you here myself," Alwin said from behind Edson. He was definitely dead. "You should have a guide for this first time. Farris took me here when I was about your age."

"Why didn't you?" Edson had so many questions for his mentor but remembered his mother's warning about him not being able to see her or the other one for much longer. He was trying to organize his thoughts, but the questions were renewing their assault. "Why did you release me so soon?"

"That's an important question. The answer to that isn't what I'm here to give you though. You'll have to find that on your own."

"Why are you here then?"

"To remind you of your obligation to the boy. You agreed to be his mentor. Honor me by serving that role well."

"Perter?" That still didn't sound right. "I've been working

with the lad. He barely needs me."

"Porter." That was it! "He needs you more than you know. Just remember what you owe him, and you'll make me proud."

"Wait," Edson pleaded as Alwin began to fade away. "Who killed you? Was it Kodran?"

Alwin opened his mouth as if to reply but vanished before any words were formed. Edson screamed again, and let the questions take over. He fell to his knees as they flooded through his mind. Answers sprang forth as well but not always to the questions being asked. They came too fast for any sense to be made of it all. The flow slowed and eventually stopped. Edson was fully on the ground by then, sobbing and wishing he could just end it all.

"Are you lost?" A woman asked. He looked up but couldn't see more than a few inches in front of his face. Either the fog had intensified, or the questions had distorted his vision. "Can I help you find the way?"

"Please," he pleaded. She took his hand in hers and pulled him to his feet. His hand hadn't passed through hers, so she had to be real. Didn't she? He still couldn't see her, but the scent of flowers trailed behind her as she pulled him along through the fog. Was she Fayme? His mother? Someone else? Whoever she was, she began singing in a language he didn't recognize. It was beautiful, despite being a bit haunting. He wondered what the words meant.

His vision slowly cleared, and he eventually saw that she had long hair, so dark in color that it was almost pure black. He couldn't see her face, as her back was turned, but was mesmerized by simply watching her walk from behind. She stopped as they came to a stream and turned to face him. Her skin was dark, from hours in the sun, and her eyes were the color of a hazelnut. She smiled and everything was right with Edson's world. He was now sure this wasn't Fayme, for he would remember a face this beautiful if he had ever seen it before. Who was she then?

"We'll rest here for a bit," she said as she sat down beside the stream. He sat beside her, searching his mind for memories that might show him where he was and why he was there. "You can drink from the stream if you're thirsty. It's safe."

Edson cupped some water into his hands and quenched his thirst. Wine would be better.

"Where are we?" he asked. "Who are you?"

"I am called Chesna," she replied. "We're on the outskirts of my tribe's camp."

"Tribe?" That brought back memories of dancing around a fire. "You're of the Wahahgma tribe then?"

"Yes, and you are Edson Pye, guest of my father. You're the singer everyone is talking about."

"You're quite the singer too. What was that song you sang as we walked?"

"There are no words for it in your language."

"It was beautiful." He felt the questions returning and fought to hold them off. It was a fight he couldn't win. "I'd love to hear you sing it again."

She smiled and humored his request. He tried to follow the song but soon became lost in her eyes and a barrage of questions. The song finished, but he couldn't move. She called his name and said other words he couldn't understand, but he was unable to respond. The questions had him. He barely noticed as she wrapped her arms around him and held him tightly, as his mother had once done. As Fayme had once done.

Nestled within the blowing winds of the questions was a safe haven. It was small and didn't offer much protection, but it was all Edson had. He put all of himself that he could in this spot and rode out the storm. The questions passed through his mind without catching hold, with him barely understanding any of them. One question stood out though. It plowed through the barriers of his sanctuary and burned itself into his consciousness: Why had Alwin released him from his apprenticeship so early?

* * *

The questions were gone when Edson woke up, but Chesna wasn't. They were both naked now, and her arms were wrapped around him. Flashes of memory from the night before took up the void where the questions had been, leaving him wondering how much of what he remembered had really happened. Unless he had somehow lost a day, he still had two days until the last show before his break.

"We should get back to the camp," Chesna said, startling Edson. He had thought she was still sleeping. "It wouldn't be good for us to be found like this."

"What about like this?" Edson asked before kissing her. She laughed and seemed to abandon the thought of returning. Edson wasn't about to argue, though perhaps he should have, as they were reawakened nearly an hour later by her father and two other men.

"This is how you thank me for my hospitality?" Chesna's father asked as Edson was grabbed and held by the two others. "I give you honor as a guest, and you take advantage of my daughter?"

"He did no such thing, father," Chesna said. "He was lost in the fog of mescal. I brought him here to give him water and keep him safe. After he fell asleep, I must have dozed off too."

“Why are you both naked?” Her father asked. Edson had no answer for that, for he had been dressed when he got to the camp of the Wahahgma tribe. He had no idea when or how that had changed.

“He was that way when I found him,” Chesna replied. That seemed to be the truth, as Edson's clothing was nowhere in sight. “I undressed to help make him feel normal, in an effort to bring him out of the fog.”

“Is this the truth?” her father asked, looking at Edson.

“It fits in with my memories,” Edson said. There were other memories not being mentioned, but he wasn't about to volunteer anything. “I have never experienced anything like this fog before. What is it?”

“A gift from our cousins to the far south,” Chesna said. Her father couldn't have possibly bought her story, so Edson was hoping to change the subject. “They call it mescalito. It comes from a plant called a cactus.”

“Who put you into the fog?” her father asked.

“I have no idea,” Edson replied. It was the truth. He knew what a cactus was and found it hard to believe eating part of one would be something he would forget. He did remember something bitter. Had that been it? “I remember eating dinner with you, and then passing around that long pipe. After that, I don't remember much of anything.”

“I want to believe you,” the man replied. Edson couldn't remember his name. “I can't be sure though. You will stay with us until Jeznar returns to our camp. He will know if you are telling the truth or not.”

“Who is Jeznar, and when is he supposed to be back?” Edson asked. He couldn't miss a scheduled performance, especially his final show before the break.

"He's our shaman," Chesna said. The fear in her eyes told Edson all he had to know. Jeznar would know they had lied. "He'll be back tomorrow."

"I guess all we can do is wait then," Edson said, forcing a smile to his lips. "Unless there's breakfast, that is."

* * *

Edson was back in a cage. It was actually just the chum where he should have spent the night, but it might as well have been a cage. Guards were posted outside, and he wasn't allowed to leave. They had given him breakfast, but it had only been porridge and a bit of hard bread. At least he had his citole this time, as well as Alwin's flute. The rest of his instruments were back at the inn with Porter. If Edson's fate turned out as he feared, the lad would inherit the lot.

Being imprisoned for the bulk of the day had given Edson time to think about his encounters with the ghosts of his mother and Alwin. Had that simply been part of the fog, or was it something more? His mother had pleaded his father's case. There was no way Edson could have imagined such a thing, fog or not. And what about Alwin? He had known Porter's name, when Edson hadn't been able to remember it himself. Why was Alwin so concerned with the lad, instead of bringing his own killer to justice? In some ways, it made perfect sense. Alwin had taken his responsibilities seriously with Edson, which was probably something he had inherited from Farris. Despite the fact that Edson hadn't been his first apprentice, Alwin had often called him his protégé. What about his early release though? Given Alwin's dedication as a mentor, what would have compelled him to release Edson early?

Another mystery was where Alwin had been for the year after Edson had been released. He hadn't gone to Rov, and Edson had heard no mention of him throughout his journeys in Aern. Edson had asked Alwin while they were drinking together on the night he was murdered, but he hadn't answered. There was little chance that the two questions weren't connected but were they also part of the reason Alwin was killed?

A shout disturbed Edson's thoughts. He looked out the flap that served as a window. The entire tribe seemed to be moving toward the center of the camp. Only one of his two guards remained in place. It might as well have been a hundred, as Edson had no chance of overpowering the plainsman.

"What's going on?" he asked the guard.

"The glav of the Penhar tribe has demanded an audience with our glav," the man replied. Edson knew from Alwin's teachings that glav was the name for the leader of each tribe. The Penhar tribe was the largest and most powerful tribe among the plainsmen. A demand from their glav wouldn't be taken lightly. "She has brought her entire force with her."

"Is that normal?"

"Not at all," the man replied. His tone said it all. He was a proud warrior but was terrified. Edson couldn't think of anything else that might give the man heart, so he picked up his citole and went into one of Alwin's more upbeat numbers. The guard didn't complain, so Edson kept playing.

"Quiet," the man said while Edson was beginning his third song. "Our glav is coming this way. Their glav is with him, along with a young man. He's one of your people."

"That's Porter," Edson exclaimed as he peeked through the

door flap. He had never been so happy to see another man before in his life. The glav of the Wahahgma tribe was a big man and fit the appearance Edson had imagined for one of their leaders perfectly. His counterpart, from the Penhar tribe, didn't fit the mold at all. She was a golden apple, left on the branch in late autumn. Slightly overripe but delicious all the same. Edson grimaced. His passion for women would be the death of him one day. Hopefully, today wouldn't be that day.

"Release the prisoner," said the glav of the Wahahgma tribe.

"Yes, glav," the guard said as he held the flap open. As a cage went, the chum wasn't bad. Edson smiled as he stepped out, his citole across his back and Alwin's flute at this side.

"Porter, my dear friend," Edson said. "I can't tell you what a pleasure it is to see you. I'll be forever in your debt for the return of my freedom."

"Nobody said you were free," said the glav of the Penhar tribe. She was more than a mere apple. Perhaps a peach, softened up perfectly, and ready to explode with flavorful juice. "I traded two dozen horses for you. You're mine until you work the cost of them off."

"I'll buy you three dozen horses to repay the debt."

"That's not the deal I made. I traded the horses for you, not for three dozen horses. You'll serve me, as I see fit, until the debt is satisfied, or I'll have your head."

"I am your humble servant, my lady," Edson said, bowing with a flourish. Why was it always his head? "I live to see to your every whim."

"Your apprentice tells me that you have one more show to play before taking a break. Is this true?"

"It is, my lady." Not a peach. There was nothing soft about

this one.

"There will be no break," she said. "You are free until the morning after your show. Pack your things then, and come to my camp. Bring young Porter along, though he will be free to come and go. You will not."

"Yes, my lady." He managed a smile. Perhaps a pepper. Pretty and full of color, but a world of agony when you bite in.

* * *

"I once had a girl, with golden hair,
And eyes the deepest of blue.
Her lips were full, her skin was fair,
I loved her, she loved me too.
I bought her a ring, to show that I care,
It was the least that I could do.
But when I came home, she wasn't there,
For she loved another man too."

Edson was playing a packed house, in what would be his last performance before boarding a ship for home. After spending most of the winter serving Theda, the glav of the Penhar tribe, Edson was more than ready to leave Aern behind. She had worked him hard for the first couple weeks, before taking him to her tent one night. After that, he had only served her at night. Not that this made his task any easier. She was the most demanding lover he had ever had and the least likely to care about his own needs. She was definitely a pepper. Fortunately, a fur trader from the Surchu Mountains had caught her eye and she had released Edson from service, calling his debt fulfilled. There had been no encounters with Chesna's father or anyone else of the Wahahgma tribe.

“I once had a girl, with eyes of green,
And the voice of a nightingale.
Her legs were long, the longest I've seen,
And she was as thin as a rail.
I bought us a home, I'd make her my queen,
Happily ever after, as if in a tale.
But things fell apart, if you know what I mean,
And so now it's just me and my ale.”

Porter was playing his lute, while Edson had his citole. While Edson was singing, the lad would join in for the chorus. He had made a lot of strides over the winter and was well on his way to becoming a bard. His natural gift for music made that part of the training easy and he was doing well with the lyre. The same couldn't be said for the flute Edson had recently bought the lad. Getting him to be able to juggle had also taken a lot of work. Storytelling was another area where he had struggled, yet had made some progress. Even with all that, he would be a big hit in Vonst, especially with the ladies.

“I've tried to be fair, I've tried to be true,
I'm a fool for the ladies, I must confess.
I've given up on love, I swore this to you,
Yet I'll probably fall for the next lass in a dress.
Yes, I'll probably fall for someone new.
She'll break my heart, at least that's my guess.
I just can't be alone when each day is through,
And that's why I'm always in this mess.”

Edson had added six songs to his rotation over the winter. Four were his originals, including the one they were singing. One of the others was a local favorite, and the last was Porter's first song. It wasn't great but was far better than Edson's first attempts had been. The show was getting close to being what Edson hoped, though there was always room for improvement. There was no way Kodran was going to win for a third year in a row.

Scene Nine:
Sails and Songs

As much as Edson had anticipated visiting Bithe, he was thrilled to watch it shrink in the distance. In a few days, he would likely regret his haste in getting out of sight of land. That was a problem for later. He was looking forward to a peaceful journey back to the mainland.

The Mouse was another cog, much like The Merda, though slightly bigger. Only two captains had been willing to carry Princess across the sea, and neither had room for two horses. Dawn's Darling wouldn't be leaving for another week, which had made Edson's choice easy. The horse hadn't been happy as she was brought aboard the ship and was likely miserable in the hold. Edson had been unable to leave her behind. Her, Porter, and a few songs were all the good that had come out of his trip to Aern. Edson hoped the horse he had promised to buy Porter would get along as well with Princess as the one they had left behind.

"Does the ship always bounce around like this?" Porter asked. He was looking pale. This was his first time aboard a ship, and he looked to be heading toward the same type of experience that Edson had suffered through.

"For the most part," Edson replied. "It might take a day or

two, but you'll get used to it."

"I'm not sure I'll survive a day or two.

"You'll be fine. Just stay near the sides or keep a bucket handy. There are plenty around."

Porter merely nodded. He would be in for a rough couple of days. While Edson empathized with the lad, he had no desire to witness the ordeal. There was a crew to entertain and get to know. Edson had used that in his negotiations for their passage. He was expected to keep the crew happy and working hard.

"I'll leave you to your suffering," he said as he came to his feet. "Hopefully, it won't be as bad as mine was."

Porter only groaned as Edson walked away. The lad went right to the side. Edson had removed his shoes immediately after boarding and was already getting his sea legs. He went first to his cabin—a little bigger than the one he had been given during his time aboard The Merda—to get his citole and a new pipe he had bought in Bithe. He thought of Kari every time he played it. Was she alright? Was she still singing and making music with the pipe he had given her? It would be nice to leave at least one good thing behind as a memento of his trip. Perhaps he would find her after Porter's apprenticeship was over and make her his protégé. That would mean returning to Zorbelix though and possibly Fayme.

A bit of wine drove off the despair that always accompanied thoughts of her. Would she haunt him for the rest of his life? How had she managed to wedge herself so deeply into his heart in such a short time? Unwilling to go down the path those questions were leading him toward, Edson swallowed a bit more wine before grabbing his instruments and returning to the deck. Perhaps a few cheerful songs would chase Fayme from his head.

* * *

"More rum, more rum,
We've got to have more rum.
Fill our cups and keep them that way,
For my friends and I could drink all day."

Edson danced across the deck, singing and playing his citole. Porter kept the beat on his lute but wasn't used to the movements of the ship enough to join in the dancing. His bout with seasickness had lasted a day longer than the one Edson had suffered through. This was the first performance for the crew that the lad had taken part in. A sailor named Jer also played along on a pan flute. He had entertained the crew before Edson came aboard and insisted on being part of the performances. His timing was slightly off on most songs, but he had a decent voice and was a better juggler than Porter. Of course, that wasn't saying much.

"More wine, more wine,
We've got to have more wine.
Tap a new cask and another after that,
For my friends and I could drain a vat."

From what Edson could tell, the crew was lazy. Despite sharing the trait, it worried him greatly. A ship was no place for laziness. Too much could go wrong. Edson had spoken with the captain about it, but the man didn't seem to care. He had inherited the ship when his father-in-law died and knew almost nothing about the sea. His first mate was an able man, but his advice seemed to be ignored for the most part. Edson was beginning to regret his hasty departure from Bithe.

“More beer, more beer,
We've got to have more beer.
It's really demeaning to make us beg,
For my friends and I could drink a keg.”

At least the voyage would be shorter than the one Edson had taken to get to Aern. That had been another part of Edson's motivation for wintering in Bithe. The city was at the furthest point east on the continent. Cronar, their destination, was the furthest point west on the mainland. Even with a lazy crew, the trip would be over quickly. He and Porter would follow the coastline south to Vonst and an appointment with Kodran. Edson was looking forward to that confrontation.

“Hey, Ho! Tickle my toe,
Pour me a drink before I go.
Hey, Ho! Feel the wind blow,
Leave a few coins if you like the show.
Hey, Ho! Look high and look low,
Look everywhere, 'cause you just don't know.
Hey, Ho! Don't say no,
Never look back, just go, go, go!”

The song was one of Alwin's older numbers. It was silly but got a good reaction whenever Edson played it. The crew seemed to like it, and Edson didn't mind a little silliness now and then. Alwin had seemed to thrive on it with his earlier songs. When and why had that changed? He wrote a lot of songs about broken hearts but that was bread and butter for most minstrels. A huge bundle of unanswered questions was building up about Alwin, forcing Edson to realize how little he had really known about his mentor.

* * *

"These have shaved edges," Edson explained, holding a pair of dice in his hands. "If you look closely, you'll see that two of the faces are bigger than the others. You'll land on one of those edges most rolls."

"Won't people notice?" Porter asked. Edson was teaching the lad some other ways to make coins on the road.

"Not if you're careful," Edson replied. "Use the sleight of hand tricks I taught you to swap the dice in and out of play. Lose nearly as much as you win, but win a good majority of the big pots. Act surprised when you win and never take anyone's last coin."

"I don't know why I'm even asking, but isn't this unethical?"

"Only if you get caught." Edson was growing tired of explaining such things. The lad would benefit immensely from a few weeks of going hungry. Ethics wouldn't stop one's stomach from growling. "You worry far too much about such things."

"One of us has to. You don't seem to worry about it at all."

"Worry about what?" Jer asked as he stepped into view. The man had an annoying habit of turning up anytime Edson and Porter were alone. He also asked too many questions. "Is something wrong?"

"The lad thought he saw a storm cloud on the horizon." Edson threw a wink toward Porter in the hopes the lad wouldn't think it was unethical to play along with the lie. "I was just telling him not to worry about it."

"Storms are nothing to take lightly at sea," Jer replied. There would be no getting rid of him now. Edson wouldn't have minded if the man were trying to take advantage of having a bard aboard the ship and aiming for free lessons, but that wasn't Jer's motivation. He offered countering opinions to almost everything Edson tried teaching Porter. "I've been nearly killed in more than a few of them."

"I'm sure we'll be fine," Edson said, not giving Porter a chance to blow the false story. "The crew seems solid enough. Speaking of which, I was thinking about giving an extra performance this afternoon. Are you two up for it?"

"I am," Jer quickly replied. He would never allow Edson to perform without him. "I just have to grab my flute."

"I'm up for it," Porter said. Now that he was getting his sea legs, he was eager to play for the crew. "Should I get my flute too?"

"Not unless you want to be thrown overboard." Porter needed to be able to play more than just the lute and lyre, but Edson was starting to doubt the lad would ever pick up the flute. "Just keep practicing in private until I say otherwise."

The pair rushed to get their gear, while Edson opened a flask of wine. He hadn't really planned on an extra performance, but it had worked to change the subject. All of Edson's fun would be ruined if word were to spread to the crew that he cheated at dice. In fact, it might be him who would be thrown overboard if that were to come to pass. At least they wouldn't cut off his head first. That was an improvement.

* * *

The groans and creaks of the ship seemed louder than the

magically amplified performances Edson had put on in Zorbelix. They were becalmed, which was a word Edson had never heard before earlier in the day. It basically meant they weren't moving, and that everyone was in a piss-poor mood, especially Edson. He just wanted this voyage over with. His wine supply was running dangerously low. Each hour they spent not moving increased the odds of him running out before they reached port.

"Very soon, we'll ride the wind once more,
And we'll reach that far and distant shore.
Very soon, we'll run together in the night,
And we'll race until darkness yields to light."

Edson was visiting Princess, who was in as foul of a mood as he was. Not that he could blame the horse, she had been cooped up in the hold for the entire voyage. He had run out of carrots to give her and could do little to improve her lot. Misery loves company though, so there he was, singing songs to a stubborn horse named after three women he had been forced to leave behind. Why then was he instead thinking of the one who had left him?

"Very soon, we'll dance together once more,
And we'll sing songs just like we did before.
Very soon, we'll take what's ours by right,
And we'll race until Vonst comes into sight."

He had written a tune for which he had no lyrics and was improvising as best he could. As always seemed to be the case, his singing improved Princess's temperament. If only someone would sing to him and do the same, though the only three people he would want to do that were out of his reach. His mother and Alwin were both dead, and Fayme had left him. A drink of wine escorted the next line into his head.

"Very soon, we'll have lots of wine once more,
And we'll drink until we pass out on the floor.
Very soon, we'll no longer be alone each night,
And we'll race until everything turns out right."

Princess bobbed her head with the beat, being unable to dance in the small pen she was confined to. It would take some time to build her strength back up when they reached the mainland. As long as the wind came fairly soon, this wouldn't be an issue. Edson had planned to set a leisurely pace for their journey north. They would reach Vonst just before the start of the Bardic Challenge. Just in time to deny Kodran a third victory.

* * *

Edson raced across the deck, yet the fight was still broken up by the time he reached it. Jer and Porter exchanged a couple more blows as they were pulled away from one another. The lad would have a blackened eye, but he had given far worse. Blood flowed from Jer's lip and nose, while both eyes showed signs of swelling. Perhaps the lad wasn't as soft as Edson had thought.

"What's this all about?" asked one of the sailors who had broken up the fight. "Fighting over who wrote a song?"

This brought a laugh from most of those around. Edson wasn't laughing though. Alwin had told him of some deadly fights that had truly been over who wrote a particular song. That couldn't be what the fight was about though. Porter had a long way to go as a songwriter, and Edson would be surprised if Jer could write a word, let alone a song.

"Me and the lad were just playing," Jer said. "I guess we got a bit out of hand."

"Is this the truth?" Edson asked Porter, who nodded, but wouldn't even look at Jer. Something more than mere horseplay had happened. There was no point in pushing it further though. Instead, he would question the lad later, in private, assuming Jer gave them a moment alone. "There you have it then. After three days of sitting in this same spot, we're all on edge. How about we put our energy toward singing some songs to cheer everyone up?"

There was a light bit of cheering for this, which was all the prompting Edson needed. He pulled his pipe from his belt and jumped into a song. Jer joined in and was quickly followed by Porter. Soon, they had the whole crew cheering them on. Edson responded, giving a performance that would have made Alwin proud. Porter and Jer seemed to push each other to new levels as well, matching Edson's effort.

After three days sitting motionless, even the lazy crew of The Mouse had exhausted their list of chores. As a result, the entire crew formed the audience for this performance, including the captain. Edson was dripping with sweat but kept going. He was in the middle of the second playing of *The Sailor's Life* when it hit him. He had never felt something so wonderful. The crew felt it too and began to cheer. Even the captain was on his feet, yelling with the rest. The show came to an end, and the crew showed no signs of their previous laziness. Underneath it all, they were sailors. There is only one thing sailors love more than the open water and that was the thing that stopped Edson's performance. The wind had returned!

* * *

"Oh, If I were a betting man,
I wouldn't bet on you.
I would search for better odds,
It wouldn't be hard to do."

Edson was singing to Princess again, but his thoughts were on Kodran and their pending reunion. There had to be a way to prove that he had either killed Alwin or hired someone else for the task. The motive was clear. Alwin was the only real competition Kodran had in the Bardic Challenge. Edson had been touted as a contender, but nobody had really believed he had a chance. Alwin and Kodran also had a long-standing rivalry, but Edson had never asked how that had started. Could that be a key to this?

"Oh, If I were a fighting man,
I would search for you.
I wouldn't stop until you fell,
It would be so fun to do."

Princess was more anxious than normal. She stomped her hooves and complained endlessly. Edson did what he could to calm her, but nothing shy of getting her off the ship was going to do that. He was anxious too. The bottle of wine next to him was his second to last. After that, his daily allotment of rum would be the only thing getting him through each day. That and his hatred of Kodran.

"Oh, If I were a wiser man,
I wouldn't think of you.
I would move on with my life,
It wouldn't be easy to do."

The festive and hardworking mood of the crew had quickly worn off. If this were The Merda instead of The Mouse, they would already be in port, even though the ships were fairly comparable. Princess would be enjoying herself in a pasture, while Edson would have all the wine he wanted, along with a woman to keep him company. Unless they all flocked to Porter again. Too bad he couldn't keep the black eye that Jer had given him. With Edson's luck, the ladies would just feel sorry for the lad.

"You have quite a bit of anger in you," Jer said from behind Edson. How long had he been standing there? "Who pissed in your wine bottle?"

"It's a long story," Edson replied, "and one I don't feel like telling. What brings you down here?"

"I wanted to apologize for the scuffle with the kid." Jer produced a carrot and gave it to Princess. Where had that come from? Edson had begged the cook for anything Princess might look at as a treat, but the man had insisted that he had nothing to give. "I was just playing around."

"No harm done," Edson said. Porter's version of the story had Jer insulting Edson and trying to convince the lad to stay on the ship when they reached port. "I'm sure that won't be the last fight the lad finds himself in."

"Still, I feel bad. He's just a kid." Princess nudged Jer, who produced another carrot. Trying to steal Porter apparently wasn't enough for Jer, he had to go after Edson's horse as well. "He handled himself pretty good though."

"I would expect nothing less. Part of being a bard is being able to hold your own in a fight." Why had he said that? The last thing Edson wanted to be involved in was a fight. Jer was just dumb enough to enjoy the barbaric activity.

"It's the same for sailors." Jer made his meaning clear with his eyes. He had some sort of issue with Edson. Hopefully, it wouldn't boil over before they reached port. With Edson's luck, the odds of that were slim.

* * *

Edson was the first person to step off of The Mouse and onto the docks in Cronar. Porter was right behind him. Edson carried his citole, while Porter had his lute, lyre, and Alwin's harp. Edson also had his tambourine and pipe, along with Alwin's flute, in his pack. The remainder of their belongings remained on the ship, along with Princess.

"Wait here for our things and Princess to be unloaded," Edson said as he tossed a pouch of coins to Porter. "I'll go find an inn and secure us rooms. Don't leave the docks. I'll come back and find you."

"What's this for?" The lad held up the pouch.

"Throw a few coins to the unfortunate sailors assigned to getting Princess off the ship." While Edson would love to stick around for that show, it had been five days since he had even a small taste of wine. "Use the rest to get yourself something to eat."

Cronar was a trading port. It was the gateway to the north. Ships came from Vonst, Zorbelix, Rov, and nearly every other coastal city of Elraon. Edson had been there twice before, both times with his father. The first visit had been before Edson's mother had died. She had been with them too. It was one of Edson's few happy memories of his childhood. The second came the year after her death. There had been little joy in that trip or the rest of his youth.

Walking through the city streets brought back memories of both trips. He passed the toymaker, where his father had bought him a wooden puppet. Edson's smile was wiped away as he remembered the puppet burning away into nothing. His father had caught him playing with it after his mother's death and had told him the time for playing was over.

A building across the street had a sign with a pair of mugs and a bottle painted on its face. The place was nearly empty, which wasn't surprising considering the time of day. It was early afternoon, and most people were still about their daily business. He took a seat at a table and smiled at the approaching barmaid.

“The cooks don't have anything ready yet,” she said. Her accent brought Edson's mother's voice to mind. “Bread and cheese are about the best I can offer.”

“A taste of wine and a smile on your lips is all I'm looking for, darling,” Edson said. Her lips turned slightly upward, but no teeth showed.

“What's that?” she asked, pointing at the citole Edson had set on the table. “Do you play it?”

“It's a citole, and I've been known to strum a chord or two. Do you like music?”

“I love it,” she replied. “I sing with the choir in Zain's temple every Fifthday.”

“That's wonderful,” Edson said, though he thought the opposite. He had been hoping to talk her into a few snuggles and kisses. Small chance of that. "What's your favorite song?"

"Morning Bloom," she answered, surprising Edson. It was one of Farris Dent's ballads. Edson had expected *She Dances Under the Moon*. "I've loved that song since I was a small child."

"It's a classic. I'll play it for you if you spot me my first flagon of wine."

"Only if you promise to pay for the second. I've had more than my share of freeloading musicians."

"I'll do even better," he said, the smile returning to his lips. "Join me and I'll buy the bottle."

That brought a real smile. The tulner he tossed on the table widened it and brought the joy to her eyes. Her hips swaying as she went to get the bottle was the most pleasant sight Edson had seen for months. He had his citole tuned by the time she returned. He sang Farris's song as Alwin had taught him. In an odd way, the song felt as if it belonged to Edson by right now. He had inherited Alwin's music. Alwin had done the same with Farris's collection.

They were on the third bottle when Porter walked in. He didn't look happy as he stormed over to Edson's table.

"I knew I'd find you drunk," the lad said. "I've been looking all over the city for you. Princess is outside. She's even angrier than I am."

"Princess?" The barmaid's eyebrows went up, as did her hand. It came down in a slap across Edson's face. "You didn't mention her."

Edson started to protest, but the idea of a woman being jealous of his horse brought only laughter, which did little to help his case. She poured her wine glass in his face and stormed off. Edson continued laughing even as he wiped his face clean.

"I don't find this to be funny," Porter said. "You could've

sent word. I was afraid something had happened to you."

"I lost track of time," Edson replied as he stood up. At least none of the wine had gotten on his citole. "I'll make it up to you. Let's find an inn and get something to eat."

"Jer's outside too," Porter said. He seemed less happy about this than anything. Edson wasn't thrilled about it either. "He says he's going to travel to Vonst and try to make the lists in the Bardic Challenge."

Edson laughed harder at this than he had about the barmaid's jealousy. The sailor had about as much chance of making the lists as Alwin did of coming back from the grave. The prospect of traveling with the man was horrifying, but Edson wasn't going to let it ruin his mood. He was back on the mainland and would soon have a chance to pay Kodran back. Nothing was going to spoil that.

Scene Ten:

Traders and Traitors

"I'll do three nights," Edson said. He was negotiating with Hallis Gort, who was the owner of the Green Room. It was the most prestigious music hall in Cronar. Edson had expected to be met by Jayme or one of his associates and was annoyed at having to handle his own bookings. "No more than that."

"Five would be better," Hallis countered. He was a large man, with nearly no hair remaining. "I'll settle for four."

"Three is all I'm offering. Take it or leave it."

"I guess I'll take it. I'll need a few nights to promote the shows."

"That's fine," Edson said. He needed time to prepare anyway. "As long as I can be on the road within a couple weeks, I'll be happy."

"I'm sure we can make that happen," Hallis replied. He picked up a small bell from his desk and rang it. "Let us celebrate the arrangement."

A young woman came into the room, carrying a tray with a pair of glasses and a decanter of wine. She poured a glass for both Edson and Hallis before leaving. While he was eager to conclude this business and be about his day, Edson never said no to a free glass of wine. Especially when it was a man such as Hallis offering. His type rarely drank the cheap stuff. Edson held no such qualms, but it was good to have the top shelf vintages from time to time.

"I've been told that you were Alwin Floyd's apprentice," Hallis said after the girl had left the room. "Is this true?"

"Yes." Would the reminders ever stop? "He was my mentor for three years."

"We were friends for a long time, though we didn't speak for over fifteen years. That's why I was surprised to see him last spring."

"He was here in the spring?" This was the first clue Edson had found about where Alwin had went during their year apart. "Was he alone?"

"Was Alwin ever truly alone? He had different lovers nearly every night."

"Did he happen to mention where he spent the winter?"

"He didn't say, but he came into Cronar on a ship out of Zorbelix."

Zorbelix? That made no sense. Why hadn't Edson heard anything about Alwin during his time there? With the way they had reacted to Edson, he could only imagine the response a visit from a bard such as Alwin would generate. Yet nobody had mentioned him at all. Something wasn't adding up.

"How long was he here?" Edson asked. He would take any bits of information he could get. "Did he leave by ship or horse?"

"He came in to port nearly a year ago to the day, and left on horseback. He was in Cronar for nearly a month. Long enough for seven shows. You should consider doing the same."

"I thought that was already decided. You'll have to make do with three, though I'm sure I'll return in the future. Alwin taught me to always leave them wanting more."

"He was a master at that," Hallis replied as he lifted his wine glass. "I'll miss the bastard. There was a time when I would have taken an executioner's axe for him. He would've done the same for me."

"I miss him more with every passing day," Edson said, raising his own glass. "All I can do is honor him by being the bard he told me I can be."

The wine was all that Edson had expected. Someday, when he retired from the road, Edson would have a wine cellar comparable to those held by men such as Hallis. Until then, the cheap stuff would have to do.

"I've been told that you have two apprentices. That seems unusual."

"I only have one. Unfortunately, I'm also stuck with a sailor who thinks he can be a bard. Short of sticking a knife in his ribs, I don't know how to get him to go away."

"Will he be part of your performances?"

"If I don't include him, he'll just find a way to weasel his way in. I'll give him a role simple enough for him to take on."

"There are ways of making people go away," Hallis replied. All mirth was gone. He was serious. "Just say the word, and your sailor won't bother anyone ever again."

"He's not that bad." In truth, Edson was tempted. Jer was one of the most annoying men he had ever met. "If he does anything stupid though, I might come see you."

"You'll find that I'm a reasonable man. A few extra shows could make all your problems go away. Alwin and I made many such deals over the years."

"I'll keep that in mind." Had they made such a deal the past spring? There were many other questions Edson wanted to ask, but was afraid to. “I think he'll decide to go back to his ship eventually though. Sailors rarely lose the itch for the sea.”

“Let us put this behind us then,” Hallis said as he reached for the wine decanter. “We'll get drunk and share stories of Alwin.”

“I'm on board with that,” Edson replied. Perhaps a few drinks would loosen the man's tongue enough to pry a few more clues out.

* * *

“Edson,” someone shouted. Edson turned and saw Garrett Rend running toward him. Garrett was a gambler. He and Edson had worked together to take a few wealthy fools for small fortunes. What was he doing so far north? He hated the cold and typically spent his winters in Rov, which was where Edson had last seen him.

“Garrett,” Edson said as the man reached him. “What madness brings you here?”

“A bet,” Garrett replied. “What else would drive me to such horrors?”

“I should have known. What's the stakes?”

“Your life. Mine too, most likely.”

Edson waited for the punchline, but none came. Garrett wasn't serious often, but this seemed to be one of the rare occasions where he was. Edson tried to think of who might want him dead and was astounded at the number of names that popped into his head. Kodran. King Jondar of Eblok. The big lass from the Broken Jaw Inn. Her father. The entire Wahahgma tribe. Not to mention countless husbands and boyfriends.

“It sounds like you have a story to tell me for a change,”

Edson said. Garrett wasn't much for music but loved stories. "It also sounds like I'm going to want a drink handy while I hear it. Let's find a tavern."

"There's one a couple streets over, follow me."

Edson trusted Garrett as much as one could trust a cheating gambler, which was little, if at all. Still, he was intrigued, so he followed the man. They cut through an alley and eventually came to a tavern called the Wayward Prince. The hairs on the back of Edson's neck stood up as he entered. There was something off about the place. Every man watched him, while trying to make it look as if they weren't. Two moved in front of the door, blocking the way out.

"What's this, Garrett?" Edson asked. The gambler simply shrugged his shoulders and pointed toward an old man seated in the corner. It couldn't be! Edson had seen enough paintings to recognize the man but had assumed he was dead. "Farris Dent?"

"Alwin said you were a smart one," the legendary bard said. Edson had never understood how someone could be starstruck before this moment. "Come over here and sit down. I'm too old to stand up, and we have a lot to talk about."

"What about me?" Garrett asked. "Am I free to go?"

"Yes," Farris replied. "You've satisfied your end of the bet. Just remember what I said, tell nobody about this."

"My lips are sealed," Garrett said. "Are we good, Edson?"

"As good as always, Garrett." It wasn't really fair to hate a snake for being a snake just because you were dumb enough to think they were something else. "May your dice always roll the way you need them to."

"I make sure they always do. You do the same, my friend."

Edson sat down across from Farris. He wanted to ask the

man so many questions but didn't want to look like a fool. This was the man who had taught Alwin. He was perhaps the greatest bard ever born. Edson remembered his foolish thoughts about inheriting the man's songs. So much for that.

"Do you know who killed Alwin?" Farris asked after Garret was gone.

"I don't have proof, but I suspect Kodran Novius." Edson had been sure of Kodran's guilt when he left Vonst. He still suspected the man but wasn't ruling anything out. "Do you know something I don't?"

"I know you were falsely accused of the crime. I wouldn't put it past Kodran. He and Alwin were the two finalists when I was looking for an apprentice. He never forgave Alwin for being the one I chose. I tried explaining to Kodran that his envy and spitefulness were the reasons I picked Alwin over him, but he couldn't accept that. He instead pointed to Alwin's wealthy family as the reason he was denied the opportunity."

"Alwin's family was wealthy?"

"Is wealthy. His father was Cerwin Trieb. Floyd was only a stage name. His true name was Alwin Trieb."

"Of Trieb Consolidated?" They controlled nearly every avenue of freight and transportation in and around Vonst. Why had Alwin never mentioned this?

"The same," Farris replied. "Alwin never wanted anything to do with his father's wealth. This arrangement suited his brother, Fedwick, just fine. He controlled the family company and fortune right up until his death."

"When was that?"

"Almost two years back. Just after the Bardic Challenge."

"Who controls the company now?" Edson asked. That was

just after Alwin and Edson had parted ways.

“Fedwick had no children. Alwin's sisters and their children are fighting for control.”

“Is it possible that one of them had Alwin killed?”

“Anything's possible. There's something else you need to know too. Someone wants you dead. There's a contract out for your head.”

“Who?” Edson asked. Always his head.

“I don't know. One thing to consider is that you would have some legal claim to being Alwin's heir. Perhaps the same people who killed him are now after you.”

“Great. Just what I needed. Got any other good news? Is my father waiting outside to point out how right he was about how my life would turn out?”

“Not that I'm aware of,” Farris said with a smile. “It's not as bad as you think. At least you know they're after you. Alwin never got such a warning. You haven't heard the worst of it yet. Pour me another glass of wine and I'll tell you the rest.”

* * *

Edson flattened himself against the wall. He had caught Jer's voice through an open window of a building just before passing. There were other conversations taking place, but Alwin had trained Edson to focus on only what he wanted to hear.

“Make sure he sticks to the coastline,” said the man Jer was speaking with. He had a rough voice. “It'll be easier for us to find him that way.”

“Why don't you just kill him here and be done with it?” Jer asked. Edson nearly kicked himself for not letting Hallis get rid of the sailor. Was it too late to change his mind? "Then I can go back to The Mouse."

"You're not being paid to make suggestions," the other man replied. "What about the kid. Can we count on him to play his role?"

"He won't be a problem." Porter was involved in this too? Edson felt as if he had been punched in the stomach. After all he had done for the lad, this was his thanks? "Edson's the one you need to worry about. He's not stupid. One mistake and he'll turn the cards on this whole scheme."

"We'll take care of him when the time comes. Just keep him to the coast. He can't be allowed to reach Vonst."

Edson waited, hoping to hear something to incriminate Kodran in the conspiracy, but his name wasn't mentioned. How far back did this scheme go? Had Fayme been part of it? If she hadn't stolen his pay for the Zorbelix gigs, he wouldn't have even considered taking on an apprentice. Was anything in his life as it seemed? Was anything real?

At least he was armed with the knowledge of the scheme against him. He had a chance to do something about it. The only question was, what to do? He would have no problem shoving a dagger into Jer's chest, but the thought of harming Porter bothered him, even knowing he was a rat. Edson had promised Alwin he would look after the lad. Had that been real though?

There was only one place he could turn to for help. Hallis Gort was the type of person best avoided, but Edson was already tied to him. Asking him for help would mean a longer stay in Cronar, but that beat dying on the coast. It was too bad Porter had gotten himself mixed up in this mess. The lad had the potential to be a great bard. Wasting such talent hurt Edson nearly as much as the betrayal.

Hallis drove a hard bargain, but a deal was reached. Edson would give him his seven shows. In return, his problems would be taken care of. He would have to drink a lot of wine to get rid of the bad taste the deal had left in his mouth, but again, it would beat dying. He wished he could go back to the simple year he had spent singing for his supper. Nobody had wanted to kill him then.

* * *

“We're all set for the final show,” Porter said. If only he knew how final it would be. “It's a full house.”

“And you said it was mistake to stay for seven shows,” Edson replied, as if that had been his plan all along. It was hard to even look at the lad without growing angry, tearing up, or both. His and Fayme's betrayals had each cut nearly as deep of a wound. Trust would come hard in the future, and Edson would likely never take on another apprentice. “We could always save some time by traveling inland instead of following the coast. Playing the small fishing villages isn't going to do much for my reputation.”

“Jer says it's safer following the coast,” Porter said. The pain grew stronger with each betrayal. “He said there are bandits on the inland roads.”

“I don't care what Jer says. What do you think?”

“I really don't care. Whichever way you decide is fine.”

“We'll worry about that after tonight. Are you sure everything's ready?”

“Yes,” Porter replied. “All of the instruments are on stage. There are three stools, and drinks for each of us.”

“Very well then,” Edson said. “I guess that's all I need for now. Give me a few minutes alone before the show starts."

"Is everything alright?"

"It will be. I just need a few minutes."

The shouting started just after Porter left the room. Edson had no idea what Hallis would do with Porter, or even Jer. Edson had insisted that the lad be kept alive, but that had been the only concession Hallis would make. There was no way of proving he would even honor that. Edson shouldn't have cared but couldn't stop himself. He felt responsible for the lad. Was it his promise to Alwin or was there more to it?

Edson was halfway through his second bottle of wine when his door opened and Hallis entered the room. His smile reminded Edson of a hungry stray, eyeing everything that moved as a potential meal or threat. One more show, and Edson could wash his hands of the whole situation.

"Your problems have been dealt with," Hallis said. Edson grimaced and pushed away the second thoughts that were flooding his mind. The lad had earned his fate. "You'll never see either of them again."

"Remember your promise," Edson replied. "The lad is to be kept alive."

"I'm a man of my word. Both of them will be kept alive, though they may wish otherwise at times."

"I don't want to hear the details. I feel bad enough already."

"You're only protecting yourself. The boy betrayed you."

"That doesn't make it any easier," Edson said. He had made promises to Alwin and the lad's mother. Edson didn't have much to offer, but his word had always been good. Sure, he had stretched it a little bit with the ladies from time to time but that was different. He had promised to protect Porter and had instead sold him to a man who would just as soon slit his throat as give him a hand. "Just promise me the boy will be safe."

"Put your worries aside. He'll live to a ripe, old age."

Edson sighed as Hallis left. The man's reassurances did little to instill confidence. Edson could almost feel Alwin's disapproval. It hurt nearly as much as the lad's betrayal.

* * *

"There once was a man, whose name I forget,
For the sake of this story, I'll call him Regret.
Regret was a farmer, with a wife and a son,
He loved to work but also loved to have fun."

The Green Room was full to capacity, yet seemed empty to Edson. He had nearly left the stage three times to find Hallis Gort and ask him to return the lad. Each time, logic won over emotion, and Edson continued his performance. No matter how many times he told himself that the lad had earned his fate, the guilt remained. Having Porter's lute and lyre on stage next to the other instruments wasn't helping. Selling the instruments was tempting but keeping them would serve as a reminder of both the lad's betrayal and Edson's reciprocation.

"There came a day, when Regret had enough,
He sold his farm and packed up all his stuff.
Regret said goodbye to his wife and his child,
He said it was his time to be free and run wild."

Edson just wanted to get the show over with. For the first

time in his memory, he wasn't putting everything he could into his performance. He was trying but couldn't muster the passion needed. What would Hallis do with the lad? Would Porter ever forgive him? Would Alwin? For that matter, would he ever forgive himself? Would he always wonder what had become of the lad? Did Edson's father wonder such things about him? Did he even care?

"There was a woman, who Regret did chase,
He couldn't resist her long legs and fair face.
Regret spent the fortune he had got for his farm,
He put his best leg forward and put on the charm."

He had been thinking of his father a lot of late. That and the words of his mother's ghost. He had already shunned the advice of Alwin's ghost. He would need to do something unexpected to throw those hunting him off his trail. What could be more unexpected than for him to go home? It was somewhat on the way to Vonst, even if it was well off the beaten path. Would his father welcome him or turn him away? If his mother's words were true, Edson's father loved him. Wouldn't that guarantee a welcome? If nothing else, it would prove whether her words were true or not. At least then he would know. It would be one less regret in his life.

"There was another man, who she loved more,
She took Regret's gold and walked out the door.
Regret went back home, but his wife wasn't there,
She had found another whose life she would share."

Edson had bought a new horse for Porter, which he would instead use as a pack animal. He would avoid most towns and cities, so he had secured a good bit of supplies. Even though he had grown up in the area, he had bought a map. He had armed himself too. Alwin had given him lessons with a short sword, but Edson had never been comfortable with the weapon. He needed something with some range. Getting close in battle was a quick path to the grave. His father had taught him to shoot a bow, but it had been years since he'd done so. Still, it would be his best option.

"There was a rich man, who had bought Regret's farm,
He said he needed a man who was strong of arm.
Regret went to work on the farm that once was his own,
But he no longer loved work and lived out his life alone."

A lass near the front was trying hard to get Edson's attention. To his surprise and dismay, he had no interest in her. She was pretty, stunning even, but that did little to distract Edson from his racing thoughts. Was Kodran actually innocent in regards to Alwin's death? Not long ago, even thinking such a thought would have seemed absurd. Edson didn't know what to think anymore. He only knew one thing, he had to make it to Vonst without being killed. He owed Alwin at least that.

"So, if you feel as if everything has gone bad,
And you're unhappy with the life you've had,
Think of Regret, and the choices he made,
He would still have his life if he had stayed.
His wife would still love him, as would his son,
Instead he cries alone when each day is done.
Take my advice, and appreciate all you get,
Thinking any other way brings only Regret."

The audience clapped lightly, which was about all Edson deserved. He pushed himself harder on the next song, and the one after that, but soon lost interest again. Finishing the show on a high note still left the audience unsatisfied. Edson shared the sentiment.

* * *

Edson left Cronar in the middle of the night. After wiggling free from the arms of the lass from the front row—he was only human after all—he had grabbed his bags and set out. Princess was on her best behavior, so Edson was able to quietly leave the city behind. He rode through the night, and the following day, before stopping at a roadside inn. His instruments were concealed on the pack horse, and he paid for his room and meal. It wouldn't do to leave any sort of trail to be followed.

He kept his drinking to one bottle of wine, half of which he drank in his room. Morning put him back on the road and led him to a decision. Continuing on the road would take him on a fairly direct route to the south, avoiding the coastline and his father. Taking the road that veered to the east would also keep him away from the coast but would lead him right past his childhood home.

"What should we do, Princess?" he asked, not expecting an answer. He was surprised when she trotted down the eastward road, making the choice for him. "Alright then, but remember this was your decision. Don't complain when you're in a leaky barn with a bunch of work animals and cattle. The other path would've led to a series of comfortable and dry stables."

Princess's reply was echoed by the pack horse. Her trot wasn't something any other horse could ever duplicate though.

Edson could only laugh and enjoy the ride. Porter still haunted his thoughts, as did the possible coming encounter with his father, but his mood still improved as the day went on. Very little about the road was familiar. Would it be the same with his father? Would they even recognize one another?

Edson spent one night camped in a valley, near a stream and another in an abandoned cabin. The route became more familiar with each mile, and the years seemed to vanish. He had nearly broken his arm climbing an apple tree they passed. His father had taught him to fish in the river that ran beneath a small, wooden bridge they crossed. The bridge had seemed so large when he was small.

Finally, the farm came into sight. It was as if nothing had changed. The barn was a little more worn, and the house wasn't nearly as big as he remembered, but otherwise it looked like he had gone back in time. An older man came out of the barn and started walking toward Edson. As he came closer, Edson saw him better. It was his father! The years had taken their toll, leaving him gray and wrinkled. Edson climbed down from his horse as his father approached.

He stopped about ten feet from Edson and put his hands on the hilts of the knives hanging on his belt. Edson's mother had been wrong. His father didn't love him. He was just another man who wanted to kill him.

“I'll tell you the same thing I told the rest of them,” Edson's father said. “He's not here. I haven't seen my son in about a decade and don't expect him to ever come home. You've wasted your time coming out here.”

“Have there been a lot of others?” Edson asked. His father didn't even recognize him! That hurt almost as much as rejection.

Almost.

“Three so far, not counting yourself. You don't have the look of the others though.”

“I've been told I look like my mother. Too much so, according to some. Especially my father.”

“Edson? By Zain's eyes, I didn't recognize you.”

“You don't seem overly pleased to see me,” Edson replied. Coming here had been a mistake. “I can go if I'm not welcome.”

“I'm just surprised.” A tear ran down Edson's father's cheek. “I never expected to see you again. You are always welcome here.”

“That wasn't always the case.” Edson fought back his own tears, as well as the anger he had held onto for far too long. “You said that you wished I had never been born.”

“I'm sorry, my boy.” Edson's father took a step forward. “I was too blinded by my grief over losing your mother to see what I was doing to you. You do look like her though. I'm sorry that once angered me. I'm sorry for a lot of things.”

“I'm sorry too, father,” was all Edson could say as they embraced. Tears ran down both of their cheeks, and Edson's anger started to melt away. He had come home, and his father had accepted him. It didn't fix everything, but it was a start.

Scene Eleven:

Reunions and Realizations

"This is good," Edson said after taking a drink of the pear wine his father had produced. "You made this?"

"Last year," his father replied. "It's one of the best batches I ever made. I'm surprised you don't remember me making this every year. It was your mother's favorite."

"It's good that you can talk about her now without getting angry," Edson said as he passed the jug back to his father.

"I still get angry," his father replied before taking a hearty drink and passing it back. "I've just finally realized that I was blaming everyone around me for something that wasn't their fault. Unfortunately, it took you leaving for me to figure that out."

"We can't change the past. If I hadn't left, I'd have never met Alwin and never become a bard. Without meaning to, you drove me into becoming what I was meant to be."

"Your mother would be so proud of you. She always loved music. I don't think I would've ever won her heart if not for playing her a song on my flute."

"You play the flute? I don't remember that."

"Not very well, especially now that my hands cramp up now and then, but I do enjoy it. Playing makes me remember your mother, and the times we danced together."

"I'd love to hear you play."

"We'll need to drink a good bit more of that wine before that happens."

Edson was more than happy to go along with that. They passed the bottle back and forth, sharing stories of their lives since parting. The jug was nearly empty when his father took up his flute. He actually wasn't bad. Edson soon joined in, playing his citole. They were up half the night, playing song after song, and drinking pear wine. They even played a couple of Edson's originals. This was a side of Edson's father he had never known existed.

Just before going to bed, Edson thought he saw his mother's ghost, peeking in the window. He smiled at her, and she smiled back before fading away. At least one ghost would be satisfied. This brought thoughts of Porter to Edson's mind and kept him awake for a while. When he finally found sleep, his dreams were haunted by visions of the lad. He awoke after a particularly bad dream and found that his father was gone.

* * *

"This, I remember," Edson said as he approached his father, who was on his knees, planting seeds in the ground. "You always were an early riser. Why didn't you wake me?"

"I've heard stories about the hours musicians keep," his father replied. "I wanted to get more of the planting done before it gets too hot."

"Show me how you're doing it," Edson said as he dropped down beside his father. "We'll get more done together."

"Shouldn't you be on the road soon? The bounty hunters

will return eventually."

"I spent the last decade angry with you and thinking you hated me. I can stay for a day or two to visit. We'll figure something out if they show up."

His father smiled and demonstrated how to plant the seeds. They spent the morning doing that and the rest of the day with other chores. By the end, Edson was exhausted but was also pleased. This is what his life would have been if he had never left. He had always looked at it as a horrible existence that he had been fortunate to escape. In an odd way, he now felt as if he had missed out by running away. It was a simple way to live, but one that he thought he might have been able to eventually enjoy.

They sang as they worked. At first, it was just Edson, but his father eventually joined in. He had a fair voice but had no control of it. Still, Edson enjoyed himself. He would never have imagined himself singing with his father. They spent another evening drinking together. Edson woke up in pain the following day; his body wasn't accustomed to physical labor. He still managed to hobble out to join his father in the planting.

Watching his father work drove home how much he had aged in the time Edson had been away. He wouldn't be able to manage things alone much longer. While Edson had gained some satisfaction from working with his father, he had no desire to inherit the farm. He might not hate the life as he once had but still didn't want to live it. A smile came to his face as he thought of someone who might enjoy such a life.

As the day wore on, their moods began to change. It began with small things. Edson would plant seeds in the wrong manner or something similar. They snapped at one another over everything and were barely speaking by the end of the day. The arguments grew louder as they opened another jug of pear wine. The happy reunion was no more, and Edson saw again the father he had hated for over a decade. Eventually, the old man passed out. Edson considered leaving then but decided against it. He gathered his things though and left everything ready for an early departure. He had clearly overstayed his welcome.

* * *

Edson was woken by the sounds of people talking. He was disoriented for a brief moment but eventually was able to focus on the conversation.

"He's not here," Edson's father said. "I've told you just like I told the others. I haven't seen him since he left home, almost ten years ago. You're wasting your time here."

"How do I know you're not lying to me?" The man asking the question had a Vonst accent. Edson would guess that he had attended at least a year or two at the university. That seemed unusual for a bounty hunter. "Perhaps we should have a look around."

"While you're at it, do some of the chores around here. Some haven't been done since he left. Look around at this place, would it look like this if my son were here to help out?"

That stung a little even if it did seem to be intended to dissuade a search. Edson regretted not leaving the night before. He didn't want to drag his father into his mess.

"We'll take your word for it. Try to detain him if he shows up, we'll cut you in on the reward."

"I doubt he'll ever come here again. How much is the reward though? It would be nice to dream."

"Five hundred tulners," the man replied. How rich was Alwin's family? "We'll cut you in for a hundred if you lead us to him."

"Like I said, it'll be nice to dream."

"We'll be in town for a day or two, just in case. Find me if your son shows up."

"You could wait there for a year or two, it wouldn't increase the odds of Edson coming here."

"Be that as it may, find me if he does."

Edson waited until he was sure the men were gone before coming out of his room. His father was watching them ride away through his window.

"They'll be back," he said. "It'd be best if you were gone before then."

"What about you?" Edson asked. "They might get rough if they don't believe you."

"I can take care of myself. It's you they're after."

"Still, it doesn't feel right leaving you to deal with my mess."

"That's what being a father is all about. You'll learn that someday. Hopefully, you'll be a better one than I was."

"Let's not get into that again," Edson said. He didn't want to leave on a bad note. They had spent one decade hating one another, the last thing he wanted to do was spend another one that way. "They'll be watching for me to leave. Go out and do your planting for the day. I'll sleep most of the day and slip out during the night."

"Do you think you'll be able to sneak past them?"

"I'm a Pye, I can do anything." Edson just hoped Princess would cooperate.

* * *

“I'll come back after this is all settled,” Edson said. He was surprised at how sad he was to be leaving. How quickly things had changed. “In the meantime, you need to take it easy.”

“I'll be fine once the spring planting is done,” his father replied. “All the bending gets to me.”

“You need help.” Edson would do all he could to provide that help, short of doing it himself. “I plan to send you someone. Promise me that you'll accept their help and treat them with respect.”

“I'll promise that if you promise me grandchildren someday.”

“Someday I can do,” Edson said. He was bound to produce a child at some point in his life. “Just don't expect it anytime soon.”

“As long as you make it to Vonst and back, I'll be content to wait until I'm on my death bed. I hope it's a bit sooner than that though. I'd like to be around to spoil the tot a bit.”

“I'll sneak through without them even knowing I was here. Like I said, I'm a Pye.”

“I'm proud of you, son.” The words nearly brought a tear. Edson couldn't remember ever hearing them from his father before. “Your mother would be too. Go to Vonst and win the Challenge. The other stuff will sort itself out.”

Edson nodded, though he doubted it would be that easy. He embraced his father one last time before slipping out. Princess and Lackey, the pack horse, were waiting. A light rain fell as he left, making the going slow. Princess cooperated, with Lackey following behind as if he were her loyal servant.

They rode through the night, stopping only when Edson had

to relieve himself. The night was clear and the moon was nearly full, giving him plenty of light to travel by. It was almost dawn when he reached the town of Drey. It had grown a bit since he was a child but otherwise looked the same. Edson was tempted to get a room at one of the two inns and sleep the day away but couldn't take the chance of a bounty hunter figuring out who he was.

He was wearing one of his father's old jackets and had all of his instruments covered on Lackey. He had left Porter's lute and lyre in his room at his father's house. If everything went as planned, both would get a lot of use once more. Edson stopped only for a bite to eat and a bit of supplies, before moving on.

* * *

Edson couldn't sleep. The night was cool, and he had found a flat spot for his bedroll but couldn't clear his mind. He blamed a lack of wine for his insomnia more than anything. That and those looking to kill him, even if he was growing accustomed to that. Not to mention worry over his father and Porter.

Fortune placed a stone under Edson, and he rolled over just in time to see someone moving toward the camp. It was too dark and too late for him to consider using the bow he had purchased, but his dagger was within reach. He held it tightly, even though he wasn't a strong knife man. He wasn't much for fights at all and hoped this wouldn't come to one. It was the only chance he had though. His heart seemed as if it would soon leap out of his chest as the person came closer. He pretended to sleep as they knelt beside him and stayed still until the last second. His knife hand moved fast, and he laid his dagger to rest across the stranger's neck.

“I'm going to stand up slowly,” Edson said. He could see

enough of the stranger to see he was a man. His eyes were wide and his head was bald. “You stay on your knees. Who are you, and what are you doing sneaking into my camp?”

“I thought you might be someone I'm looking for,” the man said, “but you don't really match the description.”

“I'm looking for someone too,” Edson replied. There was a little truth to the statement. Not much but a little. “Maybe we're looking for the same person.”

“Who are you looking for?” the man asked. Edson still held his dagger at the man's throat.

“A singer named Edson Pye. His head's worth a small fortune.”

“There's nothing small about it. I'm looking for the same man. Maybe we can work together?”

“I'm afraid that's not going to be possible,” Edson said as he sliced open the man's throat. The bounty hunter wasn't the first man he had killed, but it was the first time he had done so on purpose. He was surprised to feel no regrets about the action. Despite the fact that the man had been hunting Edson, with the intent of killing him, it was odd to feel nothing for the man's death.

He covered the man's body with some branches and broke camp. Many bounty hunters worked in pairs or even teams. Edson didn't want to be around if any others showed up. His luck had saved him once, but he couldn't count on it happening again. He changed his direction, heading more east than south. There were many roads leading to Vonst. The trick would be to find one that wasn't being watched.

If he could reach the city, he should be fine. Killing him on the road would be easy to paint as an act of random violence. Killing a favored bard during the Bardic Challenge for the second year in a row would draw scrutiny. The bounty hunter Edson had killed had failed to recognize him, but that might not always be the case. He needed to find a better way to disguise himself. First, he needed to find a town. He had moved beyond the range of the map he had purchased and only knew the direction he needed to go. It would have to be enough.

* * *

Edson sat in the sun, combing his hair. He had mixed the dregs of a couple bottles of white wine with some olive oil. Alwin had given him a few recipes for changing hair color. This one had been the only one he had the ingredients for. If what Alwin had said was true, Edson would end up with golden-colored hair.

After four days of riding mostly east, he was turning south. He had avoided towns, and people, since the encounter with the bounty hunter but was running low on supplies. He was also growing tired of sleeping on the ground. To remedy this, he was using one of the first lessons he had learned about hiding. The obvious places to hide were the best.

The bounty hunters were looking for a dark-haired singer who played the citole. Edson would become a blond-haired singer who stuck with the harp and flute. He would keep his citole hidden and would pretend to be a devotee of Alwin Floyd, playing only his music. There were many such acts around, imitating all of the popular bards. Edson often wondered if anyone was covering his songs yet.

The final part of his disguise was his voice. Edson was working on singing with a deeper voice. Most people couldn't tell one singer from another, but some had trained ears. With his luck,

Edson wasn't taking any chances. He was changing anything that might give away who he truly was. He had even moved the packs to Princess and the saddle to Lackey. The former wasn't very happy with the change, while the latter didn't seem to care either way.

The original plan had been to gradually move up the coast toward Vonst, playing shows in every town. He would've reached the city at the start of the Challenge, with word of his performances proceeding him. He didn't have that option anymore. Instead, he would appear unexpectedly, with no word of where he had been. He would need a gig right away, so his first stop would be Jayme Naral's office. Edson was tempted to send the man a message but didn't want to risk it being intercepted by those who were hunting for him.

Princess complained when Edson climbed into Lackey's saddle. She refused to move at first, so Edson sang her a song. That did the trick, but she stopped again as soon as he did. He needed practice with his new voice anyway, so he kept singing. If it kept her moving, he would sing the day away.

Scene Twelve:
Alehouses and Assassins

"Louisa was a pretty lass, as anyone could see,
The men followed her around, she had not one, but three.
She tried to pick one from the group, to set the others free,
But she couldn't decide just who that one should be."

Edson was singing in a small, roadside inn. It was simply called The Hook. Nobody seemed to know where the name had come from. According to the locals, there had been an inn with that name in that spot for over a hundred years. There were a few patrons who looked like they might have been around for the grand opening. At least none of them looked to be bounty hunters.

"Brent was the first of the three, he was a weaver's son,
He owned his father's business, which was left for him to run.
He promised her a steady life, though one without much fun,
If only he could loosen up, he might just be the one."

Impersonating Alwin came naturally to Edson, but it came with a cost. Throughout the performance, Edson had felt the eyes of Alwin's ghost upon him. Sending Porter away was a mistake. If he could do it over again, Edson would have had Hallis take Jer but leave the lad. With the plot exposed, Porter would have been forced to confess his role. He would have never been able to trust the lad but that was better than living with the guilt.

"Sheldon was the second man, a fisherman by trade,
Unlike Brent, he loved his fun and spent every coin he made.
He promised he would treat her well, each time he was paid,
If only he could save a coin, he might just make the grade."

It was good to be playing small gigs again. The large venues had their benefits, but there was nothing Edson enjoyed more than connecting with an audience. Well, maybe wine and women but nothing else. He wished he could play one of his own songs, but it wasn't worth risking. There were still a lot of miles between him and Vonst. The mere mention of someone sounding like him would draw the bounty hunters, and Edson would never make it. Playing Alwin's songs was the next best thing. In some ways, playing his music felt as if a part of him were still alive.

"Francis was the final man, and he ran a butcher shop,
He would dance with her all night, until she feared she'd drop.
But Francis didn't like to bathe and always smelled like slop,
If only he could change his scent, he might just be on top."

Edson was looking forward to a night in a bed. He had hoped to find someone to share it but didn't like the odds. The few lasses in The Hook were either older than Aileen or with their husbands. He had enough problems to deal with already. Adding another husband to the list of people trying to kill him wasn't something Edson was willing to consider at this point.

* * *

The barn door opened, prompting Edson's eyes to do the same. It had taken him some time to get used to the noises of the barn, and he had barely fallen asleep. Had the farmer forgotten some chore, or worse, changed his mind about Edson being allowed to sleep in his barn? He had been chased off of his share of farms in the past. At least both of the farmer's dogs were friendly and too old to be much of a threat.

"Dag," a woman called. It was the farmer's wife, and Dag was the name Edson was using. "Where are you?"

"Over here," he said. He had made a bed atop a pile of hay. She held out a lantern to see as she made her way to him. She held a blanket in her other hand.

"I wanted to make sure you were comfortable," she said as she reached him. "The nights are still a little cool."

"Thank you," he replied. "After spending most of my nights outside lately, this is more than comfortable."

"I grew up playing in this barn," she said, plopping down beside him. "This was my father's farm. We inherited it when he died. Lightning got him."

"That's a bad way to go." There weren't many good ways that Edson could think of. Most involved wine and women. "Your husband seems like a fine man though."

"He's a bore, but I needed someone. The choices around here aren't very good. I would've held out if I knew someone like you was going to pass through."

"You wouldn't want someone like me," Edson replied. "I

can't even stay in a town for more than a week without getting antsy."

"You might be surprised at the things I want," she said. One of her hands slid across the hay and onto his lap. Trouble was knocking once again. "Funny thing is, I always get those things."

"What about your husband?" Edson asked. He wasn't sure he wanted to test his theory about the man's dogs. "What if he finds us?"

"Simon? He sleeps like a log. It would take a lot of screaming for him to wake up. I'm sure you're good but not that good."

"What about your son?" They had a boy of around six or seven. Edson had tried to teach the boy to play the pipe, but he had no interest in it.

"He's as bad as his father." She pulled her dress over her head. Her breasts were firm and large, but Edson could only think of her family. He didn't want to be the one to wreck that. Where had these thoughts come from? He had never held any such qualms before. Why now? "It's just you and me."

"I don't think we should do this," he said. She didn't seem to hear, as she began rubbing his leg and kissing his neck. He pushed her away. "Stop. This isn't right."

"I don't care about what's right," she said, pushing back. "I've heard stories of wandering singers. You're the first one to come my way, and I will have you. You can play along, or I'll scream loud enough to wake Simon. I'll tell him I brought you a blanket and you assaulted me."

"You wouldn't dare."

"Simon," she shouted, not quite loud enough to reach the house. "The next one will be twice as loud. Shall I count to three?"

"There's no need," he replied. The woman was crazy. Sometimes, he thought they all were, but this one definitely was. "I believe you."

"Get those pants off then and prove it."

Edson went along, though his performance was comparable to his final show in Cronar. He tried thinking of Fayme but even that didn't help. Finally, it was over, and she left, after making it clear how disappointed she was. Edson wasn't happy with himself either. Beyond the threat of angry husbands, he had never before cared that a woman was married. What had changed? Could it be changed back, or would he be forever plagued with morals? The thought was horrifying and kept him awake for hours. Finally, he gave up and gathered his belongings. Not wanting to face the farmer, his wife, or their son, Edson was on the road before the sun made its first appearance of the day.

* * *

The wind was knocked out of Edson's lungs as he was slammed against the wall of the Hunter's Arrow Inn. A pair of large, bearded men stood in front of him. One of the two had done the shoving, though Edson didn't know which. He had been on his way to piss and was having trouble stopping himself from doing so.

"What's your name, boy?" the man on Edson's left asked.

"Dag Stemp," Edson replied. The false name almost came to his lips naturally.

"I never heard of a bard named Dag," the second man said. "Where are you from?"

"Cossell." It was a small town further to the east. Edson's father had taken him there once, before his mother's death. "I wouldn't expect you to have heard of me before. This is my first trip to Vonst for the Challenge. I'm hoping to get lucky and make the lists."

"You look a little old to be just starting out," said the first man. "Is that your real hair color?"

"Yes, it's my real hair color. Who would dye their hair this awful color? As for starting late, you got me there. I never really planned on doing this. I was going to marry Elsie Densor, but she chose another. I left the next day."

"What do you think?" the first man asked the second.

"I still think he looks a little like Pye. We should take him just in case."

"Pie? I don't even like the stuff. I'm more of a cake guy." Edson hoped the joke might loosen things up. He didn't know what else to do at this point. Fighting either one of the two men would be suicidal. "Wait, you mean Edson Pye? I've heard of him. He was Alwin Floyd's apprentice. I heard he killed him."

"I don't know about that," the first man said, "but we plan to catch him before anyone else can."

"If he killed Alwin, I hope you find him."

"We will," the second man said. "This guy isn't him. Sorry about pushing you. You really do look a little bit like him. He's a bit taller though, now that I think on it."

"Let's go then," the first man said, after smacking the back of the other man's head. They walked away, shoving and hitting one another until Edson couldn't see them anymore. He had to nearly run to the jakes to relieve himself, but his luck had held out once more.

* * *

"I know who you are," a woman said from behind Edson. He turned and saw a woman nearly a foot taller than him. She was wide too but not fat. There was something frighteningly attractive about her. "I saw you at Tabara Hall in Vonst last year."

"I think you have me mistaken for someone else," Edson said. "I've never been to Vonst."

"Others might believe that, but I know the truth, Edson. I also know that a lot of people are looking for you."

"It's Dag." Edson looked around, but nobody was close enough to have heard her. "I don't know this Edson fellow."

"Keep up the lie if you insist. It would be a shame to have to share your secret though."

"I'm not saying I'm him, but what would it take to keep you quiet?"

"A private show for my husband and me, back at our estate."

"I love private shows." That was a complete lie. He fed off the energy of audiences but had to stay alive to do so. "I'm free tomorrow night."

"I was thinking tonight, after your show here."

"I won't be able to give you my all after performing," he replied. He was on his first break in a tavern called The Mixing Bowl. He couldn't remember the name of the town. "You'd be much better off waiting until tomorrow."

"We're busy tomorrow. I guess I'll have to share your secret then."

"No need for that." Edson didn't think she was bluffing, but it was hard to tell. The woman had better gambling eyes than Garrett Rend or Captain Janson Matia. "I'll do your show tonight.

Just don't expect my best."

"I'm sure you'll be fine. I'll have a carriage waiting for you outside. Don't think you'll be able to slip away either. One mention of your name and the area will be flooded with bounty hunters."

"The thought hadn't crossed my mind." It had, but he had already ruled it out for the same reason she gave. He had to give her and her husband the best show he possibly could and hope they honored their end of the deal. She walked away, leaving him wondering what kind of man could be both lucky and cursed enough to marry such a woman. He finished his break, and his set, in both fear and anticipation.

The carriage was nicer than any Edson had ever seen, other than perhaps Seynia's magical coach. The seats were comfortable and didn't bounce as they moved. After four attempts, Edson gave up on engaging the driver in conversation. He was either mute, rude, or both. The ride to the estate took almost an hour. Edson napped for half of that. He was impressed when they arrived, as the place was nearly as big as the university in Vonst. Who were these people?

A butler met them at the gate. He was only slightly more talkative than the driver, as he led Edson to a waiting room. A wooden stand held a carafe of both red and white wine. Edson poured a glass of the white and sat down. The woman came into the room a few minutes later, accompanied by a man nearly half a foot shorter than Edson. He was thin, nearly rail-like.

"I'm glad you decided to come, Edson," she said. He started to protest, but she laughed. "Your secrets are safe here. In fact, this might be the safest place you've been in some time. It's the last place any of the bounty hunters will look."

"Why is that?" Edson asked, giving up all pretense of being

Dag.

"You don't know who I am, do you?"

"No. Should I?" There was something familiar about her.

"Probably not, but it's funny that you don't. My name is Terra." Bells went off in Edson's head.

"You're Alwin's youngest sister," he said, remembering a couple stories his mentor had told him. Why hadn't he remembered those stories before now? Farris Dent's warnings came to mind. "Why did you bring me here?"

"Don't worry, we're not part of the group who are looking to kill you. I inherited enough from Daddy. I don't need Fedwick or Alwin's shares."

"Who's trying to kill me? How do you know about that?"

"Relena and Lethina were always greedy." They were Alwin's older sisters. He hadn't told Edson any good stories about either of them. "I've had a spy watching both of them for years now. They're afraid you'll have a claim to Alwin's share of Daddy's fortune."

"Why am I here then? Surely not for a private show." Were Relena and Lethina responsible for Alwin's murder? What about their other brother? How had he died?

"No, that was a ruse. Would you have come if you knew who I was?"

"Probably not. I considered not coming as it was." Running away as fast as possible would've been a smarter move.

"I'm glad you did. We have a lot to talk about. Alwin told me quite a bit about you. He looked at you like a son. I guess that makes me your aunt."

"He told me a couple stories about you too."

"Probably none of the good ones. He always tried to keep

his family name a secret. I can't say I blame him. My sisters are rotten, and their children are worse. Fedwick was greedy but not overly so. Alwin was the best of us all."

"I miss him more with every day."

"Me too," she said. Her husband still hadn't spoken. He looked as if he were afraid to. "That's why I'm going to help you. I'm having your horses delivered to an inn on the road to Vonst. My driver will take you there tomorrow morning. We'll use tonight to give you the information you need to beat my sisters at their own game."

* * *

Princess seemed happy to be the one wearing the saddle again. Lackey was, as usual, content to simply trot along. After riding in Terra's carriage for two days, Edson was glad to be reunited with his horses. He was even happier to have Princess cooperating. He was still keeping up the disguise as Dag and had too much on his mind to have to keep the horse entertained as he rode.

After hearing a brief history of Alwin's family, Edson could understand why he had kept them a secret. As a child, Edson had dreamed of growing up as a member of a wealthy family. It didn't hold as much appeal anymore. His issues with his father seemed minor in comparison. Alwin and his brother weren't the first to suffer mysterious deaths.

The remaining journey to Vonst would be the most dangerous. Alwin's family would have every possible way into the city watched, but Edson had spent the latter part of his childhood learning how to get into places where he wasn't wanted. He would find a way.

His wine supply was low again, so he was hoping to find a roadside inn. Instead he found a village. Both inns already had singers, so he rented a room and paid for a meal. Since it had been awhile since he watched another singer's performance, he found a seat in the common room. The performance wouldn't begin for some time, which would give him plenty of time for drinking.

He had finished nearly a bottle when the show finally started. The singer was young, not much older than Edson was when Alwin found him. He had talent but seemed to lack training. There were at least five instances where he failed to pick up on the audience's mood and played the wrong type of song. He needed to learn to read the crowd better. His originals were really good, but again, he played them at the wrong times.

Edson was thoroughly drunk by the time the performance ended. The singer made his way through the room, accepting the well-deserved praise. Finally, he reached Edson's table.

"Thank you for attending my show," the lad said. He had a hat in his hands for coins. Edson took a couple finners off of his table and threw them in.

"You're pretty good," Edson said. "Have you had any training?"

"Not really. My father was a bard, but he died young."

"What's your name?"

"Terren Genfry."

"Is this your first time going to Vonst for the Challenge?"

"Yes. Is it that obvious?"

"Not really. You've got the skills. You need to learn a few of the nuances though. Buy me another drink and I'll teach you how to leave the audiences screaming for more."

The lad seemed to doubt Edson's words but still called over a barmaid and ordered a pair of drinks. They were the first of many, as Edson went through everything he had noticed and more. He taught the lad how to pair his songs up to build the mood he wanted, and how to read what the audience would want to hear. He crammed many of Alwin's teachings into a single lesson and hoped the lad would retain half of it.

In the end, Terren couldn't keep up with Edson's drinking. He passed out at the table while Edson was explaining the best ways to close a show. With the help of the barkeep, he carried the lad to his room and deposited him in bed. Terren would do well to find a mentor, but Edson wasn't ready for such things yet. He doubted he ever would be again.

* * *

Edson nearly cried when Vonst first came into view. He was going to make it! All roads leading to the city were flooded with people. There were only five days left before the festival would begin. He needed to find a spot to lie low until then.

It took nearly a day to reach the gates, which were closed for the night. The city had long ago grown beyond the walls, so Edson began looking for a place to stay. The first two inns had no rooms available. The third one had a single one left. It was barely big enough to hold the small cot and cost more than three times what a full-sized room should have cost. It was better than finding a spot in the bushes though, so he paid without complaint.

After a few glasses of cheap wine, he grew restless and decided to wander a bit. There were people everywhere, and some of the shops were still open. Edson stopped at a few, before coming to one that had a small collection of musical instruments for sale. His eyes nearly came out of his head when he saw his rebec among them. There was no mistaking it.

“Where did you get this?” he asked the shopkeeper, holding up the instrument.

“A young woman sold it to me three days ago,” the man said. “Do you want to buy it? It plays much better than it looks.”

“How much?” Edson was thrilled with the man's assessment of the instrument but didn't know what to think of the prospect of Fayme being in Vonst. It made sense. She had enough skill to place fairly high on the lists.

“Ten mensers,” the shopkeeper replied.

“Answer a few of my questions and you can have this for it.” Edson held up a tulner. The man nodded and held out his hand. Edson knew better than to pay before getting his answers though. “What did this woman look like?”

“She was beautiful. Her hair was dark, and she had eyes the color of emeralds.”

“Was she with anyone?” Edson managed after a moment. Seeing her face in his mind brought her scent to his nose, her breath on his neck, and her magical voice to his ears.

“Not that I saw. She came in here alone. She said she needed coins to keep her going until she could find a gig.”

“You said three days ago?”

“Yes. She's probably in the city now.”

“Probably.” Edson said as he tossed the man the coin. The rebec was in perfect tune and looked the same as it had the day she stole it. Edson carried it almost reverently back to his room. She was here. He had never dreamed of the possibility.

Scene Thirteen:
Homecomings and Husbands

Edson was the second one through the gates in the morning. He would have been first, but he was stuck behind one of the few people he had ever met who wasn't willing to give up a spot for a few coins. Edson hadn't slept. Thoughts of Fayme forced everything else from his mind. How did she continue to pull at him after the way she had betrayed him?

His hair dye was starting to wear off, but Edson didn't care. He wouldn't need it much longer. There were a few things he had to take care of that would be easier done incognito, then he would scream from the rooftops that he was back in the city. Oh, to be a fly on the wall when news of that reached the Trieb family. Or when the news reached Kodran. Or Fayme. Especially Fayme.

There were already singers on nearly every corner. These were mostly young musicians who had never served as apprentices or had any other sort of training. There were a few others mixed in, mostly those who had spent all their coin to get to Vonst, leaving none to provide them with shelter or food. Edson had been at that point the previous year. Pride had forced him to go hungry until the festival truly began.

No reputable inn, tavern, or hall would feature performances until then. Still, many singers, including some of note, would do an impromptu show in Docktown. Their purpose was to get people talking. Sometimes this backfired and painted these performers as desperate. None of the favorites took such chances. Edson wasn't about to go against that tradition.

Would Fayme be playing an early show? She had no reputation on this side of the sea and would likely struggle to find gigs once the Challenge began, but the proprietors of the inns and taverns of Docktown would fight one another to sign a singer as pretty as she was, and the sailors in port would line up to watch her show.

Before he could even consider a trip to the docks to see if he could find her, Edson needed to secure lodging and a gig. For that, he needed to visit Jayme Naral but was afraid his offices would be under surveillance by Alwin's family. Instead, he went to a tavern nearby. He paid the barkeep to send someone to deliver a message to Jayme, before settling in a dark corner with a bottle of wine. Jayme arrived a half hour later.

"I was beginning to worry about you," he said as he sat down at the table. "The last word I had of you was from Cronar. I was afraid you were dead. Where's the boy at?"

"What boy?" Edson asked

"Porter," Jayme replied. "My contacts in Cronar sent word that he was with you."

"What do you know of Porter?" Edson asked, growing suspicious. Was Jayme involved in this whole mess too? Did the plot go back even further than Edson had suspected?

"More than you can imagine and probably more than you. You haven't answered my question though. Where is he?"

"He double-crossed me so I got rid of him."

"You did what? Is he dead?" Jayme nearly came out of his

seat.

"Not if Hallis Gort held up his end of the deal. Why do you care?"

"Porter is Alwin's son," Jayme replied. His words hit Edson like a thrown brick. He was stunned. There had always been something familiar about the lad, but Edson had never made the connection. His mind went to work. If Porter was Alwin's son, was the tour of Aern simply a ruse to connect him and Edson? "He's his true heir."

"How long have you known this?"

"Alwin came to me two years back and told me the story. There's more to it though. His mother isn't the woman you met in Zorbelix. His true mother is Aileen Sager."

"Are you kidding me?" Edson asked. This was nearly as big of a stunner as Alwin being the lad's father. "Does her husband know about him?"

"Yes. He paid the couple that you met to take him across the sea and make him disappear. Aileen finally told Alwin about it a couple years back, but she had thought the boy was dead. Thomas confessed the truth to Alwin. That was when he released you. He wanted to find his son. He made arrangements with me to send you to the boy if anything ever happened to him."

"Why didn't you just tell me?" Was Alwin the man who had taught Porter in Zorbelix? That would explain a lot.

"Alwin said that you would have run away if we told you to take on an apprentice."

"That's probably true. So, what now?"

"I'll send word to Hallis. He and I go way back. In the meantime, I've been fielding inquiries for months from the biggest halls in the city. I've heard from everyone except the Diamond

House. Kodran Novius is booked there for the entire festival."

"Book me at the Amber Stallion again," Edson replied. They had treated him well enough. "I'll need lodging and stable stalls for two horses as well."

"I have a loft nearby that you can use until everything is secured. The owner of this place is a friend, I'll convince him to let you keep the horses here until then. Be careful though. Once word is out that you've returned, you should be fairly safe. Until then, the Triebs will stop at nothing to find you."

"Do they know about Porter?" Edson still couldn't believe the lad was Alwin's son. No wonder Alwin's ghost had been so angry. "Will they try to kill him too?"

"I don't think they even know he exists. Let me worry about the boy. You need to focus on winning the Challenge."

"I can do that." What did Jayme think he had been focused on for the past year? "I need one other favor from you though."

"Name it."

"I need you to secure a gig for another singer. Nothing major, any gig will do."

"That shouldn't be a problem. What's his name?"

"Her name is Fayme Lobel. She's somewhere in Vonst, but I don't know where."

"Trying to win back a lost love?"

"Something like that," Edson replied. If only it were that simple. "Just let me know where she'll be playing. I'll find her."

"I'll make the arrangements. I can also have people watch for her, and send me word when she's spotted."

"That would be great." Would it really? Did he really want to find her? What would he say to her? "I'm going to check the taverns in Docktown. She might be desperate enough to take a gig there."

"That's a definite possibility," Jayme said as he poured a glass from Edson's bottle. "Tell me about the boy though. Is he like his father at all?"

"He is." Edson had just never realized it. "He's got a lot of talent. I just hope Hallis didn't kill him."

"If Hallis gave you his word that he wouldn't, we don't have to worry about it. His integrity means more to him than anything else. It always has. Did he make any other promises?"

"No, I just asked him not to kill the lad."

"He likely sold him then. I'll track him down. You worry about avoiding the rest of his family, beating Kodran, and finding your lost love."

"That should take up my afternoon. Got any dinner plans?"

Jayme laughed and asked a few more questions about Porter. Edson gave him a rundown of his adventures in Aern, and Jayme promised a full accounting of the revenue from the various shows. Edson was surprised to find that he still had pay coming. He had spent nearly all of the coins he had received already, other than the letters of credit for Porter's apprenticeship. Edson wasn't comfortable drawing on those, so this was timely news.

* * *

Docktown was the most crowded part of the city. With few places offering entertainment anywhere else in the city, this was the biggest part of the festival for this area. Add the crews from the ships lining the docks, and there was nearly no room to move about. Edson had his pipe in a pocket but had left the rest of his instruments in Jayme's loft. He carried two small pouches of coins, both hidden away from the prying fingers of pickpockets, who were as big a part of the festival as the singers.

He went from tavern to tavern, having at least a glass of wine at each. He saw jugglers and singers, storytellers and fire dancers, sword swallowers, and street magicians, and every other form of entertainment one could imagine, but he saw no sign of Fayme. He did see someone he knew though, Welby Dinan. Edson followed the carpenter from a distance. Welby avoided most of the revelry but did watch some of the musicians. Edson suspected he was eyeing the instruments more than the singers though.

After a while, Welby headed toward the harbor. Edson followed. He waited until Welby was alone on the docks to close the gap between them. This caused Welby to turn on him, blade in hand, likely suspecting he was about to be robbed or worse.

"Easy, Welby," Edson said, pushing back the hood that had covered his head. "Is this how you greet an old friend?"

"Edson? Is that really you?"

"Yes, but keep it down. There are some people looking for me."

"I know," Welby replied. "Some of them came to the ship a couple days ago, asking all sorts of questions. With the amount of coin they're offering for you, I wouldn't be showing my face around here if I were you. I'm tempted to turn you in myself."

"It should all be cleared up soon." Edson couldn't see Welby betraying him. Coins held little value to the man where friendship was a treasure. "How long will you be in Vonst?"

"We'll ship out a few days after the festival is over."

"Returning to Aern again?"

"Most likely. I leave that up to Captain Matia."

"If you do, I have a favor to ask, and a commission for

you."

"Why don't we find a quiet spot to talk," Welby said. "You can tell me all about it, along with your tour of Aern."

"Let's go back to the loft I'm staying in. It's probably the only quiet place we're going to find."

* * *

Edson took a deep breath. He had to time his entrance perfectly. It was opening night of the festival, which meant the time had come for him to make an appearance. Bards in his position, as one of the favorites to win, rarely played opening night, yet were expected to attend an up-and-coming musician's performance in a show of support. Edson had hoped to attend Fayme's opening, but neither he or Jayme had been able to find her.

Instead, he was going to Terren Genfry's debut. The young singer had secured a gig at the Red Vase Room. It had once been a room of prominence, but the area around it had faded, taking it down as well. It was still a solid gig for a debut singer. Edson wanted to see if the lad had incorporated his advice into the show.

His own opening would come later in the week. As was the case with many of the bigger venues, the owners of the Amber Stallion hadn't announced who would be performing. In the morning, a full listing would be posted throughout town. People would line up to see who was playing where. Some would leak the knowledge, as was the case with Kodran. Everyone knew he would be at the Diamond House.

The back door of the Red Vase Room opened, revealing Jayme and the owner of the room. They smiled and waved for Edson to follow. As was custom, the owner slowly led Edson to a private booth, where Jayme joined him. As they passed, word spread of who he was. Soon, people were pointing at him and yelling out for him to play a song. The room's staff quickly put a stop to that, leaving Edson to enjoy the show.

The lad had not only taken Edson's advice, he had added two instruments, a flute and a rebec. The show was brilliant, leaving Edson wondering how this young man had learned so much in such a short time. He wouldn't be playing the Red Vase Room long and might end up as a long shot to win the whole thing. Jayme was equally impressed, and pushed Edson for information on the lad.

Terren came to Edson's booth after making his rounds of the room. Edson smiled as the lad approached.

"Good show, Terren," he said. "I see you took my advice."

"I did," the lad replied, a wide smile on his face. "If I had known who you were, I would've listened closer."

"You did fine," Edson replied. A face across the room caught his eye. It was Fayme! She was looking right at him. "This is my friend, Jayme. He has some questions for you. If you'll excuse me, I have something I must take care of."

Edson rushed across the room, but she was gone when he got to the other side. He scanned the room and barely caught a glimpse of her dark hair as she went out the front door. He ran after her but couldn't find her when he reached the street. He called her name, but there was no reply. She had to be nearby. He ran from street to street, calling her name and pleading with her to show herself, but there was no reply. She had simply vanished. Again.

* * *

Edson stumbled to the door. He had tried ignoring the persistent knocking but had finally gave up on that tactic. Whoever it was, they weren't going away. He threw the door open, intending to scream at the offending knocker. The well-dressed, older man on the other side of the door was unexpected though, deflating Edson's anger a bit.

"Are you Edson Pye?" the old man asked.

"Yes, who are you?"

"I'm Thomas Sager. Aileen's husband."

"What can I do for you?" He couldn't be here to confront Edson about sleeping with Aileen. It had been nearly a year back, and he was hardly the first musician she had shared her bed with, nor was he likely the last. Was he here about Porter? He was the one who had paid for the lad to go to Aern. He was also Alwin's former lover.

"This is a nice place," Thomas said, walking past Edson. "I always thought the Amber Stallion was the best venue in Vonst. What made you chose to play here? You could've played any place you wanted."

"They treated me well last year."

"There you have it. Quality service. So many of the young people today forget how important that is."

"I can't argue with that. Was there something you wanted?"

"That's the other problem with you youngsters. Always in a hurry. In my day, a guest would never get this far inside without being offered a drink, or perhaps something to snack on."

"I wasn't expecting company. I have wine though. Do you want some?"

"What vintage?"

"Whatever they put in the carafe. It isn't bad. Probably not as good as you're used to."

"I've had my share of the slop they serve in the low taverns. I don't waste my time with such things anymore. I'm old and I'm rich. I'm going to enjoy myself."

"I can't blame you there," Edson said. Was there even a reason for this visit? "How about I pour you a glass and you can judge it for yourself?"

"That will suffice. In the meantime, I'd like to ask you a few questions, if you don't mind."

"Ask away." Edson poured two glasses of wine.

"My wife spent a healthy amount of my coins getting you out of jail last year. I know all about her love for singers and don't really care. What else did she ask for in return for your freedom? Did she send you looking for the boy?"

"What boy?" Edson wasn't about to give anything away about Porter. He already felt bad for handing the lad over to Hallis.

"Don't play stupid with me, son. Alwin told me how smart you are. Did she send you to look for Porter?"

"No. She never even mentioned him to me."

"Where is he now? I know you were with him in Eveltour. One of my friends saw your show there."

"I have no idea. We parted ways months ago."

"Where at?"

"Bithe." Let Thomas try to find him there.

"That's good." The old man seemed to relax, and finally took a drink of his wine. "This isn't bad either. Not as good as the stuff you drank from my cellar but not bad."

"Your cellar is impressive," Edson said. He didn't know what else to say. The man obviously knew that Edson had slept with his wife, and didn't care.

"You're welcome to come over any time and I'll give you a private tour," Thomas said. The intent was clear. Edson had spent three years fending off Alwin's similar veiled advances. "You might learn a thing or two."

"I'm sure I would, but the festival is going to keep me busy. I have pressing business to attend to after that, so I won't be in Vonst long."

"That's too bad. There's always next year."

* * *

Edson had just gotten comfortable when the knocking started again. He stormed back to the door, fully intending on giving Thomas a piece of his mind. It wasn't Thomas who was knocking though, it was his wife, Aileen.

"While it's been some time since a young man stared at me with his mouth open, I'd prefer that you invite me in." She hadn't changed much in the year since they saw one another. He stepped aside and waved for her to enter. "There we go. Was that so difficult?"

"What do you want, Aileen?" Looking at her, he could see that Porter did have some of her features. The rest came from Alwin. Edson wondered how he had missed that.

"So impatient," she said, running her finger across his cheek. "I suppose I can understand that though. Why did my husband come to see you?"

"He was complaining about the coin you spent to get me out of jail," Edson replied. "I think he knows about us."

"I'm sure he does." She laughed, which was what Edson had

been going for. Anything to get her from finding out that he had given her son to a criminal. “I might have even told him about you. I don't remember. That couldn't have been his only reason for visiting. What else did he want?”

“He brought up the wine I drank from his cellar. He said mine wasn't as good.”

“It probably isn't. Did he try to seduce you?”

“He tried. I told you already, that's not my thing.”

“That would only encourage him. Did he give you a gift?”

“No, but he offered to give me a tour of his wine cellar.”

“Are you going to take him up on the offer?”

“I told you, that's not my thing.”

“I can give a tour too, you know.”

“I'm sure you can. Is that all you came here for? I have rehearsal in a few hours and need to get some rest.”

“Is there anything else about Thomas's visit you're not telling me about?”

“Not that I can think of.” He was trying to keep all thoughts of Porter from his head. Beyond his guilt, he didn't want to get further involved in Aileen and Thomas's marriage. They had enough issues without him in the mix. “Is there something else you'd expect him to talk with me about?”

“Not really. I was just curious mostly. We can drop the subject. I believe you said something about wine and bed?”

“I said I needed rest,” Edson replied. He had missed the hunger in her eyes. Was it his status as a favorite or was that hunger simply always there? The sadness was still there as well. At least he knew the reason for that now. “I won't get that with you in my bed.”

“No, you won't.” She leaned in and kissed him. He was caught, but there were worse traps to end up in. He managed to grab the wine decanter as she pulled him into the bedchamber.

* * *

The Rose and Thorn was packed for Donovan Allenson's opening. Edson had recognized the name while scanning the schedules. He had wondered who would play the house where Alwin had been murdered. The young singer from Eber was being talked about as a possible contender. Edson wanted to see the show for himself to see if he and Kodran would have a challenger and to visit with one of the few singers he had taken a liking to.

Donovan began with an original. The song told the story of a pair of the famed rangers who protected the city of Eber from the various creatures inhabiting the wild lands of southern Aern. He followed that with one of Farris Dent's favorites. Edson still couldn't believe he had met the legendary bard, or that he was even still alive. The crowd gave Donovan a deserved round of applause. He was definitely good enough to be considered a contender.

This didn't bother Edson, but he spotted someone across the room who obviously didn't share that feeling. The scowl on Kodran's face plainly showed his thoughts on having a third name thrown into the mix. That scowl made Edson's day, where seeing Kodran in the first place had nearly ruined it. Edson couldn't stop staring at the man. He had blamed Kodran for Alwin's death for most of the past year and still wasn't convinced he hadn't played some sort of role. Even if he were innocent in that, he was still an ass.

Edson forced a smile to his lips as Kodran looked his way for the first time. Edson didn't look away, though his smile widened when Kodran's scowl deepened. The man had likely been born with a pissy look on his face. He looked away first, giving Edson a chance to regain his composure. Donovan ended Farris's song and surprised Edson by going right into *The Angry Farmer*. It was odd hearing another bard perform one of his songs. Other than with Alwin, and Fayme for a brief time, Edson had never experienced that before.

Kodran looked as if his head was going to explode. He stormed out, with his hangers-on trailing behind him. Edson cheered and waved for a barmaid. His mood was improving with every step Kodran took and every note Donovan played.

Scene Fourteen:
Debts and Doubts

Kodran absently plucked at his lute. It was all he could do to keep himself from screaming at his driver again. The man couldn't understand simple instructions. It wasn't as if his job was difficult; the horses did most of the work. He was just an idiot.

The man's lack of intelligence was really only a minor inconvenience. The real problem was Edson Pye. The Eberian wouldn't have a chance, but Edson was another matter. Alwin had trained him well. Kodran would never admit how fortunate he had been to win the previous year. Edson had been on the road for a year since then, playing for much bigger audiences than Kodran had.

"Can't you go any faster?" he asked the driver, trying as hard as he could not to scream. He just wanted to get back to his room, and the ambrosia oil he had in his nightstand. He had sworn to stop using it the day before. That was before seeing Edson. Kodran hadn't known that would happen when he had spoken the words. He wouldn't have done so if he had. Just a little to get him through the night. He would quit again in the morning.

"Not unless you want me to run people over," the driver replied. His tone was unacceptable. Kodran would have words with his booking agent over this. How hard was it to show a little respect to your betters?

"Just do the best you can. I really need to get back to my room."

"Yes, sir." That was better. Good help was getting harder to come by with each passing year. That was a big part of the reason why Kodran hadn't taken on an apprentice. That and the unlikelihood of finding one who had at least a basic grasp of manners and respect. Most of those he had met had no appreciation for tradition and rules. They were all like Alwin Floyd. At least he wouldn't be a problem anymore.

Winning for a third year in a row meant everything to Kodran. He had never gotten over Farris Dent choosing Alwin as an apprentice instead of himself. Farris was the only bard to have won the Challenge three consecutive times. Matching that feat would further prove how wrong he had been with that decision. Adding in that Edson had been Alwin's apprentice only drove Kodran further.

Kodran didn't say a word as they finally reached the Diamond House. He waited impatiently as the driver opened the door and helped him out of the carriage. The oil was calling to him. Just a little to get through. That was it. He would quit in the morning. Or maybe the next day. He could do it whenever he wanted and would if he weren't surrounded by idiots. The oil kept him from strangling them all. Perhaps he would wait to quit until after the tournament.

If he won.

* * *

Kodran's tea was cold. How was cold tea supposed to help his voice? He considered complaining but knew it would do no good. The staff at the Diamond House had been outstanding his first year, but their work ethic had taken a turn for the worst over the past two years. Cold tea was only the latest in a long string of outrages.

"Has opening night sold out yet?" he asked. No reigning champion in memory had failed to open with a full house. He didn't want to be the first.

"There's still a handful of tickets left," Erhan Prenth replied. He was Kodran's booking agent, at least for the time being. A change would have to be made if Edson or another won the Challenge. "They'll be gone by tomorrow night."

"I hope so." The man was too confident. It wasn't his legacy that was at stake. Kodran was driven to be listed with the greats. Even that wasn't truly enough. He wanted to be remembered as the best. A third consecutive win would go a long way toward that. "I want to add an extra show this year. Somewhere else besides the Diamond House. Somewhere bigger."

"We have an exclusive deal. It would be a breach of your contract to play a show somewhere else."

"I pay you to work out those details. If you can't handle such a simple task, maybe I should speak with Jayme Naral. He seems to be handling Edson Pye's bookings quite well."

"I'll see what I can do." Jayme wasn't really an option. He had turned down Kodran years back, but Erhan didn't need to know that. There were other booking agents. Most of them would sell out their own mother for a chance to represent Kodran. Especially if he were to win for a third time in a row. Even Jayme might be willing to talk if that should happen. "They're going to want something for it though. An extra show there or perhaps advance booking for next year's festival."

"I'll do the extra show but keep my options open for next year. I'm growing tired of the place."

"Hopefully that will be enough, but I'm not making any promises. Was that the only reason you called me here?"

"Did you do something about the driver?"

"He's no longer employed by Trieb Consolidated. They've sent their apologies in the form of a two-week credit for usage of their carriages. That will cover the rest of the festival."

"Just make sure they send a competent driver next time. One who knows how to follow simple instructions."

"I stressed that already, but I'll send over a reminder. Are you ready for the show?"

"As ready as I'm ever going to be."

"Have you considered my advice?"

"Yes, and I still think it's a foolish idea. Alwin Floyd was a hack, at best. I'm not about to do a tribute to him during my show."

"It's your call," Erhan said. "I just think it would help with the judges."

"I don't need any help with them," Kodran replied. He had won two years in a row without resorting to such stunts. "Did you collect on the advance for the Diamond House?"

"I did. It was barely enough to keep the wolves at bay. Your debt has really gotten out of hand."

"That's another problem I pay you to manage. Do your magic with the numbers."

"I've done about all I can. You're going to have to curb your spending at some point." That was always Erhan's answer.

"Or you can get more for each show. Did you even try

negotiating a higher percentage of the gate?"

"They bumped it up five percent from last year, which was already higher than the year before."

"Take out another loan then."

"I doubt any of the moneylenders will extend your credit any further. You need to set a budget."

"We've been over this," Kodran said. Perhaps it really was time to start considering a different manager. "People have expectations for bards with my status. I can't let them down. If I'm seen eating in some rundown diner, my reputation will take a hit. I can't afford that. Especially now."

"I'll see what I can do about a loan to get us through the festival. After that, we're going to have to make some changes. Perhaps you should consider touring Aern. The pay for shows in Zorbelix alone will surpass what you typically make in Rov."

"Those huge arenas are a mockery of what a bard's performance should be. How can I read the mood of the audience when I'm playing for twenty thousand people? It's madness. Leave such foolishness to Edson Pye and his like."

"From what I've heard, he made a fortune in his tour. You would double that. Just think about it."

"Sell the remaining seats for my opening show and book a one-night performance elsewhere, and I'll consider it, but I'm not making any promises either. There is a tradition that must be honored. True bards play in Vonst in the summer and Rov in the winter. It's just how it's done."

"Traditions change." That was one of the biggest problems with society today. Nobody respected tradition. Kodran had seen more change in his lifetime than he cared to think about. "One way or another, we have to get your debt under control. The interest kicks in on four of your loans next year. If something doesn't change, we'll be defaulting on payments by late spring."

"See about getting the loans for now," Kodran said. He was tired of this discussion, and his morning boost of ambrosia oil was wearing off. "Draw up estimates on what we'd make in Aern compared to a typical season in Rov. Unless you fail to sell the tickets for my opening, we'll meet again in two days. If those seats are empty, I'll be meeting with my new booking agent."

* * *

"In lunar light, she shines so bright,
Gliding just like a bird in flight.
In perfect tune, beneath the moon,
If you stare, she'll make you swoon."

There wasn't an empty seat in the house. Kodran wasn't surprised by this but was relieved. Edson Pye's opening was tonight as well and had sold out within hours of the schedules being released. There were a few notables in sight but also a good amount of missing faces. How many of those were at Edson's show? The judges mattered the most, but there were a few others who could make or break a performer by giving a positive or negative review. Kodran was established enough to no longer be completely at their mercy. That hadn't always been the case.

"In a dream, is how she makes it seem,
Moving just like a flowing stream.
In harmony, with all that we see,
Her movements are visual poetry."

After Farris Dent chose Alwin as his apprentice, Kodran had been forced to strike out on his own. He had other offers, of course, but none of those bards offered anything near the prestige of training under Farris. Kodran spent a year at the university, studying music history and structure. He worked odd jobs through that year, since he didn't have a wealthy family to back him, as Alwin had been blessed with. After that, Kodran had went on the road and had built his audience one show at a time.

"She Dances Beneath the Moon,
But she never dances with me.
I know I said I would leave soon,
But I can never truly be free.
She'll never hear these words I croon,
For then she'd never let me see,
When She Dances Beneath the Moon."

Aileen Sager wasn't in the audience. That wasn't a surprise but still hurt. She, too, had chosen Alwin over him. It was little comfort that she had chosen Thomas over both of them. Her constant chasing of younger singers also did little to salve his wound. Nobody besides him knew that his biggest hit had been written about her. It was a secret he planned to take to his grave. They had spent two nights together. It had been many years back but was still fresh in Kodran's memories. It was even fresher when he used the ambrosia oil. He had done a little before the show, just to take the edge off, but was thinking of little besides the vial sitting backstage. His first break couldn't come soon enough.

* * *

Kodran was fully in the embrace of the ambrosia oil. He was warm and safe there. Edson Pye wasn't there. Despite putting on what he felt was his best performance ever, Kodran awoke to find he was barely mentioned in the daily performance reviews. Everyone was fawning over Edson and a pair of newcomers, the Eberian and some child from the east. It was enough to make Kodran scream.

The only positive news of the day was that Erhan had secured Kodran a night at the Crenshaw House. It was one of the newer venues in Vonst, and the acoustics were said to be phenomenal. More importantly, it held nearly two hundred more seats than the Diamond House. Talbot Silton was booked there for the rest of the festival. He had won the Challenge nearly a decade back and had proceeded to drink himself into mediocrity. His name still drew an audience, but nothing compared to what Kodran would bring in.

The show at the Crenshaw House would be different from his normal performance. He would be auditioning singers later in the afternoon, with the hopes of finding at least a pair of competent back-up vocalists for the show. Erhan had been pushing Kodran lately to consider taking on an apprentice, but he had yet to meet one he could tolerate for three years or more. Perhaps one of those auditioning would be acceptable, providing they could cover the apprentice fee.

The thought of dealing with an untrained brat had Kodran reaching again for the oil. The auditions were the only thing on his schedule for the day, and he didn't have a performance scheduled until the following night. He had no desire to watch any others after the fiasco at the Eberian's show and no lust for anyone other than Aileen, who wouldn't even speak to him. That left him alone with the oil, his music, and his memories.

The music and oil were the only things allowing him to cope with his third companion in solitude. The memories haunted him. Whether they were of his childhood and his drunken uncle or his lonely life as an adult, memories brought pain. There were the two days with Aileen, but those memories led to pain eventually too. Winning the Challenge the past two years had added to his small stash of joyful remembrances, but those were fleeting moments. This was a new year. Talbot Silton was all the reminder Kodran needed of how quick memories faded. Winning two years in a row might extend Kodran's fame a bit further than Talbot's single win, but doing it again this year would immortalize him.

The hours drifted by, with the afternoon coming quicker than seemed possible. He prepared for the auditions with another boost of oil. His supply was running low. He had planned to make it last through the festival but would be out well before the halfway point. An apprentice fee would solve that problem, though it would breed others. Things had been so much simpler when he had been a young singer just trying to be recognized.

The auditions went better than he thought, and he found four who were acceptable. Two had potential, while his single show would be the pinnacle of the bleak careers of the other pair. He would milk the most he could out of their meager talents, while evaluating the prospects of making an apprentice of one of the other two. If they failed to meet his standards, he would discard them as well. There would be three rehearsals, with the first coming in two days.

With nothing else to occupy him, Kodran retreated to the

familiar embrace of the oil.

* * *

"Your pitch is all wrong," Kodran said for the third time. He was close to going with three back-up vocalists instead of four, as one was proving to be nearly useless. At least the others were exceeding his expectations. "Let's try it once more from the top."

Two of the singers were female, including the one he was considering getting rid of. The other one was one of the two he was evaluating as a potential apprentice. She was pretty, though far too young for Kodran, and nothing like Aileen. Her name was Fayme Lobel. She was from Zorbelix, which was a strike against her in Kodran's eyes, though it might prove to be useful if he were forced to seriously consider Erhan's ridiculous suggestion of a tour of Aern. Kahlen Anthrel was the other female singer. She would be better suited to finding another career.

Dreven Hems was the other possible apprentice. He was less impressive to look upon than Fayme, or even Kahlen, but had more control over his voice than any of the others. His father was also wealthy and could easily afford the apprenticeship fee. Kodran hadn't spoken with either of them yet about the possibility of an apprenticeship, so he didn't know if Fayme was in a position to pay the fee. That might be the deciding factor, though Kodran wished it were otherwise. He was still convinced that he had lost out to Alwin for the same reason. Brendan Stevenson was the other male singer, and was little more than an afterthought, though he was leaps and bounds above Kahlen when it came to talent.

He let Kahlen go two songs later. She just couldn't cut it. The other three were in tune by the end of the rehearsal though.

With two more sessions before the show at the Crenshaw House, his confidence was growing. Fayme and Dreven both played instruments well enough to add that to the performance. Brendan had no such skill but had grown as a singer through the afternoon.

"Good work," he said as the two male singers departed. Fayme was still changing and came out a few minutes later. She was even more stunning with her hair down but still far too young.

"Thank you for all your advice," she said as she gathered her gear. "I learned a lot. More than I ever did from Edson."

"You know Edson Pye?" This was all Kodran needed.

"I met him in Zorbelix," she replied. "We were lovers for a brief time. It ended in betrayal."

"That's what happens when you mix with the likes of him." A thought came into Kodran's head. Perhaps this might not be such a bad thing. "How much do you know about him? Can you tell me anything that might give me an edge?"

"I know Edson better than he knows himself. What do you want to know?"

"Tell me everything," Kodran said. "I want to know what motivates him, what frightens him, what his strongest talents are, and where he's weak. I want to know what he eats for breakfast, and what songs are his favorites. Don't leave anything out."

"That could take some time, and I'm starving. Perhaps you could buy me lunch and we could spend the afternoon together?"

"I'd like nothing more," Kodran said, extending his arm for her. "There's a tavern nearby that's known for its lamb chops."

* * *

Kodran looked around to make sure nobody was following him. It wouldn't do at all to be seen as he was about this business. It was bad enough that he was being forced to stoop to such a low level, getting caught would be unbearable. Not to mention the end of his career and the complete destruction of his legacy. He doubted his competitors would have any issue with doing the same thing, especially Edson Pye. From everything Fayme had told Kodran about the man, there was little he wouldn't do.

Alwin had been the same way in his youth and even somewhat as he grew older. Kodran had always been reserved and didn't enjoy most of the things other men found entertaining. He had only been with two women, besides Aileen. The first had been when he was just starting out on his own, just after Farris had chosen Alwin as his apprentice. Kodran met her in a tavern. She had been amused at his lack of experience and mocked him mercilessly. He had avoided women after that, until Aileen sought him out when he first made the top five in the lists. Following their brief fling, he tried with another woman. She had been young and beautiful, like Fayme, but that had done little to arouse him. He had barely managed to complete the task and found no pleasure in it.

Drinking also held little appeal. He had been drunk a few times, but the way he felt afterward was enough to keep him sober. Alwin had been a drunk, and it seemed Edson was following in his footsteps. Kodran didn't mind a little wine with dinner, or after a show, if tea wasn't available, but that was about it. The ambrosia oil was his only real vice. He would quit doing that after the Challenge, even if just to prove that he could.

The Croaking Frog was known for its garlic potatoes and large cuts of meat. It was normally a place Kodran avoided but was a favorite of the person he was meeting. It was the perfect place for the night's business, as the booths were private and the windows were darkened. Three heavy pouches were tied to a bit of twine that ran around Kodran's neck. Erhan would scream about the dent this put in Kodran's small reserve, but it would be worth it.

Bryce Keller was already seated when Kodran arrived. He was one of the nine judges for the Bardic Challenge. He was also in a bit of a financial pinch after his son invested most of their fortune in a trade ship that sank on its maiden voyage. Kodran couldn't come close to replacing the full amount lost, but he could provide enough to keep the man and his family afloat for a while.

"Good evening, Bryce," Kodran said as he sat down.

"Kodran." Bryce had always been a man of few words.

"I was surprised you agreed to see me. I never saw you as the type to engage in something such as this."

"I never was until now. My fool of a son has nearly destroyed me. I never thought you'd be one for this type of thing either."

"Desperate times call for desperate measures," Kodran said. He was only doing what he was forced to. After this year, he wouldn't need to resort to such measures ever again. "We're clear then? You'll vote for me in the final?"

"I probably would have anyway, but yes. You have my vote."

"No matter what?"

"No matter what. I'm a man of my word."

"I know that, Bryce. I wouldn't be here if that weren't the case. Let's get this wretched business over with and enjoy our meal." He slid the three pouches across the table. Bryce quickly swept them into his lap and hid them away. It was only one vote, but it could come to that. Better to be prepared just in case.

* * *

"I never thought I'd see this day," Erhan said as Kodran signed the paperwork formalizing Fayme's apprenticeship. A pair of bags on the table held the fee she was paying. "We should celebrate."

"I have a show tonight," Kodran said. It was hardly a reason for celebration, but Erhan often insisted on such things. Sometimes, it wasn't worth the fight. "We have rehearsals tomorrow but could probably meet with you afterward."

"I'll make reservations for us." Erhan turned to Fayme. "Will you be bringing a guest?"

"No," she replied before signing her name on the contract, making it official. "I'm all alone here."

"That's no longer true," Erhan said. "You'll be with Kodran for the next three to five years. That makes you family."

Kodran had forgotten about Erhan's taste for younger women. The man had at least five years on Kodran but had been nearly drooling since Fayme sat down. Kodran would step in if things got out of hand, but she would have to find a way to deal with men such as Erhan if she was going to make it in the music business. There were few female bards, and only one had ever won the Challenge. Fayme had the talent to be the second but had a lot to learn.

"Make the reservations for anywhere other than the Croaking Frog," Kodran said. It would be awhile before he was again ready for such a night of gluttony. He had spent half the night bringing the meal back up and wouldn't have slept at all without an extra boost of oil. "And nowhere with a singer."

“That might be hard, but I'll do my best.” Erhan had connections all over the city but always tried to make his tasks look more difficult than they were. He was a fool to think Kodran didn't notice.

“Have you been able to find out the reason why the Triebs were so interested in Edson?” Kodran asked. He would use anything he could against the man.

“It has something to do with the inheritance,” Erhan replied. “With Alwin's brother dead, there's a lot at stake.”

“It wouldn't go to Edson.” Kodran had dealt with a wealthy rival for most of his life. He wasn't prepared to have that obstacle replaced by another. “Alwin had sisters and they have children.”

“I'm just telling you what I heard.” Erhan was the source of as many bad rumors as he was good. In all, he was just a small step above useless. “They stopped asking about him and have been asking about some kid named Porter. Supposedly he was Edson's apprentice.”

“Do you know anything about this?” Kodran asked, turning to Fayme.

“He didn't have an apprentice when I met him,” she replied. “He joked about putting me in the role.”

“Keep digging,” Kodran said, looking back at Erhan. “There must be something we can use against Edson.”

They talked for a little more before splitting up. Kodran sent Fayme on a few errands, while Erhan went to file the apprenticeship forms. Kodran returned to his room and the oil.

Scene Fifteen:

Reputations and Reunions

"Oh Becca, my darling, please open your door,
For it's cold outside and I've nowhere to go.
If you're still angry, I can sleep on the floor,
Oh Becca, my darling, please don't say no."

The Amber Stallion had never held so many people. This wasn't only Edson's opening performance. The owners of the Stallion had invested heavily in expansions and improvements, and it was the first show after the remodeling. The acoustics had improved with the changes. It was now possibly the best venue in Vonst. Edson hadn't known that when he had told Jayme to book him at the Stallion. Sometimes luck was everything.

"Oh Lucia, my love, please let me come inside,
For it's getting late and I've nowhere to sleep.
If you're still angry, at the times when I lied,
Oh Lucia, my love, please don't make me weep."

This was one of the first songs Edson ever wrote. Alwin had challenged him the morning of a show. Edson had to have a new song that Alwin had never heard, or he wouldn't be allowed to participate in the performance. It had been months since it had been part of the show, but it was good to mix things up. Some singers never varied their show at all. Edson would die of boredom if he were forced to work that way. Alwin had been the same way. From everything Edson had been told, Kodran was one of those who kept a firm playlist. The man really was an ass.

"Oh Marci, my sweetheart, please may I come in,
For it's starting to rain and I've nowhere that's dry.
If you're still angry, kick me square in my shin,
Oh Marci, my sweetheart, please don't say goodbye."

Beyond the brief glimpse at Terren Genfry's debut, Edson had been unable to find Fayme. If she was playing a gig, it was in a venue too small to even draw a handful of spectators. Why had she come to Vonst if she wasn't going to book any shows? Was it just to torment him? There had also been no sign of the Triebs, but he wasn't complaining about that.

Kodran was up to something. He had added two nights to his schedule, an additional show at the Diamond House and another at the Crenshaw House. Rumor had it, he had brought in back-up singers for the show at the Crenshaw. Edson had never played there but had heard good things. He was considering attending the performance, as it would fall on a night when he wasn't scheduled to play. He had only seen Kodran perform once before and was curious to see if his show had changed at all.

* * *

“Edson, wait up,” a woman shouted. Edson turned and searched his mind for a name and other details as she approached. He made the connection at the last possible second. She was the lass from the Candlehouse, nearly a year back.

“Aubrey,” he said, displaying his best smile and hoping he had given the correct name. “It's a pleasure to see you again. I looked for you at the Candlehouse when I got back into town, but couldn't find you.”

“I didn't think you even remembered my name,” she said as Edson planted a kiss on her cheek. “You always called me darling.”

“Nonsense,” he replied, relieved that he had got it right. “How could I forget the name of such a pretty lass? How have you been, darling?”

“I've been well, though busy. I'm studying to be a nurse.”

“That's good.” One of the two bounty hunters who had cornered Edson at the Hunter's Arrow Inn was across the street, trying to pretend he wasn't watching. He was doing a poor job. Edson looked around for the other one, but didn't see him. “You should come to one of my shows. I'm at the Amber Stallion now.”

“I know. I was going to get a ticket but couldn't afford it. You've moved up in the world.”

“I'm still the same man I always was.” He spotted the other bounty hunter. The man was in a booth, eating a piece of meat on a stick, while watching Edson like a hawk. There were a lot of people in sight, but none of them were members of the city watch. If the two meant Edson ill, there was nobody to protect him. “I'll tell you what though, I'll leave a pair of tickets at the door tomorrow night. Bring a friend.”

“Thank you,” she said, wrapping her arms around him. “I have to get to class though. I'm glad I ran into you.”

“Me too, darling.” He moved in the opposite direction she did. Both bounty hunters followed him. He circled around the block three times, hoping to lose them, but they stuck with him. They didn't seem to be doing any more than watching him though, so he returned to the Stallion. He would be attending a private party in the evening, hosted by Jayme Naral. Hopefully, the two idiots following him wouldn't cause any problems.

* * *

“She could be his mother,” Donovan Allenson said as Aileen entered the party with Terren Genfry. For reasons he couldn't explain, seeing her with the young singer bothered Edson.

“She could be, but she isn't.” She was Porter's mother though. He wasn't much younger than Terren. Edson took a glass of wine off the tray of a passing servant. “I'm surprised she hasn't come after you yet.”

“She has,” Donovan replied. That bothered Edson too. What was happening to him? He had never before cared who a former lover might end up with. Why now? Why Aileen? “I've been avoiding her. I almost didn't come tonight out of fear she would be after me. I owe Terren one for keeping her occupied.”

“I'll give you the same advice Alwin Floyd gave me. Just take the plunge. She'll surprise you; I guarantee it.”

“You've been with her?”

“There hasn't been a winner of the Challenge in fifteen years who hasn't slept with her. She'll catch you eventually.”

“I don't think I want to win that bad.”

“Suit yourself,” Edson said. His wine glass was empty again. Hadn't he just got it? He waved for a nearby servant. “I've been with worse for a whole lot less."

"So have I, now that you mention it."

Edson laughed and took two glasses from the servant's tray. Each was less than half full, so he poured one into the other, returning the empty glass to the tray. Donovan asked for more rum, as there was none on the tray. Edson grabbed another glass just before the servant walked away. He should have just asked for a bottle.

"How have your shows been going?" He asked Donovan. Aileen's husband entered. He had a young singer with him too. Edson didn't know his name. "Are you still filling the house?"

"It couldn't be better," Donovan replied. "We're sold out for the next three shows. My agent says we'll have the rest of the festival sold out by the end of the week."

"Who's your agent?"

"Delby Rancor."

"I met with him. He seemed alright. Better than some of the others."

"They're all scum, but what are you going to do?"

"Drink wine, make music, and love women. What else is there in life?"

"There's the sights. Seeing the sun set over a different horizon. Plus, there's rum."

Edson was about to make a snide remark, when Fayme entered the room. She walked beside Kodran, their arms entwined. Edson felt as if his heart sank to the ground. He fought back tears, unable to tell whether they were of pain, anger, or both. How could she be with Kodran of all people? How was this even possible? Had the whole thing been some plan of his to throw Edson off? Had she never loved him at all?

“She's something special,” Donovan said. All eyes in the room seemed to be on Fayme. Edson couldn't tear his away. “Why is she with him?”

“I'd give everything I own to know the answer to that question,” Edson replied. He finished both glasses of wine. Fayme didn't even look his way. She seemed to only have eyes for Kodran. Wine wasn't going to be enough. Donovan's rum was more in order. The servant was crossing the room, seemingly moving in slow motion. Edson couldn't wait. He met the man halfway, and emptied Donovan's glass in one swallow.

“Let's get out of here,” he said as he turned back to his Eberian friend. “There has to be some place close by where we can get a bottle or three.”

“Now you're speaking my language,” Donovan said, grinning widely. “I know just the place.”

* * *

Edson nearly fell over as he took a final bow. He had played seven encores, finishing with *Edla's Rose*. Alwin's classic was always a favorite. Edson had added a verse he and Alwin had written together one drunken night. As far as Edson knew, the song had never been performed that way in public. The audience seemed to love it. Beyond their importance in beating Kodran in the Challenge, Edson barely cared what they thought anymore.

How could Fayme be with Kodran? How was that even possible? It served to lend credence to the thought that she had been involved in the plot from the beginning, and thrust Kodran back to the forefront in the list of conspirators. There could be no other explanation. Was everyone involved in the scheming? Even Jayme had to be suspected, for he had been the one to send Edson to Aern. Edson had assumed that Thierry Gant had chosen Fayme as his opener, but it could easily have been Jayme's decision. Would Joceline know? Was she involved too? Was her husband? Was everyone?

The pain Fayme had inflicted when she betrayed Edson was compounded by every coin she had stolen and his rebec she had pawned, but all of that was nothing compared to the metaphorical dagger she had shoved through his heart when she entered the party on Kodran's arm. Edson had thoroughly drowned his sorrows in alcohol. He was focused completely on two things now, beating Kodran in the Challenge and finding Porter after it was over. Whether the lad had betrayed Edson or not remained to be determined, but he was Alwin's son. That was all that mattered.

Jayme hadn't received word back from Hallis Gort. Either that or he had heard back but wasn't sharing the information with Edson. If no word came by the end of the challenge, Edson would return to Cronar and demand that Hallis tell him where the lad was. He had planned to go to Rov for the winter but would put it off until the following year if need be.

There were at least six ladies clamoring for Edson's attention as he left the stage. As always, there were a few men too. He eyed the women, for he needed someone to help him forget about Fayme for a night, and politely turned away the men. The lass from the Candlehouse was one of the six. He dismissed two of the others immediately. One was far too young, while the other was too old and reminded him of Aileen. One of the remaining three resembled Fayme. She was out. The other two were both beautiful, but his eyes kept going back to the Candlehouse lass. Perhaps there was something there worth exploring.

“Sorry ladies, I'm taken tonight,” he said to the others as he held his arm out to the chosen lass. He looked her in the eyes and forced a smile to his lips. “I'm all yours, darling.”

* * *

“You were right,” Edson said. “It is beautiful. Not nearly so much as you are but still beautiful.”

“It's even better when it sets over the water in the evening,” Aubrey said. They were sharing their fourth bottle of wine, while watching the sunrise from the eastern walls of the city. They had been given permission from her cousin who was a guardsman. It had been a magical night. Aubrey had repeatedly surprised him with a wit he hadn't known she possessed. “I often watch it and dream of the places where the sun goes.”

“I could take you to those places,” Edson replied. “I plan to see everything this world has to offer.”

“You're just teasing me now.” She had everything Fayme had, other than the voice and musical ability. And the emerald eyes that a man could spend a lifetime exploring. She was here though, while Fayme was with Kodran. “You'll forget all about me as soon as the Challenge is over, if not before.”

“I remembered you after last year's Challenge. How could I forget someone as lovely as you?”

“Why don't we keep this simple? We'll enjoy each other while you're in Vonst, and you can spare me the promises we both know you'll never keep.”

“I'm not the same man I was a year ago.” Why couldn't she understand that? He needed her.

“And I'm not the same woman,” she replied. Had her eyes

always been that shade of blue? How had he never noticed? "A year ago, I would've leaped at the chance to run away with you. When I woke up and you were gone, I didn't know what to do. I cried for days, hoping you would come back to me before the Challenge was over, but you never returned. I was a wreck for months, before I finally realized I was the one to blame."

"That's not true." He had been the one to leave before she woke up. She had cried over their parting, while he hadn't given her a second thought before running into her a few days back. Other than Fayme, he had sabotaged any chance of a relationship with every woman he had ever loved. She was his well-deserved punishment. "I never gave us a chance. I'd like to now."

"I can't let myself be hurt by you again, Edson. It took me too long to recover. If you can't accept this as what it is, two people having a little fun, then it might be best if we part ways now."

"Don't say such things." Was he that horrible? Perhaps Fayme did the right thing by leaving. He wasn't fit for anyone. His only true loves would always be music and wine. "I can change."

"I don't know what happened to you, but you've obviously been hurt. I'm sorry if I'm making it worse, but I can't go through what I went through last year ever again. After the Challenge is over, I'll be looking for a stable husband. That's just not you."

"Go ahead and leave me then," he shouted. "It's the best thing you can do. Fayme was right to leave too. They all were."

"You need to take a break, Edson," Aubrey said as she waved off her cousin, who had been watching from a distance. Was he really her cousin or another lover? They all lied. Everyone lied. "Get your head straight."

"I don't need anything. Except wine. I need that."

"I think you need to go," said her cousin or lover. He was

big, whoever he was. And he had a sword. "You're going to get me in trouble."

"Piss off," Edson said. A sword would end it. That wouldn't be so bad.

"Get him out of here, Aubrey," her cousin/lover said. Edson took a swing at the man, missing his face and punching him in the side of the head. Waves of pain tore through Edson's hand and he realized how badly he had messed up. A fist rushed toward his face. He tried to move, but it came too fast. Another followed, and another, and his world went dark.

* * *

"You're a mess," Braden Asbury said from outside Edson's cell. Cell? Why was he locked up? He remembered drinking with the Candlehouse lass and swinging at a guard. That was the reason Edson's hand was throbbing. Was the guard her cousin or her lover? Edson wasn't sure. Braden? Where had he came from? Was he even really there?

"Go away," Edson said. Real or not, he wanted no part of the trickster. "You're the reason this whole mess started in the first place."

"I warned you about the price of my magic," Braden replied. "You chose to ignore those warnings."

"Are you here to rub it in then?"

"No, I'm here to help you, if you'll let me."

"You're the last person I want help from. I'll rot in my cell. Your way out isn't worth it."

"You'll be released soon," Braden said. "That's not what I'm offering to help you with. I've learned more of my magic over the past year. I think I can correct some of what I did to you."

"Why should I trust you? Alwin died because of you."

"That's hardly true. My magic is powerful but not that powerful."

"So you say, but my life has been upside down since I met you. Alwin's dead, I sent away my apprentice and now can't find him, and my heart's been ripped to shreds. That seems pretty powerful to me."

"I'll shoulder the blame for one of the three," Braden replied. "A year ago, you weren't capable of love. Your biggest weakness in song writing was your inability to write love songs. I believe my magic saw that as an obstacle that needed to be removed. By allowing you to feel love, it opened the door to you rectifying this weakness."

"Are you saying I only loved Fayme because of your magic? Again, that seems pretty fucking powerful."

"As I said, my magic is powerful. It's just not powerful enough to take the life of another because of the choices you made."

"So, what are you offering me exactly? What will your magic do to me this time?"

"I'll simply reverse the magic of last year. You'll be the same person you were then."

"Is there a price to pay for this?"

"With magic, there's always a price to pay. I can't tell you what the price will be for this magic."

"Can't or won't?"

"Does it matter?"

"I suppose not." Was this what he really wanted? He thought of Fayme, and of the Candlehouse lass, and even of Aileen.

He had developed feelings for all three in some manner. Even further, he had named his horse after three women who he wouldn't have cared about at all before Braden's magic. What about Kari Charon? Would the child mean so much to him without the magic? Then there was his father. A year back, Edson wouldn't have even considered a reconciliation with him. Was that the magic too? If so, did he want to give that up?

It was easy to remember the pain that Fayme had caused him, but what about the good memories? He wouldn't have those without the magic. Were those memories worth the pain? Was Kari? Was his father? Edson thought of his night with the Wahahgma tribe, and the questions that had plagued him. Was that the drugs or the magic? Or both? If the magic were reversed, would he no longer care about Porter's fate? What about Terren Genfry or Donovan Allenson? Without the magic, Edson feared he would see them as threats to be dealt with, rather than as friends to help out and look after. He would be no better than Kodran.

"Go away," Edson said, knowing there would be times he would regret this decision. "I don't want to go back to what I was. I'm better now than I was then."

"Are you sure? The magic will be more difficult to reverse with the passage of time. This may be your last chance."

"I'm not sure, but I think it's for the best that I stay this way."

"Very well then. Farewell, Edson."

"Farewell, Braden."

The card reader faded away as if he hadn't truly even been there. Edson wasn't really sure that he had. A guard came a few minutes later, telling Edson that he had been bonded out and was free to go. Edson almost laughed at that. Was anyone ever truly free? He found Jayme waiting outside with a carriage to take him back to the Amber Stallion. There was one thing that would never change. No matter what happened, the show must go on.

Scene Sixteen
Bards and Bastards

"What happens now?" Edson asked. He hadn't seen Jayme since the day he had been released from jail. Finally, after three days, a carriage had arrived with a letter telling Edson that they had to meet. "Will I go back to jail?"

"Everything is taken care of," Jayme replied. "All of the charges have been dropped. Word of your arrest won't even reach the ears of any of the judges."

"That's the best news you've given me in some time," Edson said. "What's it going to cost me?"

"About a tenth of your take for the festival. I hope it was worth it."

"Not really. My hand still hurts, and I'm betting the lass won't want anything to do with me now."

"If she has half a brain, that's a safe bet. Not that it matters. Her cousin insisted that the agreement include a provision blocking you from ever speaking with her again."

"Did you call me here just so you could antagonize me?"

"No, but I'm not going to pass up the opportunity."

"Why am I here then?"

"I received a message from Hallis Gort," Jayme said. Why

hadn't he started with that? “He shipped Porter to the salt mines to the east. Along the way, the boy escaped with a pair of his fellow prisoners. One of them has been caught but doesn't know where the others went.”

“Good for him,” Edson said. “I guess he doesn't need rescuing.”

“I wouldn't assume that. We don't know anything about the man he's with, assuming they're still together. Porter could be in a much worse situation now than he was.”

“What can we do then?” Edson asked. He had spent one off-season touring Aern. Spending the next one searching the eastern wildlands for Porter wasn't what he had in mind. Still, the lad was Alwin's son. “He could be anywhere.”

“For now, I'm putting the word out with the few contacts I have in the east. We'll meet again after the Challenge is over and decide what to do. We might have to send some search parties out though. If word reaches the Triebs that he's roaming free on this side of the sea, they'll have bounty hunters all over the place.”

“I still have that pair trailing me from time to time,” Edson said. He caught glimpses of the two nearly every day.

“I wouldn't worry too much about them. They won't do anything in the city.”

“That's easy for you to say. Have you thought about my suggestion?” Edson wanted to do a free performance with Terren Genfry and Donovan Allenson. His idea was to take over the section by the fountains in Stensor Park. The park had been named after Sterling Stensor, who had financed the first Bardic Challenge many years back. There was plenty of room there for a large audience, and sound carried well in the area. Alwin had always talked of putting on a show there. Edson planned to dedicate the show to him.

"I have. At first, I was against it, but I'm starting to come around. You need something to counter the stunt Kodran is pulling tonight. My only concern is that this will shine a light on both Terren and Donovan. The boost could give one of them the victory."

"As long as Kodran doesn't win, I'm fine with that."

"You really hate him that much?" In truth, Edson barely knew his rival. Most of his opinions were based on things Alwin had told him. "Even knowing that he wasn't likely involved in Alwin's murder?"

"I'm not convinced of that yet. He could easily be in league with the Triebs. Even if he's not, he stole Fayme."

"I doubt that's the case," Jayme replied. "He's registered her with the university as his apprentice. I don't think there's anything else there besides that."

"Why didn't you tell me that before?"

"I just found out earlier today and hadn't gotten to it yet."

"That doesn't really change anything though. She could be his apprentice and his lover. I can't count how many times Alwin tried to convince me to go to bed with him."

"That's Alwin. I loved the man like a brother, and cried for hours when I heard he'd been killed, but he never met a person who he didn't want to stick his cock into. Kodran has a lot of faults, but that isn't one of them. I wouldn't be surprised if Aileen was the only lover he ever had."

"I still hate him." Was it possible that they weren't lovers? Was she just learning from Kodran? Was that any better? "Enough about him though. Are we going to do the show with Terren and Donovan or not? If so, we need to start planning. If not, I need to come up with something else."

"Let's do it. I'll speak with Terren, if you'll talk to Donovan. I can get the permit for the park and start putting the word out."

"Let's keep it quiet for now. We'll let the word out the morning of the show. I want to blindside Kodran with this. Otherwise, he'll be able to plan a counter move."

"That's a good idea. I'll bring in a bunch of criers that morning. We'll post them all over the city."

"Thank you. Is there anything else? I've had a song in my head all morning. I want to get it written down before I forget it."

"Nothing that can't wait," Jayme said. "We need to start thinking about your winter plans, so I can start making arrangements. Especially if you're going to Rov."

"That was my plan, but it might depend on Porter being found."

"We'll find him. I don't have a lot of connections in the east, but those I have are reliable."

"I hope so." Porter being Alwin's son almost made him Edson's little brother. He had always wanted a sibling growing up. He dreaded facing the lad but would do nearly anything to find him. "I don't know if I can live with myself if something happens to him."

* * *

Edson joined in the applause. As much as he hated to admit it, Kodran's show was fantastic. Two additional singers had joined him and Fayme on stage. One of the two showed some talent and would surely be snatched up as someone's apprentice. The other played his role well yet was obviously limited. Fayme's performance was stellar, making Edson want her even more. Kodran was outstanding, showing why he had won two years in a row, and clearly re-establishing himself as the favorite once again.

"I've seen enough," Edson said. Donovan nodded in agreement. It had been a last-minute decision to attend the show. Edson had spent a fortune for the tickets and owed Jayme another favor for finding them. "Let's leave before the encores."

"It's your coin," Donovan replied. "I would've been just as happy drinking in the nearest rundown tavern."

"Me too, but I wanted to see what we're up against. Are you still in for the show in the park?"

"More than ever. Someone needs to beat Kodran. Are you sure Jayme will be able to convince Terren?"

"He's meeting with the lad and Aileen tonight. There's no downside in it for him though, so I don't see why he wouldn't. Besides, Jayme is really good at convincing people to do things. I wouldn't be surprised if Terren comes out the meeting thinking the whole thing was his idea. Do you think Delby is going to have a problem with you doing this?"

"If he does, I'll fire him and convince Jayme to represent me."

"That would be something," Edson said as they reached the exit. Their seats had been far to the back. The Crenshaw House had impressed him nearly as much as the performance. "We could convince him to book a tour together. We could even go to your home and do a show."

"I'm going there for the winter this year anyways. Delby has booked me for Eblok and Zorbelix. I'll go west from there to Voctoro and Eber."

"Will you make it back here in time for the Challenge next

year?"

"Barely, but it'll be worth it. I haven't been home in six years. How about you? What are your winter plans?"

"I was hoping to go to Rov this year," Edson said. "I might end up wandering the east looking for Porter."

"Why the east? Have you learned something new?" Edson and Donovan had told each other much of their life stories the night of Jayme's party. Edson hadn't updated his friend since then. He tried to remember how much he had told, and what he had kept secret.

"He was being taken to the salt mines but escaped. That's about all I know. Hopefully, he turns up. There isn't much to the east. Spending the winter wandering the wilderness isn't in my plans."

"Spend some time with the rangers in Eber and you'll grow to love such opportunities. I'd join you if I wasn't going home."

"I'd rather join you."

"If he turns up, perhaps you can. What about tonight though? What are we going to do with ourselves?"

"Let's find that rundown tavern you were talking about. I feel a need for a night of drinking, singing, and dancing."

* * *

Nearly half the population of Vonst seemed to be at Stensor Park, but Edson only saw one face. Fayme had come to his show! Even better, Kodran wasn't with her. Edson stared at her as he sang *Nightingale*, his tribute to Alwin. Donovan and Terren accompanied him, letting him have the lead for this song. They had shared that role for the most part, though Edson had a larger repertoire of songs, which put him in front more often than not.

"Thank you," he said as the song came to an end. He smiled as an impulse came over him. He switched his citole for his rebec and started playing, slowly at first, encouraging Donovan and Terren to pick up the tune and join in. It wasn't one they had rehearsed, but the beat was fairly simple. Donovan's lute quickly joined in. Terren's rebec followed shortly after. Edson kept his eyes on Fayme. She wasn't looking away. As Edson's friend, Garrett, often said, it was time to throw the cards on the table. Still playing, Edson walked toward her. "This song has only been performed once before. I wasn't planning to do it tonight, but the woman I wrote it with is in the audience. Her name is Fayme Lobel. If you were fortunate enough to see Kodran Novius's fantastic show at the Crenshaw House, you'll remember her well. Give her a big hand and maybe we can convince her to join in."

The gathered crowd shouted and cheered. Most of them likely hadn't attended Kodran's show, but everyone had at least heard about it. They also knew that Edson and Kodran were the favorites, with Donovan and Terren also in contention. Edson stood in front of Fayme, staring into her eyes as he began to sing.

"I remember crying myself to sleep,
Wondering if you were really there.
I remember and I start to weep,
As I run my fingers through your hair."

She glared at him through the verse. Donovan and Terren kept the beat perfectly. Edson smiled at her and swore to himself he would forgive everything she had done if she would simply sing with him. He wanted much more, but that was all she owed him.

Just one song. His heart raced as her part approached. Would she abandon him again? He closed his eyes, unable to bear watching if she remained silent.

"I remember thinking you were a dream,
Something I made up in my head.
I remember and I want to scream,
As I hold you tightly in our bed."

Edson opened his eyes and smiled. He reached out his hand and was surprised when she took it. He pulled her forward and danced with her back to the stage, as he sang his next verse. Their eyes remained locked through the song and the long round of applause that followed. At the end, he kept his vow and released his anger with her. She hadn't done anything he hadn't done himself in the past. He gave her one more smile before she returned to the crowd. She returned it with one that gave him hope for the future, despite the obvious obstacles in their path.

With a large, dark cloud removed from Edson's life, his joy in performing returned completely. He pushed Donovan and Terren to levels they probably hadn't known they were capable of reaching, as they put on a show that wasn't likely to be forgotten anytime soon. All three of them were drenched in sweat at the end. He hugged both of them as the audience gave their thanks for the performance. He looked around for Fayme but couldn't find her. She had given him a song though, that was what mattered. She would return or she wouldn't. He would love her either way.

* * *

For the second year in a row, Edson was rushing to make it in time for the announcement of the winner of the Bardic Challenge. He wasn't alone this year, as Donovan ran alongside him in a mad dash to reach the university lawn. Despite barely avoiding numerous collisions, they made it just as the dean was starting to climb the steps. Terren smiled as Edson and Donovan took spots on either side of him. Kodran scowled and looked away.

"Cutting it a bit close," Terren said. "I was beginning to think you wouldn't make it."

"Not all of us had the luxury of Aileen's carriage," Edson said. The lad blushed a little, but his smile widened. There was at least twenty-five years between him and Aileen, but they seemed to make each other happy. What more could one ask for in this life? "Besides, I wanted to give Kodran a chance to think he had it wrapped up."

Edson didn't hear Terren's mumbled reply, as he had noticed Fayme standing nearby. He smiled at her, but she either didn't notice or ignored him. He would have to find out which later, as the dean had reached the podium. The crowd went silent in anticipation.

"We come to the end of another outstanding festival," the dean began. "We entered the competition with two clear favorites and emerged with four contenders. Kodran Novius put up a stellar defense of his title, highlighted by an unforgettable night at the Crenshaw House. Not to be outdone, Edson Pye shined night after night at the Amber Stallion and unselfishly shared the stage with both Donovan Allenson and Terren Genfry at Stensor Park. Donovan is the first singer from Eber to be listed in the top five, doing so in only his second Challenge. Going even further was young Terren, who came out of nowhere to capture the hearts of everyone. Can we please have a hand for everyone who competed this year, and for the judges who had the difficult task of picking a winner?"

Edson closed his eyes, just as he had when he waited to see if Fayme would join the song at Stensor Park. He didn't care which name was called, as long as it wasn't Kodran. Even if it was, would that really be so bad? Would it really matter? There would be a Challenge again in a year, and another a year later. Edson was young and would have plenty of opportunities to win. He had friends, he had his father back, and would hopefully someday have a chance with Fayme. What did Kodran have?

"I'm pleased to announce that Terren Genfry is the winner of this year's Bardic Challenge. Congratulations, Terren!"

Edson turned and embraced the lad, while Donovan patted him on the back. Kodran scowled and looked as if he would rather be anywhere else in the world. Fayme smiled for a brief moment, while Kodran was looking the other way. Edson smiled back, before joining Donovan in pushing the lad forward to claim his prize.

* * *

Edson breathed a sigh of relief as the carriage ride came to a merciful end. After a long night of celebration with Donovan and Terren, he wasn't happy when Jayme sent the carriage with a message for Edson to come immediately. The dreadful ride had ended in front of Jayme's office. Aileen's carriage and another were parked in front. Edson didn't wait for the driver to open the door, waving the man off with a forced smile.

The entryway was empty, but the sound of voices came

from the back room. Edson whistled a tune he had stuck in his head and went down the hall. He froze immediately after entering. Kodran was in the room with Fayme beside him. Across from them, Aileen sat beside Terren. Jayme was on the other side of the room, along with Thierry Gant and a man Edson didn't know.

"What's going on?" he asked, looking at Jayme. He looked over at Kodran. "What's he doing here?"

"The Triebs know about Porter," Jayme replied. Aileen sobbed at this. Terren leaned in to comfort her, drawing a scowl from Kodran. Was he holding a grudge against the lad for winning? "We need to act fast or he'll soon be dead."

"That doesn't explain Kodran being here." So much for a winter in Rov.

"I'm here to help Aileen find her son," Kodran said. "If I had known about him, I would've done so long ago. Unfortunately, the task fell on you and you decided to pawn him off on a criminal."

"I didn't know who he was," Edson replied. Aileen's scowl was a near match for the one Kodran wore. "I never would've done that if I'd known he was Alwin's son."

"Thomas told me the boy was dead," Aileen said. "He insists it was to protect Porter from the Triebs, but I don't believe him. He always resented that I had a child with Alwin."

"He isn't the only one," Kodran said, just loud enough for Edson to pick it up, but not for Aileen to hear. Could this be the true root of the rivalry?

"What are you proposing we do?" Edson asked, looking at Jayme.

"I'm suggesting you find him," Jayme replied. "Aileen has agreed to finance the effort."

"You expect me to find him before the army of bounty hunters the Triebs will send? I appreciate the confidence, but even I'm not that cocky."

"You won't be alone," Terren said. "I promised Aileen I would help. I'm from the east. People will talk to me. They're not going to trust you."

"I'm going too," Kodran said. It was Edson's turn to scowl. "Someone needs to keep you from drowning in a wine bottle."

"I go wherever he goes," Fayme said. Edson felt the scowl melting away.

"What about you, Jayme?" Edson asked. "And Thierry? Will you be going with us?"

"We won't," Thierry said. He nodded toward the stranger next to him. "Gravis will represent us. I think you'll find him to be quite helpful."

The man's smile told Edson all he needed to know. Gravis would be the muscle of the group. That was fine with Edson. The last thing he wanted to do was get in any sort of fight. Could he travel with Kodran though? And Fayme? At least Terren was a decent lad, and Gravis had the look of a man who wouldn't say no to a night of drinking. It wasn't as if Edson could say no. Porter was Alwin's son. Porter was Edson's brother.

"When do we leave?" he asked.

"Tomorrow morning," Jayme said. "Everyone will meet here at dawn."

* * *

Edson was halfway to a good drunk when he saw her. She was tall, only an inch or so shorter than he was, and had red hair.

He had always had a weakness for red hair. Or any color for that matter, as long as it came with a pretty face, as was the case with this one. He smiled and she smiled back. She kept her eyes locked with his as she approached his table.

"I know who you are," she said as she sat down. She smiled again before emptying his wine glass in a single swallow. "You're Edson Pye, the famous singer."

"I don't know about famous, but I am Edson Pye. You have me at a disadvantage, as I don't know your name."

"You can call me darling, just like you do all the others." Did he know this lass? She didn't look familiar. "I can promise you'll remember me above all of them though. In fact, I'll bet this is a night you never forget."

"You're using all of my lines," he said. What did he have to lose though? After the meeting at Jayme's office, Edson had finally gotten a chance to speak with Fayme. She had made it clear that any romance between them was a thing of the past. He would be stuck with her and Kodran for the near future. Why not enjoy this night? "I'll play along though, darling. What did you have in mind?"

"About three more bottles of wine and a big bed."

"I can provide both if we go to the Amber Stallion."

"That's what I was hoping you'd say."

Edson threw a few coins on the table and led her to the door. The Stallion was only a few blocks away, so he didn't bother calling for a carriage. Walking would give him a chance to work off the wine he had already drank. About halfway there, she stopped and pushed him against the wall of a tailor shop, kissing him passionately.

"I can't wait," she said. "Take me in the alley."

"Not the best place, but I've done the deed in worse spots." He laughed and unbuttoned his trousers as she pulled him into the alley. He pulled her toward him and kissed her again, but she pushed him away. A half dozen men stepped out of the shadows, along with a pair of older women.

"I told you I could get him to come to us, Aunt Relena," said the redhead. Edson groaned. If one was Relena, odds were, the other woman was Lethina. That made the lass Alwin's niece. That also put Edson in a tough spot.

"Nice work, Kethel," one of the women said. He assumed she was Relena. "What are we to do with you, Edson? I would've been happy to give you enough coin to keep you drunk for the rest of your miserable life, but you had to stick your nose where it doesn't belong. Tell me where Porter is and I might still do it."

"I don't know," Edson replied. "The last place I saw him was Bithe."

"That's a lie," Relena said. She nodded at one of the men. He raised his fists and stepped forward. Edson tried to defend himself, but he was no fighter. He found himself on the ground three punches later.

"Okay, he was in Cronar." The truth couldn't really hurt at this point. Porter wasn't likely to be anywhere near there. "I have no idea where he is now though."

"But you're trying to find him," Lethina said. "We can't have that."

"I'm doing no such thing," Edson insisted as the puncher loomed above him. "I'm getting ready to leave for Rov for the winter."

"That's two lies." Relena nodded again and the looming man reached down and pulled Edson to his feet. He cocked his arm back for another punch, but a shout from behind drew his attention. The two bounty hunters from the Hunter's Arrow Inn ran into the alley, crashing into the first men they came to. Edson tried to pull away from the man holding him, but couldn't.

"Leave him and get us out of here," said Lethina. The man threw Edson back to the ground and started leading the three women away. The rest of the men were occupied by the bounty hunters, so Edson started following the women. He didn't get far before Kethel turned and smiled at him.

"Where do you think you're going?" She strode toward him with a confident swagger. She looked nothing like Alwin, or even Porter.

"I'm just trying to get away. We can dance some other time, darling."

"I look forward to that," she said as she burst forward, "but I can't have you following us."

He barely saw her fists coming, as she landed nearly a dozen blows in what seemed to be only a couple seconds. He fell again, with pain exploding throughout his body. She was gone by the time he reached his feet, but the pair of bounty hunters had reached him. They had left Alwin's sisters' men scattered on the ground behind them.

"You're coming with us," one of them said as the other grabbed hold of Edson. "You could've saved us all a lot of trouble by just telling us who you were back when we first found you."

"Who are you working for?" Edson asked. He had assumed they were lackeys of Alwin's sisters. Were they instead Kodran's men? Someone else's?

"We serve Fedwick Trieb," said the man holding Edson.

"I thought he was dead." Alwin's family was far too

complicated. No wonder he never wanted anything to do with them.

"He is, but he left us with a task," said the first man. "That's where you come in. We need your help."

"What do you need me for?"

"You're going to help us find Porter Trieb before anyone else can."

"What are you going to do with him?"

"We're going to protect him," said the man holding Edson. "He's the rightful heir to Fedwick and Alwin's estates."

"I'm supposed to be leaving with another group in the morning to find him. We should all work together."

"That's not how this is going to go." The man tightened his grip on Edson. "You're leaving now with us. If anyone finds him first, we're going to finish what those men started with you. I won't serve Relena or Lethina."

"I can sympathize with you there." Edson wasn't really looking forward to traveling with Kodran, or even Fayme. Perhaps this would work out for the best. "Can we at least stop at my room to get my things? I don't even have my citole with me."

"We'll make a quick stop," said the man who wasn't holding Edson. He looked to be slightly older than his companion. "Don't get any ideas though. We'll be watching your every step."

Edson had a lot of ideas, none of which were likely to improve his circumstances. His bags were already packed, so it just took a few minutes to load everything onto Lackey. The horses ridden by the bearded men towered over Lackey and Princess. The latter seemed intimidated by the big horses and displayed none of her usual stubbornness. As always, Lackey went along without complaint.

They arrived at the gates just as the city watch was

preparing to close up for the night. A couple coins from Edson's older companion granted them passage, and the hunt for Porter began.

Coda

Joceline eyed the letter nervously. A sailor had delivered it to her, claiming it was from an old friend. She didn't have any friends who were sailors, though she wouldn't mind being friends with the man who had brought the letter. He was quite a specimen. It was hard to focus with the beautiful man watching her, but she smiled as she saw that the letter was from Edson Pye. She hadn't thought of the singer in some time but had fond memories of their brief fling. Perhaps he would be returning and could provide her with more pleasant distractions.

"Do you know what this says?" she asked after reading the letter.

"I didn't read it," he replied, "but I know what he meant to ask you. Can you help or not?"

"I can try, but this won't be easy." From what she remembered, nothing with Edson ever was. "How long will you be in Zorbelix?"

"We'll be leaving in ten days. Will that be long enough?"

"I hope so, but I'm not promising anything."

"Can I help at all?"

"I doubt it, but maybe you should stay here just in case I

need you for anything."

"I have to return to the ship every third night to stand watch, but I'm all yours for the rest of our stay."

"Be careful what you promise. A woman could get ideas."

"Edson warned me about your ideas and of your arrangement with your husband. I've been at sea a long time and would welcome those ideas."

Joceline smiled and put down the letter. A few hours delay wouldn't hinder the task too much. With her husband away on business, the sailor and Edson's request would be a welcome distraction. Especially the sailor. She took his hand and led him off to explore some of her ideas.

* * *

Welby ran his hands across the body of the citole. It was as smooth as glass. All that remained was putting the pegs in and adding catgut strings. He would have it ready well before they docked in Cronar. It was slightly smaller than the one Edson carried but was similar in design. It was easily the most beautiful instrument Welby had ever crafted.

The test would be in how it played. Unfortunately, he didn't know how to play a single chord. Neither did the person the citole was intended for. If things worked out Edson would provide lessons in the future. If not, Welby had promised to find someone else for the lessons. He said a quick prayer to Zain in the hopes of that never happening.

The pegs went in without problem, but he waited to add the catgut strings. That was one lesson he could give, and one memory he wanted to share. He smiled as he searched the ship. It brought back memories of his time in Zorbelix with Joceline. Their search had been frustrating from the start, but they eventually had success. The same was true of his search of the ship, and he was soon back in his workshop, demonstrating the proper method of stringing the citole. The sounds it made were beautiful, even if he wasn't sure it was in tune.

It fit perfectly in the hands it was built for, and the sounds were even more beautiful, despite being the first efforts of an unskilled beginner. Everyone had to have a beginning. Welby was thrilled to share in this one.

* * *

"I'm coming," Edward Pye shouted, in the hopes of calming whoever was banging on his door. He hadn't had visitors in some time. Even the bounty hunters had stopped coming to see if his son was home. The lad had promised to return, but there had been no word since then. Perhaps this was him, though, if it was, he needn't have knocked. It was his home too.

The farm grew lonelier with each day. Edward had been nearly at the point of giving up when his son had returned. He was approaching that point again. With Edson pursuing life as a bard, there was nobody for Edward to give the farm to. His son's promise of grandchildren was likely hollow. Edward hated to think he had spent his life building the place just so it could rot away when he was gone.

"I said I was coming," he shouted as the knocking began again. People had no patience these days. He threw open the door and found a small girl standing on his porch. She smiled up at him as if he should know her. He started to smile back, but gave up on the effort. At his age, his teeth were nothing pretty to look at. Instead, he bent down and looked her in the eyes. “Hello, darling. Are you lost?”

“Not anymore, grandfather,” she said. “My name is Kari. Edson sent me a letter saying this is to be my new home.”

Edward couldn't stop the smile then. He didn't know if this was really his son's child and didn't care. Edson had kept his promise and gave him a grandchild. That was all that mattered. “Welcome home, Kari. I'm Edward.”

“I like grandfather better.”

“Me too, darling. Me too.”

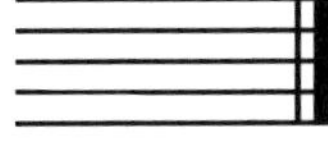

The forests of Northern Michigan were an ideal setting for Jeff Pryor's childhood. He developed a love and respect of nature at an early age, before moving to the more populated metro Detroit area in his teens. Spending formative years in both urban and rural environments contributes strongly to his stories.

Jeff began telling stories as a young child. Reading and writing were early passions, but Dungeons and Dragons was what eventually led him to fantasy. Many years of telling his stories around the gaming table eventually stirred his writing passion. 'Chosen of Trees and of Talons' was published in 2016, followed by his first poetry collection, 'Whispers of a Broken World', the following year. 'Strings of Chance' begins a new story, with many still to come.

Jeff still lives in Michigan, the place where people point at their hand to show where they're from. He lives with his adult (whether she wants to admit it or not) daughter and a jerk of a cat named Tarot. Northern Michigan is a second home, with the call of the forest always in Jeff's ear...and his stories.

www.pryorwords.com

www.facebook.com/pryorwords

www.twitter.com/pryorwords